Running before the
Prairie Wind
An Historical Novel of Southwestern Minnesota

RUNNING BEFORE THE PRAIRIE WIND

Copyright © 2009 by Anne Ipsen.

All rights reserved. No part of this book may be reproduced in any form whatsoever, by photography or xerography, or by any other means, by broadcast or transmission, by translation into any kind of language, nor by recording electronically, digitally or otherwise, without permission in writing from the author, except by a reviewer, who may quote brief passages in critical articles or reviews.

ISBN 978-0-578-02731-9
Library of Congress Control Number: 2009930334

First Printing: September 2009

A portion of a letter from Mary Carpenter is quoted at the beginning of Chapter 8 with permission of the Minnesota Historical Society. Sara Davenport's lovely watercolor, found on www.thelegacystudio.com, inspired the cover image and was adapted with permission. Ranch windmill image by Alison Pfaelzer. Photo of the author by Carol Weston. The book was designed by Steve Glines of ISCSpress.com.

ibus press
Newton, Massachusetts

For more information or to order, visit
www.ibusgroup.com

Bookseller and special sales discounts available.

For Alison, my first reader,
because she wanted to know what happened to Karen;

To my Minneapolis friends for patiently listening;

And to Jay, always.

Also by Anne Ipsen

*A Child's Tapestry of War,
Denmark 1940-45 — a memoir*

Teenage Immigrant — a memoir

*Karen from the Mill,
a novel from the golden age of sail*

For more information visit the author's website:
www.AnneIpsen.com

Running before the Prairie Wind

An Historical Novel of Southwestern Minnesota

Anne Ipsen

ibus press
Newton, Massachusetts

1
Running before the Prairie Wind

[The Pilgrim was] going along at a great rate, dead before the wind, with studding sails out on both sides, alow and aloft, on a dark night, just after midnight, and everything as still as the grave, except the washing of the water by the vessel's side; for being before the wind, with a smooth sea, the little brig, covered with canvas, was doing great business, with very little noise.

Two Years before the Mast
Richard Henry Dana, Jr. (1816-1882)

August 1890

Karen Larsen was waiting for her husband to come home—again. It didn't really matter whether he came in time for dinner, one more or less of the eight that usually sat around the table would not make a difference, and the girls would put a plateful aside for him. But Karen liked to know, liked to plan. If Peter came home all tired and hungry, this evening would not be a good time to talk about naming the baby. Not that he wasn't thrilled; they both were.

"Just in time for our anniversary," he had said when she told him last month.

"The baby is due end of March, not in February," she corrected him, thinking of their fifteenth wedding anniversary.

"Yes, but we left Denmark in March," he had pointed out. "We can celebrate the baptism and our ten years in Minnesota at the same time."

He had kissed her then, and soon his tenderness turned to passion that pushed away all plans.

Karen looked again at the page in front of her, blue pencil poised to correct the next grammar error or replace a dull phrase with a more colorful description. Peter was a skillful writer, but this article on the design of a modern silo for fermenting corn silage was too prosaic, even for a newspaper column.

"It's for information, not entertainment," he would say when she pointed that out.

Yes, but it does no good to put our readers to sleep, she thought, rehearsing her argument. *You need to put in something more personal, more human interest.*

Too hot and restless to stay indoors, Karen put the draft aside since it was for next week's edition and could wait. Rising from her desk, she pulled out the pins that held her braids at the nape of her neck and went outside to collect lavender seeds from the plants in the flowerbeds along the front porch. Earlier in the month, she had harvested most of the fragrant blossoms for sachets to keep their clothes smelling sweet, but had allowed some of the flowers to go to seed for next year's planting. Crumbling some into her hand, she wished she could hibernate with them in the barn safe from the cold Minnesota winter to wait for spring. Even better, be tucked in a warm drawer among fragrant sachets, to sleep through the dark days and dream about the bountiful sun.

She shook her head to brush away the gloom. *This time will be different. Nothing bad will happen to any of them, not to Peter, not to the children, and not to any of the girls. The happiness of this glorious summer will carry us all through until spring.*

The problem was that since she had told Peter about the baby, he had avoided the subject, the way he avoided talking about anything that might remind of the past. Was he afraid that the wrong word would tip them over memory's edge? He was even starting to avoid her, traveling more than ever and burying himself in running the paper. Somehow she had expected that when he left the sea and they came to Minnesota, he would leave restlessness behind and settle down. Instead, he had founded a farming co-op and found a manager for their prosperous farm so he could spend time lecturing about agriculture and roamed the prairie sea instead of sailing around the world. Then last year they had started a weekly newspaper, but that meant late Friday nights in the last minute rush to put *The Lincoln Pioneer* to bed.

Not that she and the children were unhappy, quite the opposite. Peter's boundless energy and exuberance was infectious. If he just wouldn't be away so much; at least when the time came. And they needed to talk. She would show soon and then the girls would know and the children suspect—at least John. At nine, he would be embarrassed and need a wise father's explanation. Lil-Anne was too young to understand much at five, but there was no keeping secrets from her. She should be told soon so she could have the joy of anticipation, not just wake up one day and find herself replaced as the baby of the family.

A buggy turned down the lane, trailing a cloud of dust and coming to a clattering halt in front of the rambling white farmhouse. Peter Larsen was home. He glanced at the cloudless sky with the expert eye of a seaman and checked the direction of the wind by the flywheel on the windmill. *Good, the weather will hold*, he thought. *We'll be able to finish the threshing.* He caught sight of his wife kneeling in front of the flowerbeds, glowing in the late afternoon sun. With her braids down her back like that, she looked no older than when he had seen her on the dock, waiting for him to return from sailing around the world. Except then her hair was covered, saved for his eyes only.

He picked up a copy of the newspaper and waved it over his head. "It's done," he called. "We made it in time for me to come home for supper."

Karen rose and ran joyously towards him.

"Don't touch me," he grinned, holding up his ink-stained hands. *Yet*, he added to himself. Then he had to repeat the warning when little Anne bounded out the door, ready to pounce.

Svend and John came from behind the house and he tossed the reins to the farmhand and handed the newspaper to the boy.

"*Go' Javten, Kaptajn Storkeben*—g'evening Captain Storklegs," the irrepressible Svend greeted him in their nightly ritual.

"Is that any way to greet your master?" Peter shot back.

Svend was a Larsen institution. Much more than a farmhand, he was Karen's persistent follower from the winter before their wedding. Where Karen went, Svend followed, even emigrating with them across the Atlantic.

The gnome-like little man grinned cheerfully and said in his thick Danish dialect, "John and A'll take care of Blackie; you just wash up."

While Peter went to the back of the house to use the outdoor shower contraption that Svend had rigged by the barn, Karen went to the kitchen to supervise dinner preparations. As she automatically twisted her braids into a bun more practical for bending over a hot stove, a pair of brown and a pair of blue eyes turned at her entrance, the faces of the two girls pleading for acceptance of the work they had already started.

"Well Madmor, what's on the menu?" Karen asked Minnehaha who was perched on a stool stirring a bowl of meatballs. Inger, a tall Swede with a crown of blonde braids wound around the top of her head, was peeling carrots and onions onto a piece of newspaper. A basket of corn stood on the floor waiting to be husked before being steamed in the pot simmering on the stove. By the pan, the butter stood ready for frying the meatballs, and the water and coal buckets were each filled. All seemed in good order. Karen smiled and gave a nod of approval for the menu and the preparations.

"I'll chop the parsley," she offered, tying an apron around her waist.

Minnehaha and Inger were only two of the four girls that lived on the farm to learn household management; the Danish Elsbeth and Irish Bridget were across the road, helping prepare dinner for the farm hands under the supervision of the manager's wife. They had started with one girl just before Lil-Anne was born when Peter felt they needed more help for the growing household. Based on the Danish model that a girl most easily learns housekeeping from someone other than her mother, Karen had invited a young neighborhood girl to help out in exchange for room, board, pocket money, and instruction in domestic arts. Soon she added another girl to the group and then a third and fourth, as word spread that she had a way with young people and that she could teach them American ways. These were not skills the girls could learn from their own immigrant mothers who often spoke very little English and had a difficult time adapting to the strange new life. The farms were isolated and the roads poor, so becoming a Karen Girl also gave them the opportunity to learn English and socialize with other young people.

Of course, Minnehaha was not an immigrant, but she had badly needed to come to terms with her mother's Indian heritage yet be accepted by her father's people. During the year she had made huge strides in confidence, partly because the other girls, being immigrants, accepted her on her own terms and had no prejudice against her mixed background.

Karen had developed a system whereby a new girl started every three months and stayed for a year, practicing the different aspects of housekeeping by rotating roles. The following month, Minnehaha was due to leave and she was *madmor* in her last rotation. Literally translated from the Danish, the word is 'Food-mother' but really means 'Mistress-of-the-house' and as such Minnehaha managed the household and instructed Inger, their newest girl, in dinner preparations. Karen felt strongly that it's simple enough to learn how to clean and cook but the girls also needed practice in being in charge and teaching others.

The system worked well. The four current girls got along and were cooperative. Inger had been a little homesick in the beginning, but her English was improving, as was her self-confidence. Bridget, the next madmor, was coming along nicely, and Karen would be able to continue to leave the house and children in competent hands when she needed to be away from the farm. Elsbeth was a sweet girl, but a scatterbrain. It was hard to imagine her with her own brood of children at the right hand of a sturdy farmer.

I'll miss Minnehaha though, Karen mused. *I hope I can find her a good job. Nearby so we can visit.*

"Be sure to have Lil-Anne set the table and check that she counts out the napkins and forks correctly," she admonished Inger. "I know it's quicker for you to do it yourself, but she needs to learn responsibility and we can't have you girls spoiling her."

"Yes Mistress," Inger said with a quick bob that hinted that she had been told this every night all week.

"You don't need to bob. This is not a grand house in the city, and you're not a lady's maid. Or, is this your polite Swedish way of telling me that I've said it before?"

"No Mistress," Inger said, but there was a gleam in her eye and she forbore to curtsy.

At the end of the meal, Peter wiped his mouth and said, *"Tak for mad*—thank you for the food." Echoes circled around the room.

"Velbekomme," Minnehaha replied in her role as madmor. Although they spoke English at the table, they always observed the Danish custom for concluding the meal by thanking the preparer.

Strolling outside, Karen and Peter sat down on the porch swing holding hands and looking more like young lovers than well-married folks. They enjoyed the refreshing wind and listened to the crickets that insisted that the heat of the day was not yet over.

Peter sighed contentedly. "August is my favorite month on the prairie. I love the square settings of wheat drying in the sun alternating with the fields lying 'summer fallow' and the tassels of corn waving in the west wind. This morning, I saw a hawk soaring over a gray heron fishing in the creek, and the birds sang in the cottonwoods along its banks. Such an abundant land."

They sat quietly, admiring the purple clouds of the sunset, the silence only broken by the shrill fiddling of the cicadas.

Peter sighed again. "I often think of how the Minnesota prairie defines our lives. Like the seas that created the Danish islands, the Prairie Sea is ever present, sometimes bearing us on a following wind, so quietly that we hardly know how much progress we're making. This beautiful summer we've had the wind at our back and only light swells to rock us to sleep. I only pray that the winter storms will not shred our emotional sails."

"What do you mean?" Karen asked in surprise.

"Well you know how you get," Peter looked meaningfully at Karen's waist.

"Oh, I'm fine—this time will be different." She shook her head in denial.

"Don't you think we should keep Minnehaha? She's such a help and would like to stay."

"It's time for her to move on and Bridget will do well as madmor. Elsbeth is a little scatterbrained, but Inger will be very good with the baby when the time comes."

"I'm not talking about the girls we have now, but the new ones. You always take their problems so to heart. Are you sure you can tackle all that this winter?"

"No, it'll be fine. Give me something else to think about. I can't just sit and twiddle my thumbs."

"Just sitting is not you," he admitted. "But now that you're starting your column, you won't be twiddling. Have you decided whom to interview for the first edition of 'Meet your Neighbors'?"

"I thought perhaps Inger's parents would be willing."

"Some new settlers have bought the old Klepinski farm.

The Bullards are from New Hampshire. Welcoming them to the neighborhood would make a perfect excuse for you to interview them."

Karen reached up to smooth the frown from Peter's face, then snuggled closer. Not looking at him, she changed the subject, "I've been thinking. Would you mind if we call the baby Rachel?" When he didn't answer, she added, "You know, for Jesse's little girl."

"Do you think that's wise? Won't that just bring back bad memories?"

"I'd have to ask him, but I think he would be pleased."

"I was thinking of you," Peter murmured, but Karen seemed not to hear.

The two sat in silence, watching the sun going down behind the apple orchard. Peter breathed deeply, enjoying the lavender fragrance that was Karen.

2
The Bullards

We take it for granted that newcomers to Minnesota are from Scandinavia or some other country across the Atlantic, but Obadiah and Mildred Bullard hail from Nashua, New Hampshire. At the beginning of the summer they bought the old Klepinski farm two miles north of Lincoln and have begun to transform the dilapidated shack to a large, comfortable frame house. We can look forward to learning American farming methods from Obadiah, though he readily explains that the Nashua soil is far less fertile than here and the winters almost as harsh. Both Obadiah and Mildred are members of the Society of Friends, better known as Quakers, and Mildred is a preacher of the Word. She believes that men and women are equal before God regardless of station in life or family background and seeks to find the 'light within' each person. They have been called to Minnesota with a 'concern', as they term their mission, to work with Indians and orphans.

The Bullards are New Englanders of long standing. Mildred's family moved from Boston to Newport, Rhode Island three hundred years ago to escape religious persecution while Obadiah's great-grandfather was a New Hampshire minuteman during the Revolution. The couple both attended The Friends' School in Providence where they met and later married. They still retain the customs of 'plain dress and speech,' addressing stranger as well as friend by their name without Mr. or Mrs. Also by custom, Obadiah does not take off his hat to anyone, reserving such a sign of respect for the Lord.

Our new neighbors are the parents of Emily Brown of St. Peter, Minnesota and Dr. Amos Bullard of Boston, Massachusetts.

They have three grandchildren in St. Peter where Mr. Brown is a judge.

Karen Andersdatter
The Lincoln Pioneer
Saturday, August 22, 1890

The next week, Karen had Svend harness the buggy and drove up to the old Klepinski farm to welcome the Bullards, as Peter had suggested. It was still early afternoon when she pulled up in front of a half-built house and, by way of announcing her presence, called loudly, "Whoa Blackie!" She was impressed. Judging by the number of men hammering on the framing, this would be much larger than the simple 'balloon' houses that were bounding up everywhere like prairie grass after a spring rain. The setting of wheat that awaited the arrival of the threshers was small, but the beautifully proportioned stacks looked as if they had been designed by the hand of an artist. Many more fields had been newly cleared and plowed for planting next year. By spring this would be a substantial farm.

The owner emerged from the back of the former settler's shack that was evidently the family's temporary home. She saw his eyes narrow at the sight of her, a strange woman with a frilly bonnet and unfamiliar buggy.

"Welcome to Lincoln," she said. "I'm Karen Larsen. My husband and I have a farm a couple of miles south of here."

"Bullard," he returned tersely. He did shake hands with a firm grip but never raised his hat. Not very friendly.

Mrs. Bullard, hanging quilts to air on the clothesline, nodded curtly.

"What beautiful quilts. Did you make them?" Karen exclaimed.

The woman thawed. "Yes indeed," she said, her sharp intelligent eyes contrasting her plain dress and old-fashioned poke bonnet. "You're welcome to examine them."

Her work was exquisite, with beautifully matched squares and lively colors. "I only know enough about pieced quilts to admire your artistry," Karen said. "In Denmark, where my husband and I were born, quilts are purely utilitarian and just made from whatever leftover pieces of cloth."

"Here too," Mrs. Bullard countered. "Please, come inside and have some cold lemonade." After apologizing that as yet they had no parlor but must do with the kitchen of the old shack, she continued, "But there's no reason why something useful can't also be beautiful; the art is in selecting the right scraps and putting them together to please the eye. New England ladies have developed a number of wonderful patterns, but some of them have nothing better to do than brag about their latest work." She sniffed as if bragging were the greatest sin and she would never stoop so low.

"Mrs. Bullard, you have no need to brag; your work speaks for itself, even to someone as ignorant as I."

"Please call me Mildred."

They chatted for a while about the weather and the harvest. Karen tried to ask her where they were from, but Mildred kept directing the conversation back to her and her family. Without ever seeming nosy, she managed to keep her talking about Peter, John, and Lil-Anne.

"Tell me about Denmark," she said, seeming genuinely interested. "I know very little about Europe."

"Peter and I grew up on Fanø, a small island off the west coast of Denmark. My father was the town miller, but most of the men went to sea. Peter too. We married after he returned from sailing around the world as First Mate on my uncle's ship."

"Fanø sounds like Nantucket, an island off the coast of Massachusetts," Mildred said. "My grandfather was Captain of a clipper ship in the China Trade."

"After we were married, Peter and I sailed together; we too went to China, that is, Canton; as well as Japan, Hawaii, and San Francisco."

"Astonishing. Is that when you decided to immigrate? What on earth made you leave the sea and become farmers in Minnesota?"

"Oh, not until after we had returned to Denmark and John was born," Karen said, quickly steering the conversation away from dangerous waters. "We heard that some Danes had settled here in Tyler, and Peter didn't like being captain of a steam ship—too noisy and dirty, he said. Not like a square rigger."

"I hear there's a Danish college in Tyler. How did that come about?"

"Back in 1880, when the train came through here, a group of Iowa Danes bought options for land south of the railroad to found a Danish colony," Karen explained. "One of the first things they did was build a church, an elementary school, and one for young people. They called the colony *Danebod*, meaning 'the help of the Danes'. The folkschool is based on the principles of Bishop Grundtvig and schools he founded back home. He felt strongly that young people from the farms and small towns should have the opportunity for an education beyond the basic principles taught in elementary school. I went to Askov Folkschool back home before I married Peter, and I still draw on what I learned in those few months."

Education was evidently one of Mildred's passions, for she became quite animated, explaining that even in the seventeenth century New England towns were required to establish public schools for the settlers. "Of course, the early schools were only for boys, but even girls and servants were taught enough of their letters so they could read the Bible."Where did the girls learn to read, if they didn't go to school?" Karen asked.

"They were supposed to learn at home, but that didn't always work if the parents were too busy or were barely literate themselves. Soon special Dame Schools were set up for the little ones and eventually the girls were allowed to go to the public schools."

"Only in this century did everyone in Denmark have the opportunity to go to school, but most rural young people leave at fourteen, right after they're confirmed."

"Obadiah and I are members of the Society of Friends who have founded wonderful schools in Rhode Island and Pennsylvania. There's even a women's college in Pennsylvania as well as Haverford for boys."

"A friend, Elizabeth Bendixen, told me that Quakers believe in looking for the light of God in everyone." Karen said. "I think that's the best possible way to teach children and that Grundtvig would have approved."

Karen brought up her own passion. "I'm much concerned about our neighbors who come to this country with too little money, no English, and barely able to read in their own language. Especially the women are very isolated and don't have the opportunity to learn English. That's why I make my girls study in the afternoons, after our work is done."

"Girls? I thought Lil-Anne was your only daughter." And Karen explained about her four 'girls'.

Mr. Bullard interrupted by entering the room to claim a glass of lemonade.

"Oh, I almost forgot," Karen exclaimed. "I really came to

interview you for my column in *The Lincoln Pioneer.* Would you tell me about yourselves? That is if you don't mind, Mr. Bullard." She felt intimidated by the forbidding man's presence. *Perhaps if I use my notebook. That would look professional; impress them that I know what I'm doing.*

Mildred fortunately readily supplied the details of their background and Karen wrote it all down. Obadiah said nothing, except to remove the pipe from his mouth and insist, "Please, no Mister. I'm plain Obadiah Bullard."

Karen nodded sagely, making a note of his request. Then she countered, smiling, "And I don't like to be called Mrs. Larsen, plain Karen is fine. Lars was my husband's father and I'm not his son. That's why my *nom de plume* is 'Karen Andersdatter,' in the old Danish manner—for my father." *I'm babbling*, she thought and confessed that this was her first assignment. "But I have written little stories for the paper back in Denmark," she hastened to add, so they wouldn't think her a complete neophyte.

The afternoon had passed so quickly that when the grandfather clock chimed four, Karen jumped up from her seat, dropping her notebook and almost knocking her glass off the table. Before she could bend down, Obadiah had rescued the little book and handed it to her with a grunt. She was so unnerved by his manner that she almost lost her bag; but when she looked up to apologize for her clumsiness, she realized that his grunt was a smothered laugh and that he was looking at her with a friendly smile.

"Don't mind my New Hampshire Bear," Mildred giggled. "His growl is worse than his bite."

It was only when Karen went outside and saw the quilts still hanging on the line that she remembered to invite Mildred to come on Saturdays. "The neighbor women gather and bring their fancywork. I think they would be very pleased if you came. Bring your quilts and tell us how they're made."

All week, Karen worked on the Bullards' story and only finished it on Thursday, the day before they went to print. She asked Peter to edit the article.

"I wouldn't change a word," he chuckled. "I met the Bullards. Only you could have made that man of few words and his quiet wife come to life on the page."

"Don't mind Obadiah. New Englanders are reserved, but

very kind once you get to know them. And Mildred's not quiet at all."

"I'm delighted you like her. You need an older woman in whom to confide, someone who can fill the gap of family left behind. I hadn't realized that they're Quakers."

"I was waiting to surprise you." She almost said that Mildred reminded her of Elizabeth, their good friend in San Francisco, but she was afraid that she would cry. Peter would hate that.

3
The Lincoln Pioneer

Exactly every mile, the surveyors' lines slice the road running west from the county seat of Tyler to Benton Lake. Each slice defines a section road, but most are barely more than grass trails running ruler-straight north and south into the distance, cutting the land into precise mile-square sections. At the intersections lie the farms, each master of its own quarter section of land. Our little town of Lincoln is two miles west of the county seat of Tyler. At the outskirts lie a series of frame houses and, at the center, the Roman Catholic church glares across the intersection at that of the Swedish Lutherans, the only other brick buildings here being the post office and John's elementary school. A wide gravel road, dignified by a sign proclaiming it to be Main Street, runs south between this social heart of the town to the whistle stop railroad station next to the lone grain elevator. The two-block business section contains a general store, a café, and a few storefront offices, their owners residing conveniently above; our newspaper office is squeezed between that of a lawyer and a grain buyer.

Letter to Elizabeth Bendixen
from Karen Larsen
Lincoln, Minn. August 10, 1873

At the rear window of *The Lincoln Pioneer*, Peter straightened his back, aching from bending over the too-low table. He had just finished proofing Karen's column in the light from the alley, checking the title once again: *Meet Obadiah and Mildred Bullard from Nashua, New Hampshire,* and admiring the byline "by Karen Andersdatter." Finding no errors, he turned to the front page.

This sheet was always printed last, in case of last-minute breaking news, and just an hour ago the apprentice had arrived breathlessly from the railroad station waving the text of the speech Governor William Merriam had delivered that morning in Marshall. That article had been set just fine, but there was a mistake in the contents section in the lower right hand corner. They usually did not correct minor typos since changing even one word might mean that much of the column had to be reset; but this error was not minor and fortunately was at the end of the line.

Chuckling Peter called over the young man and pointed to the offending 'dottir' in the sentence 'See page 4 for the first of a regular column by Karen Andersdottir.' "Karl, I'm sorry but we have to fix this. As much as Mrs. Larsen likes you, she'd be upset at being made into a Swede." He would have teased the boy more but Karl Johnson was already stammering an apology, blushing with embarrassment.

"Don't take it so hard, we all make mistakes. It's just that Mrs. Larsen is looking forward to seeing her byline in the paper, so it needs to be right."

He smiled again and to make Karl feel better said, "Why don't you come to supper tomorrow night? Isn't there a certain Inger at our house who might be glad to see you?" The boy's cheeks deepened to ripe cherries and his lips parted in a grin as he mutely nodded.

"We're expecting Jesse Schneider this weekend and I know you'll find him interesting, so even if Inger pays you no attention, your trip won't be wasted."

Peter wiped his hands on an old rag, satisfied that the last frame of type had been set and the front page corrected. Once again, the Saturday issue of the newspaper would be ready the next day when the farm families came to town for their weekly shopping. Deftly steering around the racks of drying newsprint that nearly filled the room, he said to his partner, "Well Sam, I'll leave *The Pioneer* in your capable hands."

"You say that every week. Don't worry, Karl and I'll put the paper to bed; there's little more to be done. You go home to Karen and the children."

Sam said that every week too, knowing that Peter felt guilty about leaving his partner and their apprentice to do the messy work of collating, folding, and stacking the paper into neat piles for sale and delivery early in the morning. Bachelor Sam lived above the office and since Peter had both family and farm to call him home, they had agreed on this arrangement when they started the paper last year.

The partnership with Sam was agreeable in many ways, mostly because they shared a vision of a newspaper that would bind together the immigrants from many different countries. Peter, a world traveler from his days at sea, was conversant in many languages. He had a nose for a good story and his descriptions of scenes at sea and farming on the prairie were evocative. While Peter was the visionary, Sam Quincy was the craftsman, having learned the printing trade in his youth back in Boston. He was an expert in everything from mixing ink and tinkering with the balky press to correcting spelling and editing grammar. Karen was the third, silent partner, 'silent' in name only as she regularly voiced her opinions. Unknown to most of the town of Lincoln, her contribution to the enterprise, in addition to editing Peter's reporting, was to keep the accounts and track the growing number of advertisers and customers for their print services. Using her business experience from helping her father back home, they had begun to provide the growing printing needs of the thriving community that went well beyond the publication of the modest weekly newspaper.

They picked the name *The Lincoln Pioneer* not only because it described most of the citizens of Lincoln county and its namesake town, but because it was the same word in so many of the native languages of their readers. While the bulk of the news of town and state was printed in English, the paper had, from its inception, featured a column called *News from Home*, containing clips from newspapers and letters from the 'Old World,' brought in by readers. These contributions were printed in their original language and followed by Peter's skillful translation into English. Well, at least he edited and translated those written in Danish, Norwegian, Swedish, German, or Dutch. He did need to call for help from local clergy with the occasional Icelandic, Finnish, or Czech letter.

"My hometown paper back in Denmark had a similar column, but in reverse and called *Letters to Home*, written by Fanø seamen from far-flung ports of call," Peter told Sam when they first discussed their plans. "Karen sent them some of the stories that I wrote her from my travels. Imagine my surprise when I received the first copy on arrival in San Diego back in '74. Seeing my name in print so unexpectedly whetted my appetite to write more. But Karen improved my stories, editing them so they could stand alone and adding her own touches to make them more interesting."

"Look what trouble your stories have got you into now," Sam had said, when the three of them signed the partnership agreement. "Karen, you certainly have a way of inspiring people."

"Well that's my wife for you." Peter had grinned at Karen affectionately as he scrawled his signature at the bottom of the page, next to hers. "I never know what's next and I wouldn't have it otherwise."

Peter was cleaning the last of the ink off his arms at the pump in back of the printing office when Sam stuck his head out the door. He handed Peter several newspapers saying, "Here are the first off the press. I thought you would want extras because of Karen's column; it'll be the talk of the town. The idea that women not only read the newspaper but can also write will shake up the old fogies. My mother will be so pleased to receive hers. She'll brag all over Boston that one of my partners in the wilderness is a capable woman and be tickled pink by Karen's byline. It's a nice old-fashioned tradition for a modern woman."

He watched Peter climb into the waiting buckboard. "Just think, it's only been a year since we started the paper. We're doing very well."

"Yes, we've been lucky," Peter agreed. "Karen tells me that next month we'll be in the black."

Grinning, he flicked the reins lightly. As he turned out into Main Street, several friends greeted their popular neighbor. "Be sure to get tomorrow's newspaper," he called, holding the paper triumphantly over his head. "We have a new feature, written by Karen."

Once on the open road, he said to the horse, "Helmsman, set the course due east. We have a following wind and homeport is less than a league away. We'll make it before two bells and Madmor's call to dinner." The mare needed no encouragement to set off at a brisk trot, knowing from the lowering sun that they were homeward bound and being well-accustomed to her master's peculiar turn of phrase.

Peter relaxed in his seat; the warm August sun and light west wind was at his back, the limitless prairie spread before his contented eyes. The silk tassels of the corn rippled in the breeze; the man-high prairie grass in the swampy areas glowed in the late-afternoon light against the blue sky. "I'm a lucky man," he sighed. "Life is good; family and food wait at home, our beautiful home."

4
The Jewish Peddler

A road ran past the southwest corner of the homestead. It was no more than a prairie trail but its two parallel paths were already worn deep by the hoofs of many horses and oxen and the wheels of many wagons. The road came from the southeast and trailed away towards the northwest. There was much vacant land—school sections as the phrase went and railroad land—and the first roads ran where they would, often diagonally across the mile-square tracts of prairie.

A Human Life, Memories of a Pioneer by his "Oldest Boy"
Willard Dillman (1872-1938)

Minnesota, August 1890

Jesse Schneider was calling on his last few customers and looking forward to his Sabbath rest at the Larsen farm. The peddler's sun-browned face and hands bespoke his itinerant life, although his slight frame and narrow shoulders looked more like those of the scholarly rabbi that he had once been.

His final stop was at a small Norwegian homestead. The farmer, not knowing what to make of his black suit and hat, asked him in accented English whether he was a preacher.

"Just Jewish—a Jewish peddler," Jesse answered, his life's story being too complicated for casual explanation. Although he seldom spoke of his past, he always freely admitted being a Jew. Yet, so as not to call undue attention to his strangeness, he had cut his traditional side curls and he tucked in the ritual fringes on his undershirt whenever he was on the road. Like other newcomers to the Minnesota prairie, he was trying to live in peace within two cultures.

"Vat name?" one of the farmer's children asked in halting English, pointing to the mare.

"Bessie," he answered, breaking an apple in half and showing her how to feed it to the horse on the flat of her hand.

"Tickles!" she giggled and rubbed the soft muzzle.

Jesse smiled. The gentle mare was his secret weapon for breaking the ice. He saw the farmer's eyes narrow as if he were speculating whether this strange looking man, who was stupid enough to give a cow's name to a horse, was stupid about money also.

The mother emerged from the soddy and the little girl made her come and pat Bessie's silky mane. After a few words they concluded a trade of a cooking pot in exchange for some embroidery. "Hardanger," the woman called it, promising more on his return trip in a few weeks. Bartering like this had made his Marshall store flourish. Knowing the settlers were often cash poor, he traded necessities for farm produce and the work of their wives' hands. *Customers back in town will like this fancywork*, he thought.

Back on the road, Jesse barely had to twitch the reins before Bessie picked up the pace. She knew the way to the Larsen farm and was as anxious as her master for the green pastures and day of rest that awaited them with their Christian friends.

He thought about when he had first met Karen. *Was it really fifteen years ago?* The peaceful town in Ribe on the west coast of Denmark had been a welcoming refuge for his parents when they fled north from the unrest in Europe, but he had felt isolated and friendless in this new culture. Until he met Karen.

She was from the nearby island of Fanø but lived for a time with her aunt in town, and one day she entered his father's weaving shop to buy silk scarves. Jesse and his younger sister Hanna were at the counter, helping their mother who spoke little Danish. Although he was used to the strange looking women from Fanø coming to buy their traditional head covering, he had immediately sensed that Karen was different from the usual customer. Her hair was as modestly covered as his mother's, yet she carried herself with pride and the light in her eyes dreamt of adventure. With an air of independence that he had never seen before in a woman and curiosity about everything, she accepted his Jewish strangeness without fear.

That winter, they had become friends, albeit they made odd companions and never met without the company of his sister. Karen was tall and thin and, at her mother's insistence, still wore traditional Fanø dress with a scarf tied in a peak on her head that made her even taller. He was pale and, even then, he looked the Jewish scholar with corkscrews curling along a chin barely covered by a sparse beard. When Karen confided that she was hoping to marry First Mate Peter Larsen when he returned from sailing around the world, Jesse confessed that he was engaged to a girl in Lithuania that he had never met. Despite the difference in religion, over the years their friendship grew, surviving marriages, separation, and tragedy and enveloping both their families.

When Peter had told Jesse that he and Karen were emigrating from Denmark, Jesse realized that he too should seek a life in the New World. Eventually, Karen had persuaded him to leave the crowded streets of New York and move west to the fresh air of the Minnesota prairie with his family of wife, two children, sister Hanna, and her husband Saul.

"I'm no farmer," he had protested, but she had pointed out that Marshall was a fast-growing town, only 30 miles north of Lincoln. She was right, their store was doing well. *As always,* he mused. *Sarah and the children are happy; Saul is an excellent partner and businessman. Hanna has married a good man. If only her pregnancy goes well.*

That same afternoon, Karen and Lil-Anne climbed to the attic to ready the sewing room that was also their guestroom. They never knew exactly when Jesse would arrive, but today was Friday and when he was on the road, he liked to spend Sabbath with them. At the Larsen farm no one would question his strange ways and he could enjoy the privacy of the little room after days sleeping in the back of his peddler's wagon.

"It's so hot," five-year-old Lil-Anne complained, speaking Danish because they were alone.

Karen smoothed the crocheted counterpane and went over to open the window. Mother and daughter stood for a moment enjoying the cool breeze.

Lil-Anne stared down the road, trying to conjure the peddler's wagon. "No Uncle Jesse," she said, disappointed.

"He probably won't be here until later. About when Papa

comes home," Karen said. She tugged at the starched white curtain and smiled down at the impatient child. "Go pick some flowers. Ask one of the girls to put them in a vase."

Back downstairs, Karen opened the chest in the front hall. "John, come help me raise the flags."

"Aw, do I have to?" the nine-year old whined. "I just got home from school...."

"Jesse's coming," Karen explained, handing John the folded flags. The Danish flag was a present from home the first Christmas after she and Peter had settled in Minnesota, and they bought the Stars and Stripes when Lil-Anne, their American child, was born.

They walked down the drive to one of the two staffs flanking the entrance to the farm and she unwrapped the halyard. Tying the ends of the American flag and taking the Danish one from her son, she handed him the rope. "You raise it. Don't let it touch the ground!"

"I know, I know," John protested, pulling the flag to the top of the mast. "Let's just do this one."

"No, we do both. It's important that we remember who we are."

"For my birthday next month, I just want to be American," he insisted.

"We'll see."

"Aw, you always say that when you mean 'No'!"

By mid-afternoon, Karen looked out the kitchen window every few minutes, seeing the children impatiently wandering out to the road.

Finally, the dusty wagon turned the corner. She removed the pins that held her bun and shook out her corn silk hair until it fell most un-matronly down her back. Taking off her apron and smoothing the skirt of her favorite lavender shirtwaist, she wondered if he would notice the slight bulge. Although Jesse never looked directly at any woman other than his wife, he always saw everything.

Running out the door, she was just in time to hear the children's happy cries to get Jesse's attention. She couldn't make out the words but knew exactly what was said, because the exchange was always the same.

"*Onkel Jesse, så kom du da endeligt*—Uncle Jesse, you finally came!"

Jesse woke from his daydream and found that Bessie had automatically turned down the tree-lined lane towards the white clapboard farmhouse. Anne was jumping up and down by the side of the road, flanked by her more dignified, older brother.

"Nu Bessie, look who came out to meet," Jesse said in English, exaggerating his accent. " Zo Anne, come give Uncle Jesse a kiss. John, run tell your vonderful Momma vee is here."

"Aw, Uncle Jesse, you always forget how to speak Danish when you first get here," Anne teased, climbing up on the wagon and giving him a big smack on his whiskery cheek.

"I thought you were supposed to speak English during the day," Jesse grinned, this time in excellent Danish.

"Nah, only when anyone's around that don't speak Danish," Anne said. "Anyway you're special and your English ain't so good."

"Mom already knows you're here," John said jumping to sit beside his sister. "Move over, little squirt."

"Only Mama gets to call me little," the girl protested.

Noticing Karen standing in the doorway, Jesse called out, "Is that really you? Has the shy young girl that I met so long ago bloomed into this self-assured woman?"

"And is this tanned peddler, my scholarly friend?" Karen countered. "The children have been looking for you all day. Peter'll be home as soon as they get the newspaper to bed." She was about to give him a welcoming hug, but Jesse backed away, reminding her in time. Instead, she took the wheel of cheese that he handed her and said that she would fetch a chicken for his supper. Because of the Jewish dietary laws, Jesse would not eat at their table.

He turned to unharness Bessie but saw that Svend had beaten him to it. "I'll do that," he protested, knowing it was useless.

Svend grinned cheerfully and said in his thick Danish dialect, "John and A'll take care of Bessie. We'll wash the wagon up good, the way you likes for your Sunday. Later, A'll show you where A's fixed up a new bath place where Rabbi can wash."

"Thanks, but don't call me Rabbi," Jesse said automatically, also grinning.

"Enough rabbi for the likes of me," Svend mumbled as he gave John a whisk of straw with which to rub Bessie down.

Karen returned, laughing at the familiar interchange. "I put some fresh picked corn by the fireplace." Handing a squawking chicken to Jesse, she turned to the children and admonished, "You two, stay out of the way and come inside when Uncle Jesse tells you."

Jesse went to the back of the barn, the chicken struggling in his arms. Sharpening the ax, he expertly chopped off the head and hung it by its feet to let the blood drain. As a young man in Lithuania, his wife had insisted that his rabbinical studies exempted him from such domesticities, but on the prairie he had learned to butcher chickens to give him a change from the bread, cheese, and eggs that formed the bulk of his food on the road. But, wielding the ax always brought back that dreadful day....

Anne sat down next to him on the stoop of the back porch, hugging her rag doll while they chatted and he plucked and gutted the chicken. When he had swept up the stray feathers and congealed blood and buried them in the trash heap, he split some logs and piled them on the outdoor fireplace. A stick served as a spit for the chicken and he placed a pot of water on the lively fire for the corn. Retrieving dough from the back of the wagon where it had been rising since lunch, he divided it into rolls and put them on the shelf of his camp oven.

Satisfied that his solitary dinner could progress on its own, Jesse took a box of books from under the wagon seat and carried them up the stairs to the attic.

Anne tagged along, carrying a vase. "Me and Mama made your room ready, in case you came," she explained. "And I picked the flowers. They're called zinnias, but they don't smell as good as lavender."

"Yes, but they are so colorful," Jesse pointed out. He exchanged his hat for a yarmulke and found a towel and clean shirt. Hand-in-hand they went back down the stairs.

"Now, I need to get ready, so I'll see you after dinner." He looked fondly after the child as she scampered away.

Back outside, Svend proudly showed him his bath contraption by the barn. "Just pull this chain on side of the tank and you'll be in a summer rain," he explained. "A's warmed the water in the sun, so as Rabbi won't freeze his butt," and he laughed immoderately at his little joke.

"That's quite an engineering feat," Jesse said, admiring the handiwork. "Where would Karen and Peter be without you?"

"And where would A be without *Mistress Moon*? A'd be stuck shoveling shit back in Riwe," Svend answered bluntly. He always called Karen 'Mistress Moon', her nickname from the winter in Ribe when they had all met. It was the only English he ever spoke, perhaps not realizing that it was from the title of a Wordsworth poem.

"And I'd be lost in the slums of New York," Jesse countered.

"Rabbi better take off the cap, unless he means to wash that too," Svend reminded him and stepped out of the fenced area that gave privacy to the shower.

Jesse stripped off his rumpled clothes and washed thoroughly, grateful for the cooling 'summer shower.' Drying himself, he shook the dust from his pants and put them back on. Then he kissed the ritual fringes on his undershirt and slipped it over his head, smoothed out the wrinkles on his clean shirt, and buttoned it down the front allowing the fringes to show below the hem. After combing his hair, he carefully replaced the rescued yarmulke on his head and went back to finish preparing supper.

Judging that the chicken was ready, he added the corn to the simmering pot of water. He raked the rolls out of the camp oven and put raw carrots and a drumstick onto his plate. Wine poured into a mug and a clean towel placed over the rolls completed his preparations for welcoming Queen Sabbath. A veritable feast compared to his usual fare.

Peter's buggy turned down the lane from the main road, trailing a cloud of dust. *"Go' Javten, Kaptajn Storkeben,"* said Svend, catching the reins. *"Rabbien kom*—The Rabbi came," he said over his shoulder as he unharnessed the horse.

Peter jumped down from the wagon with a bundle of newspapers in his arms. He reached Jesse in a few strides of his long legs, and noting that the guest was ready to eat his dinner, said, *"Velbekomme*—Enjoy."

"*Shalom*," Jesse said, squinting up at his friend against the lowering sun. "I just finished saying *Kiddush*," he added, handing him a mug of wine. "I was hoping you'd be home in time to share a drink with me before Karen calls you to dinner."

Peter took off his hat, washed his hands in the waiting bucket, and sat down on a chopping block. "*Skaal,*" he said, raising his mug.

The two men sat in companionable silence while Jesse ate his chicken and Peter chewed on a roll and sipped the wine.

"The farm and children don't seem to have slowed Karen at all. With her hair flowing down her back, she doesn't look much older than when I first saw her," Jesse said.

Peter laughed, "She let her hair down and raised the two flags just for you. She knows what her menfolk like." Grinning to remove any hint of jealousy, he added, "But I saw her first."

"Every time I come, this place is bigger and busier," Jesse said, ignoring the jibe. "How many girls has she taken on now?"

"It's still only four, though sometimes they seem like twice that number!"

"And this is the woman who used to complain about how hard her mother made her work!" Jesse laughed.

"She claimed her mother was teaching her enough about housekeeping to run the king's palace. That's why she insists her girls only do housework in the morning and write and study English in the afternoon. 'Exercise for both body and brain' she calls it."

"I can just hear her! Before you know it she'll make it a Danish Folkschool. Except they aren't all Danes, are they?"

"No, Karen takes any nationality if she feels they'll benefit from being here. The girl who is to leave next month is an Indian half-breed. When Minnehaha first came, the mothers of the other girls were in an uproar and threatened to take them home. We couldn't tell whether they were afraid her relatives would scalp us or that she'd bring bedbugs. They soon adjusted though and she's the best one we've had this year—and beautiful!"

After a pause, he added, "If you think this place is busy today, you should see it on most Saturdays. She invites the neighborhood women to come for lunch and fellowship. We've outfitted the old barn with tables and chairs so they can do their needlework while they talk. 'Exercise for the jaw,' I call it. You should hear them babbling away in all different languages."

"A Babel Barn?"

"Exactly! Karen will like that. Tomorrow you'll have your Sabbath peace, though; we're all going to the neighbors' for their turn at threshing. It's a good thing we're done here, that steam engine makes an infernal racket—you might find it hard to think."

"Are you threshing boss again this year?" Jesse asked.

"Well, yes. The monster belongs to the cooperative, but I'm the one who keeps it going. The engine is just as cantankerous as the one aboard my first steamship."

"Little did you know that being a steamship captain would come in handy on the prairie!"

"The harvest is especially fine this year. The co-op has built a grain elevator in town, now we only have to find a buyer."

"I know the new buyer for the new Washburn Mills in Minneapolis. I'll speak to him when I get back to Marshall."

Anne came flying out the door and climbed up her father's back, "Mama says to come to dinner." From her high perch, she turned to Jesse and added equally imperiously, "I'll come and get you when we're done. Can I light the candles?"

"We'll see," Jesse said.

After a reminding cough from her father, Anne protested, "But I don't know how to say *please* in Danish."

"It isn't so much in the words as in your tone of voice," her father pointed out.

Peter picked up the bundle of newspapers at his feet and handed Jesse a copy off the top. "Here's tomorrow's *Lincoln Pioneer* to read while you wait. It's hot off the press, as we newspaper men like to say."

After dinner, Karen said to Minnehaha, "Peter and I'll be on the porch, if you need anything. John, please tell Uncle Jesse that we're done—just as soon as you've taken out the garbage."

She grabbed Lil-Anne's arm, as she was about to rush out the door. "Not you, Young Lady. You still have to help clear the table."

"Aw, but he promised I could light the candles. He did, didn't he Papa," Lil-Anne insisted.

"Jesse didn't promise. He said, 'We'll see'," Peter told her firmly. Relenting, he added, "You can both tell Jesse that it's time."

"Girls, don't forget to put up the milk for breakfast yogurt," Karen fussed.

"Yes, Mistress" the two girls chorused with patient grins.

Peter put his arm around his wife's waist and led her gently out the door, teasing, "You've trained them well enough to fix the king's breakfast. Let them be."

As they went, they heard the children arguing, "You lit them last time," "No, it's my turn," until finally the echoes of: "mine," "no, mine" faded away.

5
The Children's Hour

Between the dark and the daylight,
When the night is beginning to lower,
Comes a pause in the day's occupations,
That is known as the Children's Hour.

A sudden rush from the stairway,
A sudden raid from the hall!
By three doors left unguarded
They enter my castle wall!

The Children's Hour
Henry Wadsworth Longfellow (1807-1882)

Karen sank gratefully down on the porch swing.

Peter set it gently in motion and whispered, "Will you also put down your hair for me, if I ask you nicely?"

"Later...," she chuckled, blowing in his ear. *He still does that to me. Makes me weak in the knees. Just with his voice.*

A procession came around the corner of the house and, blushing, she stood up to greet them. Jesse was leading, carrying the wine in his extended arm like a trophy, Lil-Anne came next, firmly clasping two candles in her pudgy hands, and John followed with the brass holders.

Peter led everyone into the dining room, but Karen drew him back into the shadows to watch. Jesse placed the candles in their holders on a little side table and sat down on a chair with Lil-Anne in his knees so the candles would be at her height. "It's a woman's job to light the candles, but you're still too young.

Instead, you and I will say the prayer together and John will light them for us."

Tenderly he draped his handkerchief over the child's head and, while John lit the candles from Papa's match, they chanted together, as he had taught her, *"Baruch atau Adonoi…"*

Guiding her small hand, Jesse covered both their eyes and prompted, his voice breaking slightly, "Now ask for blessings for Mama and Papa."

Karen blinked away tears at the sight of her friend's dark head bent over the blonde braids. She felt his pain, the pain that never quite left his eyes, and put her hand protectively over her skirt, on the life that only she could feel. *We'll tell him tomorrow, Rachel.*

Peter put his arm around her shoulder and smiled slightly. Meeting her eyes he mouthed, "Rachel it is."

Leaving the candles to burn out by themselves, they all went out to the porch where it was cooler. Jesse settled in the wicker chair across from the swing. He pulled Lil-Anne onto his lap; John sat on the floor next to him and Jesse rested a hand on his shoulder.

Peter poured wine for each of the adults and raised his own glass, *"Skaal* and welcome, friend."

"Tell us about the family," Karen prompted.

"Shining Sarah is a gift from heaven. Without her, I could never leave the boys as much as I do; they're lucky to have such a mother. Jonathan's a big help in the store, and a scholar like his Grandpa. But David.…" He sighed. "Always running off with his friends to cause trouble instead of studying. But like an angel he sings, like a real David.…"

"But he's only seven. Isn't he too young to be serious?" Peter protested.

"He does fine in school where they don't expect much, but has no interest in learning at home with his brother and me. His Hebrew's very bad."

"He'll be all right. You'll see," Karen said. "Maybe he'll suddenly catch fire, like my cousin Jens. Did I tell you he's been accepted to show at the Royal Academy of Art in Copenhagen?"

"I'm not so sure I want my son to be an artist," Jesse laughed. "A Jewish artist has problems."

"Well if my brother Christian could become a Classics

scholar at the University of Copenhagen, why not David? Or maybe he'll be a famous singer," Karen said.

"Speaking of scholars, " Peter interjected. "Pastor Jensen asked me to invite you to church next time you came. He'd like you to give another talk."

"I'd like that," Jesse replied and added with a twinkle in his eye, "I don't get to preach in a church very often, especially not in Danish."

"Perfect," Karen exclaimed. "There's a picnic afterwards, at Lake Benton. Please come." Anne jumped up and down on Jesse's lap clapping her hands in approval.

Jesse mumbled about needing to start on the road right after church, but Karen would not hear of it, "If you're worried about the food being kosher, we'll have plenty of corn and maybe fish, if the men catch anything."

John, usually the quiet member of the family, said, "And you could come fishing with Daddy and me."

"I really can't," Jesse replied regretfully. "Bessie and I have a long way to go that day."

Turning to Anne who was about to protest that she should be allowed to go fishing with the men, he said, "Tomorrow, may I borrow you for a walk. Will you come with old Uncle Jesse?"

"Can we go down to the river and pick flowers?" Anne asked eagerly. "Can we? I'm supposed to go to the Paulsen farm for the threshing, but stupid Jakob Paulsen always pulls my braids."

Karen protested, "Everyone is to help serve dinner to the crew...."

"I'll take care of Uncle Jesse," Anne interrupted. "He needs me so he won't sit in the poison ivy again."

Karen could only relent.

It was almost time for the children to go to bed but John begged a story first, "Tell us about the real David, the one who sang."

"Your Mama is the storyteller," Jesse protested. "Karen, please?" and everyone settled down to listen.

"A long, long time ago," she started, "David was king in Israel, but before that he was a shepherd boy. He watched his Papa's sheep and sang songs to the moon and the stars; songs so wonderful that we still sing them today. He was the youngest son of Jesse. One day, the Prophet Samuel came to Jesse's house and asked to meet his sons. Only the six older ones were home as David was out with the sheep."

"Where was David's sister? Was she herding sheep too, like you did, Mama?" Anne interrupted.

Jesse hugged the child closer and whispered, "Hush n' listen. There's no sister in this story."

Karen continued, "One by one, Samuel examined each boy and rejected them all. David was sent for. All dusty from the field, he came. Samuel knew this was the right one and anointed him king."

"Did he go to the palace right away and start bossing around his older brothers?" Lil-Anne asked eagerly.

"No, silly," John said. "He had to fight Goliath first."

"Samuel should've picked his sister. She was much smarter," Lil-Anne said, as usual having the last word.

Jesse laughed. "Maybe next time you should tell the story."

After the children were in bed, the adults went back to the porch. Jesse picked up the folded copy of *The Lincoln Pioneer*. "This is the best issue so far. I don't know how Peter has time to run the farm and a newspaper too."

"The secret of being a good captain is delegating to the first mate! Olaf Iverson is an excellent farm manager, leaving me free to work on the paper. Don't forget, I have two excellent partners: Sam and Karen."

"I forgot that Karen is your 'silent partner' and now a reporter. She must have taken lessons from you in delegating!"

"Not so silent! And now the public will hear her voice."

"I only glanced at her article about the Bullards. I want to read it more carefully tomorrow." Jesse shook his head and repeated, "I don't know how you both do all this."

"I've been wanting to write about our neighbors," Karen explained. "Most people don't understand the different cultures that are represented in our readership and how interesting their stories are. Mildred Bullard is a fascinating woman. So educated and intelligent. You should stop by their farm on your way home."

Jesse turned salesman. "I'll do that. See if they need anything." Then he made a startling announcement, "I'm thinking this will be my last summer on the road and this will be my last round."

Karen looked upset and Peter exclaimed. Jesse explained that the store was doing well and now that most of the settlers preferred to trade in the towns developing along the railroad, he didn't really need to travel any more. "I'll miss meeting the new immigrants though, watching them move from tiny shacks to clapboard houses, and seeing the children bloom, the parents stand up straighter. Karen'll just have to write about them in her new column and send the paper to Saint Paul. That's where we're thinking of moving."

Karen was surprised. She knew that, as much as Jesse regretted the long absences from his family, he found the silence and openness of the prairie helped conquer the daemons from his past.

"How is Hanna?" She asked, referring to Jesse's sister who also lived in Marshall. "Is she still homesick for Ribe?"

"Now that she's finally in a family way, she seems happier although the pregnancy weighs on her. I don't know what I'd do without Saul as a partner, he has such a way with the customers. But I wish he were a better Jew. He's good to Hanna, would give her anything, but has no interest in the traditions, says they're too much trouble in an isolated place like Marshall. It makes it hard for Hanna, and she worries about the child and how he is to grow up. That's one reason we want to move. To be part of a Jewish community."

"She's always welcome here. The fresh country air and food would do her good. We'd see that she had what she needs. Saul could come when her time is near."

"Don't you have enough on your hands?" Jesse said, not quite refusing. "I hear you have quite a crowd coming to your Saturday do's. And all your girls...."

"Hanna's no trouble. It would be good for the girls to hear about city life." Then she dropped what was an old un-winnable argument.

They talked quietly of the weather and the good harvest, how a cool July had helped the wheat, and that the corn liked the heat of August. The hard times around the country this past year had blessedly passed them by and they hoped the general economy was in recovery.

Finally they just sat in silence sipping the last of the wine and admiring the last of the sunset. Karen looked at Peter sitting next to her on the swing, his long legs stretched out and his callused hand covering her own. She thought he looked tired. *No wonder, he spent the morning tinkering with the threshing machine and an afternoon helping put the paper to bed.* She glanced at Jesse and was surprised to find him studying her face. He turned away to watch the heat lightening.

My two best friends, Karen thought.

6
Sabbath Peace

For the Lord thy God bringeth thee into a good land, a land of brooks of water, of fountains and depths that spring out of valleys and hills;

A land of wheat, and barley, and vines, and fig trees, and pomegranates; a land of oil, olive and honey;

A land wherein thou shalt eat bread without scarceness, thou shalt not lack any things in it; a land whose stones are iron, and out of whose hills thou mayest dig brass.

When thou hast eaten and art full, then thou shalt bless the Lord thy God for the good land which he hath given thee.

Deuteronomy, 8: 7-10

As was his custom, Jesse stayed alone in his room Saturday morning away from the bustle of the family's household chores. After reciting the Sabbath prayers and eating a Spartan breakfast, he studied *Talmud*. Then, turning to the *Torah*, he read the familiar words of Deuteronomy in which the Lord told Moses about the good land that he was going to give to the Hebrews, the land of milk and honey.

Late morning, Anne clumped up the stairs to his room to announce that lunch would be waiting for him in the springhouse but that she was not to linger and disturb his peace. Then she gave him a hug and disappeared out the door before he had a chance to thank her. Grateful for the quiet, he continued his studies until about noon when his growling stomach awoke him to the time. He went down the stairs and into the warm August day, passing Karen at the front of the house where she was supervising the girls loading hampers of food onto the big hay wagon.

Catching sight of Jesse, she smiled. "Good morning. I hope your lunch is all right. There's fresh plain bread, cottage cheese with dill, and hardboiled eggs; the plate is from your wagon."

"Bless your thoughtfulness, and have a good day," he answered, knowing that she had taken care that his lunch was kosher and proper for him to eat.

On his way to the back of the house, he passed Svend trundling a can of buttermilk down the hill from the spring house. He sat down under the shade of the elm tree that Peter had planted soon after they settled on the land. It had now reached a size to provide welcome shade from the August sun.

Above the creaking of the windmill that pumped water into the springhouse cistern, he faintly heard Karen's, "Girls, you ride with Svend. Peter and I'll follow," and then Svend's, "The Rabbi is up by the springhouse, *Kaptajn Storkeben*." The rumble of the wagon and the cheery voices of the girls faded into the distance.

Peter came striding up the path to the tree. "*Velbekomme*. May I join you?"

"Last I looked, this was your house," Jesse joked, and patted the grass beside himself.

Peter proudly handed his friend this week's newspaper folded to the proper page and said, "Did you have a chance to read Karen's debut as an American correspondent?" He ducked into the springhouse to pour himself a cup of cold water. Returning, he stretched his legs comfortably on the ground, his face anticipating Jesse's words of praise.

Jesse did not disappoint. "I saw it earlier. Her writing is very fine. Who would've thought that Michel Mogens actually managed to teach her some English back in Ribe?"

"That pretentious poet only got her started. When we lived in San Francisco, that's when she really learned."

"Karen seems to have made friends with this Mrs. Bullard. I'm delighted. She needs a *confidante*."

"I hadn't realized that Mrs. Bullard is a Quaker until I read the article. Karen didn't mention it. Wanted to surprise me. We had a dear Quaker friend in San Francisco, who was such a help during our tragic time there."

Peter shifted his legs as if uncomfortable at the memory. He changed the subject. "Watch out, she'll probably write about you next! Can't you just see it, 'Jesse, the Prairie Rabbi'?"

"I keep telling you, I'm not a Rabbi," Jesse protested but laughed.

Staring at the grass between his feet, Peter suddenly blurted, "I've never told anyone this, but I saw Karen in that lavender dress she wore to the Bishop's party in Ribe."

"You mean, her first regular dress? The one that had Michel Mogens mooning and quoting Wordsworth? She wore the dress after you came home?"

"As best I can figure, I saw her in that dress about a month before she actually wore it. You study ancient mysteries, *the Kabalah*, isn't it called? Perhaps you can explain what happened. It's way out of my territory."

"You mean you had a vision? That doesn't sound like you."

"In a way. The dress and the woman wearing it were real enough, but I swear, I saw Karen. I met Lydia Kensington the first time I was in San Francisco, a temptress that bewitched me. She looked like Karen and was wearing a dress just like that. Not that there weren't other girls—you understand about sailors and foreign ports." Peter got a dreamy look in his eyes, "Later there was a lovely little Hawaiian girl with a nut-brown body and black hair...but that's another story. Anyway, Lydia had a strange power; she appeared out of nowhere and then vanished. If she hadn't left, I might well have stayed in California and courted her. By comparison, Karen was but an innocent child. When one of her letters finally caught up with me in Australia, months later, I came to my senses. She wrote about wearing a lavender dress to a party and I saw her again, this time in a dream. I finally understood what Karen really meant to me and what a treasure she was. A large part of Lydia's attraction was the physical resemblance, but that was also what finally repelled me because she was a wicked lady—totally unlike Karen. How could I have been so dumb? Well, my mystical friend, what d'you say?"

"Even if I were a Rabbi, I couldn't grant you absolution," Jesse teased. "But if it makes you feel better to confess your youthful indiscretions, they're safe with me. Isn't it a blessing that even the young can come to their senses?"

Peter rose from the ground. "I really just came to remind you that we're expecting you to preach tomorrow."

"I haven't forgotten, friend. But I really don't know what I'm supposed to say!"

"You'll think of something."

Anne appeared out of nowhere. "Papa, Mama says it's time to leave."

"I guess that means it's time for our walk," Jesse said, rising also and brushing crumbs from his beard. "Heron, ready or not, here we come."

That evening, Jesse sat by the window in the growing darkness of the attic room, the book he could no longer see to read resting in his lap. The children came bounding up the stairs, falling over each other in their eagerness. "Nu, vat is all dis noise?" he mocked in English, smiling at the breathless children. He expected them; this was their Saturday evening ritual.

"Three stars, we saw the first three stars. The Sabbath is over," they chorused.

"Mama says bring down your cup for coffee," John added.

They watched in respectful silence as Jesse honored the beginning of the next week by taking out a braided candle and a small box of spices. He poured a little wine into a saucer and lit the candle. Inhaling the aroma of the spices, he chanted, *"Baruch atau Adonoi...."* After extinguishing the candle in the wine and putting everything away, he let the children pull him down the stairs, grabbing his cup on the way out.

There was a quiet knock on the front door just as he reached the bottom of the stairs. Before Jesse could think to open it, a blonde girl beat him to it. On the step stood a young man, bowler hat in one hand, a drooping bouquet of flowers clutched in the other.

The blushing girl was squeezing through the door, when Karen called from the next room, "Elsbeth, is that Fred? You two stay on the porch where we can see you."

"Was that really Fred?" Jesse asked Anne, grinning beside him. "I thought your brother lived here."

"Nah, Mama says he's too old now and has to live across the road with the farm hands. He's courting Elsbeth."

"I can see that."

"He's not really my brother," Anne whispered as if she were imparting a secret. "He's adopted."

"I know," Jesse whispered back. "But still, it's good to have two brothers."

"Sometimes."

Although the next day was Sunday, the farm was up with the sun. The essential chores of milking and feeding livestock were quickly done, but then breakfast had to be cleared and picnic baskets of food for the afternoon outing prepared. By the time Jesse had unwrapped the phylacteries from his arms and packed them away with his prayer shawl, the flags had been raised and everyone spruced up for their various houses of worship.

Karen came into the yard looking very elegant in a pale blue dress with little sprigs of flowers and a lace-trimmed straw bonnet. Nature had received liberal help from a curling iron to make two loose curls that softened her square jaw line and the matronly bun at the nape of her neck. The four girls followed, dignified in their Sunday best—all except Minnehaha who was barefoot. Her bonnet dangled by its ribbons from one hand and high topped black shoes from the other. Inger and Bridget crossed the road to ride with the Iversons and some of the farmhands to the Swedish and Catholic churches in Lincoln. Minnehaha and Karen were to ride with Jesse, but everyone else going to Tyler climbed into Peter's wagon.

"I wanna go with Uncle Jesse," Anne protested.

"You had him all to yourself yesterday afternoon," Karen said firmly. "Now it's my turn."

"And Minnehaha doesn't have much Danish," she whispered to Jesse as she climbed up at the front of his wagon. "We can talk in perfect privacy."

Minnehaha jumped into the back and sat with her bare feet swinging over the edge, her high top black shoes lined up beside her and bonnet safely in her lap. Turning into the road, Jesse smiled and glanced sideways at Karen. "You have your hands full with your girls. Even the quiet ones keep you hopping."

Karen laughed. Deliberately, she didn't use anyone's name so as not to be understood by their passenger. "That's why I'll only shepherd four at a time."

"I noticed the love-birds last night. Do you always keep

such a tight reign on the girls when they have callers?"

"I promise the mothers that their daughters won't get in trouble while they're under my roof, but they sometimes act a little wild in their first freedom away from home. I now understand why Mam tried to keep Peter and me as far apart as possible. I hated her for it at the time, but now I know. That's one reason I insist the girls have to be eighteen before they can come, not that they're much more sensible, but at least they're old enough to decide for themselves. Not like Peter and me—I was way too young."

"The blonde seems too shy to be wild. And was that really your foster-son? He's all grown up."

"He'll be twenty-one in the spring. It's hard to believe it's been five years since...." Karen's voice broke, but she quickly recovered. "You think the blonde is quiet, you should've seen the dark beauty, our chaperone riding back there, when she first came. Afraid of everyone, she was; like a big-eyed fawn, trying to hide in the grass by being very still. Her mother died when she was five and both her peoples have rejected her, whatever the color of their skin. Her father's done his best, but he's not much of a farmer and his new wife is as bad as Cinderella's stepmother. The girl has really bloomed in the last few months. It's almost time for her to leave us."

"Where are you placing her?"

"I'm working on the lady with the quilts." Karen laughed.

She wondered how to ask Jesse about Rachel, but he seemed to read her mind, "Speaking of trouble, when will the little one arrive?"

Her hand automatically went to her lap. "How did you know?"

"You have that special bloom about you and a way of holding your hand, as if to keep him safe."

"It'll be sometime in late March. But how could you tell? You never look at me," she protested.

She hesitated. *How does he always know everything? How best to ask him? He never talks about her. Anymore than I talk about....*

Finally she whispered, "We want to call her Rachel, but not if you mind."

Jesse's eyes clouded over, but he recovered quickly and said softly, "I'd like that." He smiled. "Are you sure it'll be a girl?"

"I have a feeling."

They rode in silence, each deep in thought, she recalling

their winter in Ribe. I *was waiting for Peter, even then.* "Remember that crazy outing on Christian's birthday, that last time we were all together?"

"How can I forget? We were well chaperoned there too. Let's see, there were your brother Christian and his friend. Then your cousins, my sister Hanna, and the soulful Michel and his sister."

"Don't forget our faithful Svend, our coachman. That makes ten with you and me. We were certainly a jolly bunch!"

"You and Michel knew all the songs."

More silence. "Michel proposed to me. Did you know that?" Karen asked. "Not then, but months later."

"Yes, he said he was going to. We became pretty good friends after that day. You were right, we did have a lot in common and when you left Ribe to go home, we had you to talk about. What did you tell him?"

"I was tempted, it was very romantic to be courted by a poet and Peter was at the other side of the world. My mother was thrilled at the thought of someone, anyone, who wasn't a seaman. Then I realized that Michel was a dreamer and not very practical. Peter can seem casual and impulsive but he really has both feet planted on the bridge. When he came home, I was glad I had turned Michel down—one look at Peter and I knew; he was the right one all along."

"I almost asked you myself," Jesse confessed. "I had a fantasy of us running the weaving shop in Ribe together, but when Michel told me he was going to propose, I realized it was an impossible dream. That was when I finally agreed to go to Lithuania and marry Deborah, as my father wanted. Then the minute I saw her, I too knew that here was my soul's mate. It was a good life, or would have been if not for...."

Karen looked at him in surprise. She envisioned herself living in Ribe and selling scarves to her old Sønderho neighbors. Jesse was in the next room, weaving at his father's old loom while small dark boys with black yarmulkes and brown-eyed girls in Fanø bonnets played on the floor. *Talk of impossible dreams! It's almost funny. All these years and I never suspected.*

"You can smile and shake your head now, but it didn't seem very funny to me then," Jesse said ruefully.

"Don't you know that I'll always love you? You're my best friend," she exclaimed, forgetting herself and squeezing Jesse's arm.

43

By this time they had arrived in Tyler and dropped Minnehaha in front of the Episcopal Church, she having transformed into a very respectable and demure young lady in black shoes and bonnet. Then they drove back across the railroad track where Peter and the Danish portion of the Larsen farm were waiting outside the Danebod church. As they all went in, Jesse hung back to sit in the last pew. He stared uncomfortably at the statue of Jesus on top of the steps to the altar. *Why does everyone always tell me their troubles? I can't even settle my own soul.*

After a hymn and some prayers it was time for the sermon, and Pastor Jensen introduced Jesse. He checked that his yarmulke was on straight and walked up the aisle. The congregation turned in their seats to see who their visitor was. Some, recognizing the peddler from his visits to their farms, smiled. A black-clad widow that he did not recognize sat in the front row looking prim and forbidding.

"Here we go," he mumbled as he passed Karen. Whether in explanation or as a prayer for inspiration, he wasn't quite sure.

He was silent for a minute, wondering how to begin. Then remembering the passage in Deuteronomy that he had read the day before, he spoke slowly and simply in Danish, "For the Lord thy God has brought us into a good land, a land of lakes of water, of wheat, and barley. That's not quite how the Fifth Book of Moses goes, but it seems fitting here on the prairie." He paused until the congregation nodded and smiled as they realized what he was saying.

"My old teacher, the Rebbe should only see me now!" he said softly. He raised his eyes and focused on the beams where motes danced in an errant sunbeam. As if he were addressing the ghost of his Lithuanian mentor, he continued, but more loudly. "Reb, this is a good land where people can be free. We may be a little short of fig trees and the hills are not much higher than the valleys, but the Lord has given us a New World and we bless Him for it, each in our own way."

Then looking at his rapt audience, he continued, "As I travel the Minnesota prairie, I see how new settlers from many lands have taken this good land and made it bloom. Especially when I visit my friends, Karen and Peter Larsen, I am impressed by how they honor the Lord's gift by sharing their joy with all their neighbors. Let us learn from them. Unlike at the Tower of Babel where strange languages separated the people, let the Lord smile at our joy as we celebrate our differences and accept our new common lives. I know no better celebration than the Larsen Babel Farm where isolation and strangeness can be forgotten over threshing and fancywork."

Even the prim widow's mouth softened as she understood his last words.

During Jesse's sermon, Karen looked at her Jewish friend standing next to the marble statue of Jesus. The Danish sculptor Thorvaldsen carved the famous original for the cathedral in Copenhagen, and this smaller reproduction had been installed here with great fanfare and many homesick tears. Jesus looked down at the congregation, holding out arms, his hands palms up in welcome as if he were calling the tribe of Danes together.

Suddenly she too felt homesick, not sure whether she longed for the sand dunes of her island home or the happy years when she had sailed with Peter. Was she like her immigrant neighbors? Was she so homesick for Denmark that she cried at the very reminder? She thought about the good land that Jesse talked about and the blending of cultures that made her new home. *Why do we think that being Danish is somehow better, our language somehow richer? Has Danebod forgotten what we left behind: the rural poverty, the lack of opportunity, and the constricting traditional society? Did we really think it would be all milk and honey and are disillusioned by the hard work? If it is all just for the children why do we strive to keep the past alive? Why are we not content?*

When Jesse finished, the Pastor Jensen rose. "Thank you, Mr. Schneider. Your faithfulness to Jewish traditions is an example to us all that, different as we are and far from home, we can be true to our own heritage and yet be friends."

As Jesse made his way back down the aisle, she heard murmurs of, "What a nice young man," "So handsome," and "I never realized Jews read the Bible." Karen looked back and saw that he had reached the door. He turned and grinned at her; he too had heard the last comment.

Pastor announced the concluding hymn, her favorite by Grundtvig about the golden mouth of morning. She looked at the statue again and, suddenly feeling at peace, reached for Peter's hand as they rose to sing. *If only we can always be this close.*

7
Calling the Tribes Together

On the Mountains of the Prairie,
On the great Red Pipe-stone Quarry,
Gitche Manito, the mighty,
He the Master of Life, descending,
On the red crags of the quarry
Stood erect, and called the nations,
Called the tribes of men together.

The Song of Hiawatha
Henry Wordsworth Longfellow (1807-1882)

The yard was humming with women's voices and the excited shrieks of children playing tag. Saturdays were the common market day when many farmers came to town and, all morning, wagons had been pulling up to the barn at the back of the house. After dropping off the women and younger passengers, the wagons proceeded into town, farmers at the reins. While their husbands were in town exchanging gossip and buying supplies, their wives met in the Larsen barn for fancywork, fellowship, and food. At first skeptical, the women had finally been impressed and delighted at how well it worked. They brought food to be shared and even the newest immigrant with the poorest English could demonstrate a skill learned in the old country: some fancy embroidery stitch or some novel way to prepare a stew. By now, the yard was humming with women's voices and the excited shrieks of children chasing each other.

Karen was in the yard welcoming each wagon when the Bullards arrived. "I'm so pleased that you could come," she exclaimed, pulling Lil-Anne forward. "Mildred and Obadiah, I'd like you to meet my daughter, Anne."

The child, knowing what was expected, gave a little bob as she shook the older woman's hand, then turned to Obadiah, still at the reins, and repeated her curtsy.

Mildred smiled. "What lovely manners."

Knowing that next the guest would ask about her age, Anne blurted, "I'm five. Mama says I'm not to call you Mrs. Bullard and that you're the quilt lady that she wrote about in Papa's newspaper."

Karen was about to apologize but saw that Mildred was amused rather than insulted by Lil-Anne's bluntness. Instead she called the girls over for introductions.

"Mildred Bullard, I'd like you to meet two of my girls. Bridget is Irish and Elsbeth's parents are from Denmark."

"It's easy to tell who is who," Mildred chuckled, looking from the blonde curls of one to the red hair of the other. "Are you from Dublin?"

"No, County Galloway. On the west coast."

"And what a charming brogue you have." Turning to Elsbeth she asked, "Are you from Fanø, like Karen? Did I pronounce that right?"

"Almost. I was born in Iowa, but my parents are from Holstebro, a small town on the mainland, north of Fanø."

"Girls, take the children down to the orchard. Lil-Anne too, before she gets in trouble," Karen said and explained that these two girls were assigned to keep the children entertained while their mothers met in the barn.

The other two girls appeared.

"This is Inger and I'm Minnehaha," the Indian girl said taking the initiative. "Inger is in charge of food and I'm to help you with the quilts."

"I brought a traditional New England corn pudding. I hope no one will think it too strange," Mildred said handing the Swedish girl her contribution to lunch. She turned back to the Indian girl, eyebrows raised questioningly.

"We call her Minnehaha although her Christian name is Ruth Samuelson," Karen explained. "We recently read Longfellow's *Song of Hiawatha* and what started out as a tease, stuck. She seems to like her new name."

"As long as I can call you Nokomis, the daughter of the Moon" Minnehaha shot back with a grin.

"Don't mind my children," Karen rasped, bending her back as if she were indeed Hiawatha's ancient grandmother. Then in her normal voice, "They've been prattling all this nonsense ever since we went camping at Pipestone by the new Indian School. We thought Minnehaha should learn more about her heritage and it's not far from here. It was a big disappointment—the Federal School has no interest in Indian culture, just in 'civilizing' the children. We've had to do our own studies."

"I never did like 'Ruth' anyway," said the object of the kidding, flipping her braids out of the way. "That's all they would call me at Saint Mary's, my American school in Faribault." She picked up a bundle of quilts from the back of the wagon and carried them into the barn. Karen and Mildred followed, carrying the rest.

"Mid-afternoon?" Obadiah questioned as he turned the wagon.

"Yes," Mildred answered and would have said more when she saw the sign over the door. "Babel Barn, indeed," she chuckled.

"Peter put that up yesterday," Karen laughed. "He wanted to write it as Babble, but I wouldn't let him. He loves puns. Just wait until you meet everyone else, and you'll see what he means."

Mildred followed Minnehaha to the back of the barn where a table and two chairs faced rows of benches along other trestle tables. The girl showed her where she had piled the quilts. "Such beautiful colors."

Mildred added her armful to the pile. "Please help me spread them out so everyone can see the different patterns."

When they finished, she sat down in one of the waiting chairs and studied the crowd as she let the babble of different languages wash over her. She glanced at Minnehaha. *What a lovely young lady. So quick and confident. I wonder....*

Karen was making her way up the aisle between the tables, stopping to speak to several of the women sitting on the benches. She stood next to Mildred's chair. "Please welcome Mildred Bullard to our Babel Barn," she announced in English, pronouncing the biblical name with a short 'a' in the European manner.

When the last echo of applause and laughter had rippled through the room, she continued, "Mildred Bullard has recently moved here from New Hampshire and has brought some of her lovely quilts. She will explain to us how these traditional New England patterns are made." She repeated each sentence in Danish slowly enough so the Swedes and Norwegians in the room could understand while others whispered translations into a scatter of other languages.

Mildred rose, and, quickly understanding the language limitations of her audience, spoke simply, pausing for Karen and others to translate. Asking Minnehaha to hold up a small baby quilt she explained, "This is the easiest and quickest to make. It is called 'Nine Patch'." She pointed to each of the squares, counting them in turn to illustrate her point. "Each square is a different fabric and a good way to use up odd scraps. Choosing them to harmonize sets the theme; this one is for my youngest grandson who likes lively colors." She went on to name the next three patterns: 'Boston Common', 'Crazy Quilt', and 'Log Cabin'.

"The crazy quilt was given to me as a farewell present when we left Nashua. Each of my friends made a square out of silks and velvets and embroidered her initials in the center. Then the squares were joined and decorated with featherstitching. Finally the wool stuffing and muslin backing were added and the three layers tied together at the corners with knots of wool yarn."

She went on to explain that the popular log cabin pattern was the most flexible. She passed around strips of fabric joined to illustrate different stages of assembly and showed how the squares could be arranged in a variety of placements by contrasting the light and dark fabrics in stripes, zigzags, or a checkerboard.

"The log cabin pattern is particularly good for a community project because much of the work can be done at home. If everyone contributes fabric scraps and the layout is planned well, the cutting of the strips can be carried out in a short time. The final joining and quilting can be completed by the group in a few sessions."

Mildred sat down to a round of applause.

Karen rose again, "Wasn't that fascinating? Perhaps we should all bring in our scraps next time and ask Mildred to help us with some quilt projects. I am quite sure that Jesse Schneider would be pleased to sell anything from the Babel Barn Ladies in his store in Marshall. Now let us eat the lovely food that everyone has brought."

That evening, everyone was crowded around the kitchen table, not just the family, but also the four girls and several of the farm hands. Sam Quincy and Karl Johnson from the newspaper had also come to supper, but Svend was conspicuously absent. He had staunchly resisted all attempts to teach him English, claiming he was too old and perfectly happy doing whatever he was told. Peter and Karen had urged him to move to town, where his gift for tending horses would have easily found him a job and he could raise his own family. "Kaptajn Storkeben is the best master that A could want and Mistress Moon's family is enough for me," he always said. His nicknames for her and Peter were his idiosyncratic compromise between respect and love for his adopted family. When Peter had told him there was to be a planning meeting after supper, he still refused to come. "Just tell me what you decide," he had said.

When everyone was seated, Peter introduced the visitors and asked each of the others to say a little something about who they were. Each of the girls gave her name and background. Then the two young men spoke. Hans was one of the hands and Fred, as Sam knew, was the Larsen's adopted son.

Five years ago, the family that owned the farm across the road had been stricken with diphtheria and all but Frederik had died. Rather than see the child sent to an orphanage, Peter and Karen had adopted the lad and taken over the farm, holding it in trust for the boy. Fred, his Danish name having been anglicized, was now a strapping young man of twenty whose eyes frequently strayed across the table to where blushing Elsbeth sat staring at her hands.

"I'm surprised to see you here," Sam teased. "I thought young men like yourselves would prefer spending Saturday evening in town."

"The food's better," Hans grinned, stealing a glance at Minnehaha. "And the scenery," Fred chuckled, looking at Elsbeth. The two girls pretended not to notice.

Maybe it's just as well that the men live across the way—separated from the girls, Sam thought.

While the dishes were being cleared and after-dinner coffee poured, Peter explained that they were to have a family meeting that evening.

"Do you want us to leave?" Sam asked.

"I'd like you to take notes. Just don't publish anything until we give you leave."

"Of course not, Partner," the newspaperman answered.

He caught Anne around the waist and pulled her onto his lap. "Hello, Lil-Anne. Remember your Uncle Sam?"

"I'm not little," the child protested. "I'm almost six and I'm going to have a little sister soon."

So that's the news I'm not supposed to publish yet! Pretending he hadn't heard, Sam said, "What if I call you *Wenonah*—that's Indian for eldest daughter?"

The child seemed to like that, but Minnehaha froze, the coffeepot in midair so the cup she was filling almost overflowed. "My mother called me Wenunah," she whispered in awe.

Just then, the Iversons came to the door, Olaf taking off his muddy work boots before coming in. Olaf Iverson was manager and his wife Helga housekeeper of the house across the road where Fred and the farmhands lived. When they adopted Fred, Peter had asked the Iversons, a childless Swedish couple, to move into the boy's home and run the two farms as one.

Olaf slapped Peter jovially on the back and boomed, *"Go' Kväll*—Good evening. *Välkommen*, Mr. Quincy, Karl" he added sticking a callused paw in front of Sam's chest and nodding to the apprentice.

Meanwhile, Helga had gone straight to the coffeepot on the stove to pour two scalding mugs before sliding her ample skirts onto the end of the bench. The large grin on her round friendly face was her only greeting.

Karl and a happily giggling Inger were whispering on a bench in the corner of the room. They tried to sneak out the door, but Karen caught Inger's eye and pointed to the bench. That was as far as they would be allowed to retreat from the rest of the company.

Peter rose at his end of the table and welcomed the assembled company. He explained that an abutting quarter section of land was being sold by a Danish family who had tired of fighting the Minnesota winter and planned to move on to Nebraska where the climate was rumored to be milder and the land cheaper.

"I warned the Johansens that Nebraska is filled with pious Danes. The happy ones stay in Minnesota and dance themselves warm in the winter," Peter joked. "Erik will not be deterred. He wants to move soon so they can get settled in their new place before the onset of cold weather, but first they need to sell the harvest and the farm to pay for the new land. I want to help them, but we can't afford their price. This meeting is to develop a plan for buying their farm." He sat down to let everyone argue.

Sam smiled. He suspected that Peter had a plan, that this plan needed everyone's cooperation, and that it would eventually be revealed by the conversation. He would wait patiently until eventually everyone came around to his point of view while thinking it was their own idea in the first place. Sure enough, after a chorus of voices argued and interrupted each other, the discussion settled down and each was allowed his or her say.

Olaf Iverson started them off. "With the thresher working well, for once, we're almost done with our wheat and the Johansens are next on the co-operative's list."

"But what about the corn, it won't be dry enough until later," said Fred.

"And we have all those new apples," John contributed.

"And the Johansens have to leave soon," Olaf added.

"Before they can sell the grain and the corn," Hans, the farmhand finished.

"What about a loan from the bank?" Karen asked.

"My daddy says once you mortgage land, you'll never get out of debt," Minnehaha declared pessimistically.

"The Johansens can't get a harvest loan if they're going to leave," Bridget added.

"There's so much corn this year, unless September turns wet or we have early frost. There will never be enough room in their tiny barn for it all."

Karl removed his gaze from Inger's face just long enough to ask, "Didn't you build one of those new-fangled round barns that we wrote about in the newspaper. The one that professor from Wisconsin invented? That's supposed to have so much room."

"Yes the King silo has plenty of room for silage. But we still have to fill it and not all the corn is ours," Peter pointed out, smiling because the arguments were obviously going in just the direction he hoped."

"We'd all help. Would that work?" Inger ventured shyly. "We're all used to working hard."

"Me too, I'll help. And Helga can cook." Anne piped up.

Sam felt it was his turn to contribute, "I don't know from

farming, but can't Peter buy the farm with whatever money he has and mortgage the harvest and land for the rest? That's how we've built the newspaper. The Washburn flourmills in Minneapolis are always looking for contracts. You can probably also sell your silage during the winter."

A few more voices were heard from and then there was silence as they pondered the large task ahead. Peter, however, looked pleased. He rose again and looked triumphantly around the room, "I believe we have consensus. If we all pitch in we can finish threshing the wheat, then harvest apples and corn from all three farms. I'll go to the bank on Monday and send a telegram to the grain buyer in Marshall. Before the month is out we can send the Johansens off with money in their pockets. Many hands make light work, and several brains are better than one."

Sam whispered to Karen, "What a flatterer. He planned this all along, didn't he?"

"A regular Hiawatha, sent by Gitchie Manito to get the tribes to act together," Karen joked. "Like a good captain he explains the situation, and the crew is up the rigging without needing to be ordered aloft!"

8
The Benson Soddy

We have a little to eat yet & perhaps some way will be provided for more when it is gone. We sold all of our cows but two & a young heifer. Our best cow was sick on the road & does not yet recover. She will be no dependance this winter. The other will give milk in a few days but we shan't have much butter to sell. The first two years here will be hard very probably. If we struggle through them, then we stand a chance to do pretty well I think. As to clothing we'll have to do almost without I guess....

I took our team last Sabbath and Mamie [daughter] & I went to meeting at Marshall. Congregational preaching in the forenoon, then S. School and Methodist preaching in the afternoon. Both the sermons were good & the S. School interesting. My shoes were too poor to go, & I had no gloves which did not correspond with the rest of my dress, but I put aside scruples and went. Geo. has no pants fit to wear, so he can't go....

Do you want to know what our carpet is? Our cabin has a ground floor and we spread green grass over it for a carpet & change it occasionally. It saves sweeping & mopping. But I would rather have a chance to do both.

Letter to Aunt Martha
from Mary Carpenter
Marshall, Minn. July 10, 1873
Minnesota Historical Society, by permission

September 1890
It was easier to place Minnehaha than Karen had hoped. After Mildred Bullard spoke at the Babel Barn about her quilts, she and the Indian girl chatted and before lunch was over, they had come to an arrangement. At the beginning of the following month, Minnehaha went home to her father's house in Faribault for a short visit; then Obadiah picked her up and drove her to their farm and her new job. At first there would be little for her to do, but since the Bullards planned to adopt some children from the next orphan train, there would soon be work enough for her capable hands.
Karen was happy that her little plot to get them together had succeeded so well. Now she only needed to work with the new girl that was to start in another week, and write her column, and worry about the children, and Peter, who was away again, and .... *It's too much. Peter is right; I can't do it all, especially when he's not here. Doesn't he know that I need him here, not gallivanting around the countryside?*

One Sunday afternoon, Karen decided to call on the Swedish family that Mildred had told her had settled just down the road from them. *I'll bring Inger in case there's a language problem. Afterwards, we can stop by the Bullard farm and Inger can visit Minnehaha. They'll both like that.*
   They packed a traditional welcome basket with bread and salt, and also an apple cake; small gifts so as not to embarrass recipients without the means to respond in kind. Svend hitched the buggy and they climbed up, Inger carrying a bouquet of wildflowers.
   On the way, Karen tried to prepare the girl, and possibly herself, for what they might encounter. "The Bensons only have a soddy, so it's likely to be cramped quarters," she said. A well-built soddy, so called because of walls that were partially made of sod blocks cut from the prairie, was a practical first shelter. Properly constructed, they were dug deep into the ground and the sod stacked carefully and thick enough to keep out the wind, but they could be too small and airless for a large family. If the chimney did not draw right the small rooms quickly filled with smoke and poisonous fumes.
   "Mildred Bullard says that the Bensons are very poor; there are too many children, too close together and another on the way. She's worried about this winter."

Inger nodded. "Last March, we saw that there was no smoke from our neighbors' chimney. By the time my father could get there, they had frozen to death."

Karen shuddered. Everyone knew stories like these. New settlers that were ill prepared for the grinding cold of the Minnesota winter, the numbing isolation. In a heavy snowstorm, drifts could cover a low house, the family unable to get out. Grizzly thought. "I hope we can help."

"Perhaps you can invite the woman to one of your Saturday get-togethers. Or maybe they'll have an interesting story and you can interview them for the paper."

Karen was skeptical. "The coming birth might provide an opportunity. Most women welcome company during labor. Mrs. Benson will be used to giving and accepting such help from home. The difference is that in Sweden she would have had a network of kith and kin; help from strangers is harder to ask for and to accept."

They turned off the main gravel road and drove along a green trail. Over a low rise, they saw the grassy top of a ramshackle soddy. It was dug into a small hill with the upper half of the house in unfinished lumber and the roof covered in more sod. At the side of the shack, a farmer was chopping wood. He looked strong but was swinging the ax slowly as if his arms were heavy, his burly frame exhausted.

Hailing Mr. Benson, Karen secured the brake and looped Blackie's reins around the post with enough slack so she could mouthe a clump of grass. He stared suspiciously at the visitors but swung his ax one more time to leave it in the chopping block. When Karen introduced herself and explained that they had come to welcome them to the neighborhood, Mr. Benson greeted them politely but glumly in Swedish. Leaving them to get down from the buggy by themselves, he walked ahead down a step through the only door into the house.

Karen looked around in dismay at the cramped combined kitchen-sitting room with an iron stove. A table was placed against the wall under the single window and a torn curtain hung at the side of a doorframe through which a bed was dimly visible. A cradle and the spinning wheel next to it were old and well made, but the rest of the furniture looked hurriedly nailed together from scrap lumber.

Mrs. Benson limply shook hands as she shooed away four

whiny children clinging to her apron. "I'm Maia," she said hospitably enough in Swedish, accepting the token gifts with a wan smile. "Please come and sit." She reached for the water kettle simmering on the stove and poured more water into the coffeepot through its cloth bag of over-used grounds. "It'll be ready soon," she promised.

Karen was relieved that Inger accepted this reuse of the coffee beans without comment.

Mr. Benson pulled the table from the wall and the two eldest children, a girl and boy of about six and seven, scrambled to sit on the bench at the inner corner. The father gestured for the guests to slide in after them. Pushing the table back, he pulled a hinged board down, blocking the door. He and the younger children climbed onto this second bench leaving Mrs. Benson nowhere to sit. Standing by the stove, she wiped two chipped enameled cups with a corner of her apron. She poured the coffee, her eyes apologizing for the thin brew, but she said nothing as she handed them out.

The children brightened when the apple cake was passed around, eagerly grabbing at their share and then fighting over the last piece. Their father raised his arm, and the two older boys cringed as if expecting to have their ears boxed. Glancing at the company, he withdrew his hand at the last minute and settled the argument by claiming the last piece for himself.

With the door blocked, the four walls of the small room closed in on Karen until she could hardly breathe. Fighting nausea, she took a sip of coffee hoping to settle her stomach. The contrast between her own comfortable Babel Farm and these miserable circumstances was overwhelming. She and Peter were well-off because of the size of their farm and the regular income they still received from their share in the family shipping concerns, but their riches were not simply material. This family looked to have no resources at all.

Trying desperately to make conversation, Karen asked, "*Hvornaar?*" She gestured at the cradle in the corner and hoped that the Danish word for 'when' would be similar in Swedish. When Mrs. Benson did not seem to understand, she repeated her question in English and asked Inger to translate.

"In five months," Mrs. Benson answered and held up a hand of fingers.

Karen mimed holding a baby in her arms and, pointing to herself, held up the five fingers of her left hand and the thumb and index finger on her right. *"Syv Maaneder,"* she said. The woman nodded and smiled weakly to show she understood. Mr. Benson remained mute, his hands lying limply on the table, his eyes unfocused.

After some gentle prodding and with Inger as occasional translator, Mrs. Benson haltingly told the family's tale. They had come from Småland five years ago with the two eldest children but little money. Oskar Benson had been a master carpenter at home, but here he was only able to find work as a farmhand. They had lived in a shack near Marshall where Oskar worked for the owner and had finally saved up enough to buy this abandoned farm for back taxes. Every weekend all summer Oskar had come the fifteen miles from Marshall to build the soddy and re-claim the field closest to the house. Finally a few weeks ago, the rest of the family had moved in. Oskar still went back to Marshall four days each week to earn a few dollars for winter supplies and worked his own land on the weekend. Maia was due in February but was feeling 'poorly'.

Well, no wonder, Karen thought; *I would also feel poorly if I were four months pregnant and lived here, isolated and with four small children!* She glanced at Oskar. He looked worn out, and she had smelled alcohol on his breath. He wouldn't hesitate to take out a bad temper on the family.

"How can we help? Is there anything you need?" she finally asked.

"I work. I take care my family," Oskar interrupted firmly, in broken English.

The language barrier frustrated Karen. Usually she could understand the Swedish and Norwegian of her neighbors well enough and they her Danish, but this stuffy room was filled with a fog too thick to penetrate. Inger tried to lighten the atmosphere with small talk, but her voice was only a rumble in Karen's ears. She clenched her jaw. *I won't be sick, I can't.*

She rose abruptly from the bench and, mumbling something about calling again, tried to get out. Oskar shoved the children out of the way so he could raise the bench and Karen beat a hasty retreat, Inger only inches behind.

Karen barely made it to a shrub at the side of the soddy, before losing the watery coffee and the only bite of cake that she had been able to swallow. As they climbed onto the buggy

Inger handed her a handkerchief. "Are you all right? You look dreadful. Let me drive. You just close your eyes."

Karen nodded gratefully and let her take the reins. Back on Marshall Road, she pointed north, "Go that way. We need a little cheer! Obadiah and Mildred Bullard live up the road a bit, and she said to call anytime."

9
Quakerly Concern

To laugh often and much; To win the respect of intelligent people and the affection of children; To earn the appreciation of honest critics and endure the betrayal of false friends; To appreciate beauty, to find the best in others; To leave the world a bit better, whether by a healthy child, a garden patch or a redeemed social condition; To know even one life has breathed easier because you have lived. This is to have succeeded.

Author unknown, often attributed to
Ralph Waldo Emerson (1803–1882)

Once away from the depressing Benson soddy, Karen felt better, but couldn't shake off a sense of doom. "I don't know what came over me," she apologized, breathing in gulps of fresh air. "I don't usually get the vapors."

She leaned against the backrest of the buggy seat, looking forward to the cheer and peace of Mildred's home. In her mind she went over and over what she should have said, what she should have done to get the Bensons to accept help. *What right do I have to complain? I have a loving husband, a beautiful family, a spacious home, and satisfying work. Yes, Peter travels more than I'd like, but it's not as if I am left by myself when he goes. Get a grip on yourself and don't panic just because not everyone is so fortunate.*

"We're almost there," she said brightly. "Minnehaha will be settled by now, and the two of you can have a nice visit. Remember, the Bullards prefer to be called by their full names rather than Mr. and Mrs. It seems a little odd at first, but you'll soon get used to it and they're very nice, even if Obadiah Bullard is a little quiet."

"Yes, Mistress," Inger muttered with a grin.

But Mildred Bullard was not quiet at all and greeted them warmly. Not as warmly, however, as Minnehaha who came bounding out of the house braids flying and enthusiastically embraced first Karen and then Inger.

Mildred, noticing how pale Karen looked, called for Obadiah to take care of the horse and wagon. Leading her guests indoors she said, "We were about to have tea. Minnehaha, please bring the pot into the parlor and then why don't you show Inger your room."

"Just imagine," Minnehaha said, "I have my very own room. Of course, it isn't really a room yet because the walls aren't in, just quilts hanging from the studs to give me privacy. But my very own!"

Soon Karen was seated with another welcome cup—this time of strong tea.

"Have a little apple pie," Mildred said solicitously. "You look quite ill." Seeing Karen hesitate, she added, "Just a little bite. It will help settle your stomach."

"I don't know what came over me. We were visiting the Bensons and suddenly…"

"That's hardly surprising, in your condition."

"I don't usually…, Even sailing through a typhoon off Japan, when I was expecting Lars, I was fine."

"Lars?" Mildred said. "Isn't your son's name John? Wasn't he born in Denmark?"

"Yes, yes, I mean John," Karen mumbled looking confused.

There's some mystery here, Mildred thought and changed the subject. "We're so delighted to have Minnehaha with us."

"She's lucky to have found such a good place," Karen replied, more composed. She looked around, admiring the beautiful home the Bullards were creating and the progress since last time she'd been here.

"Let me show you what we plan to do," Mildred offered, her voice diffident, as if afraid of showing un-Quakerly pride in earthly possessions. She led Karen through the spacious first floor, which was nearly finished, and then pointed at the stairs. "On the second floor there will be several bedrooms for the needy children we're planning to adopt. That's why we invited Minnehaha to help us. She seems capable of handling a whole trainload!"

"Speaking of the needy. I have a very bad feeling about the Bensons. Can't we do something to help?"

Back in the drawing room by this time, they sat down again and pondered the problem. Karen was comforted by the silence. Her mind wandering, she was reminded of the peace she had found in Elizabeth's parlor in San Francisco. Do all Quaker women have such grace?

The grandfather clock in the corner struck four and Mildred came back from her center.

The girls returned and claimed their tea and pie. Minnehaha pointed out the window to the skeleton of an old cottonwood tree and the stream beyond. "See that rotten tree out there. The window in my room faces that way. In the spring, we're replacing it with a weeping willow. That stream needs a willow, don't you think? Obadiah said I could pick any type of tree I wanted."

"And Mildred is going to teach me quilting," the girl rattled on. "The embroidery we had to do at school is really boring and quilts are so much more practical."

Mildred smiled at her enthusiasm. "I figure, if she can sew, she can quilt. But Karen and I were discussing how to help the Bensons. Any ideas?"

"Perhaps if we talk to the Swedish Church," Minnehaha suggested.

"I don't think they even know about the Bensons, they've probably been too busy getting settled to go to church," Karen said doubtfully. "Besides they may be too self-conscious about their poverty to feel welcome."

"Maybe I can get my mother to say something to Pastor on Sunday," Inger suggested. "We Swedes aren't as open and friendly as Danes and Norwegians but once you get to know us, we're fine. It just takes a while."

"Like New Englanders," Mildred smiled.

At that point Obadiah came and sat down after giving a dour nod to the company. He sipped the tea that Mildred handed him in silence.

"What if we offered to have Inger stay with Mrs. Benson for a couple of weeks when she's close to her time?" Karen asked.

"You could tell them that it's part of her training and point out that the Benson's will need someone to help with the younger children."

"I was there for my mother, the last two times. I know how to help," Inger said quietly.

"I knew I could count on you. But they have no room and I don't trust Oskar."

"If Inger stayed here...," Mildred offered.

Minnehaha had been following the conversation closely and now said firmly, "Inger can sleep in my room. We can alternate working here and at the neighbors'."

"What do you know of Oskar Benson?" Mildred asked Obadiah. "Karen Larsen thinks he might take his tiredness out in drink and turn on his family. Can you reason with him to see if he can ease his work a little and spend more time with his family?" She seemed to take the grunted reply as an affirmative.

Karen thought the Swede and the Quaker would make a strange pair, neither having much to say.

"I'll handle Oskar Benson," Minnehaha said. "My father used to come home drunk and angry, but I learned how to settle him down. Oskar can't be any worse."

Obadiah took the pipe out of his mouth long enough to settle the problem, "Benson can do carpentry on our place in exchange for supplies. The hands'll get them settled now, then he helps us during the winter." These two sentences seemed to exhaust his supply of words because the pipe went back in the mouth and only the sound of air bubbling through the tobacco could be heard over the ticking of the clock.

"That's very generous of you," Karen suggested.

"Not at all," Mildred answered. "This will be good for everyone. We have been reading some of Emerson's essays. He writes that satisfaction and success come from helping others. He says it well."

Minnehaha, sensing that Karen didn't know Ralph Waldo Emerson's work, eagerly quoted: "'To know even one life has breathed easier because you have lived.' Isn't that what you tried to teach us, Karen?"

They drifted onto other subjects, Inger and Obadiah listening quietly, but the rest tossed the conversational ball back and forth. Karen relaxed, grateful to leave dark thoughts behind.

Minnehaha mentioned her recent visit with her father. "He told me a bit about my mother and that they met as children.

There wasn't time for much because my stepmother was home most of the time and she hates to be reminded that Papa had an Indian wife. The last day at the train station, he handed me a slip of paper and whispered, 'Talk to him, he knows about your mother.' The paper just had the name: Chief Good Thunder."

Mildred took up the thread. "We wrote my son-in-law in Saint Peter and asked about this chief. He found out that Good Thunder went with his people when they were exiled to the reservation in South Dakota. He returned just a few years ago...."

"And has settled near here, up by Redwood Falls," Minnehaha interrupted breathlessly. "Mildred says we should write to the priest at the mission there and ask him to find out about my Dakota family."

She was silent for a few minutes and then asked, "Why do you suppose Father won't talk to me? I used to think it was all because of my stepmother and that he is ashamed of me too, but now I'm not so sure."

Mildred had a sudden inspiration. "How old is your father? If he knows Chief Good Thunder, maybe they met during the Sioux uprising."

"No he was just a boy in '62. I asked him once if he fought against the South and he told me it was over before he was old enough to join. But his father, my grandfather Samuelson, was killed at Gettysburg with the First Minnesota regiment. He won't talk about that either;.I only found out because my stepmother brags about what a hero he was. Why won't he talk to me?"

"Perhaps it's too painful, Dear," Mildred said quietly.

Karen wanted to tell them that her mother wouldn't talk to her about her grandfather drowning with his ship for the same reason, but suddenly her throat closed and there was a roaring in her ears.

After a few minutes, she managed to say, "I know so little about the Sioux uprising. Where can I find out more?"

"Henry Whipple in Faribault would know," Mildred answered. "He's the Episcopal Bishop of Minnesota and built the cathedral there. He's getting on in years but still travels around to all the churches that he founded in the Diocese, including an Indian Mission at the Lower Agency near Redwood Falls."

"I know him!" Minnehaha exclaimed in wonder. "He's the one who got me into school at Saint Mary's Hall. I didn't like it much there—the girls were really nasty to me, but he was very nice. We just called him the Bishop, so I had forgotten his name." She looked abashed and added, "We really called him 'the Bish' and his wife was 'the Second Wife'."

Mildred chuckled. "My son tells that Henry Whipple is called 'Straight Tongue' by the Indians and his first wife was 'Saint Cornelia'. Saint Mary's started in her home and moved to a bigger building after she died."

"Tell us more about when you were little," Mildred encouraged. "Do you remember your mother at all?"

"Only vaguely. I remember father crying and then she wasn't there anymore. We traveled for a long time in a wagon until we got to Aunt Dorothy's farm in Faribault. Uncle George had died some time before and Daddy took over the farm—not much of a place. Aunt Dorothy died soon after I started elementary school. The neighbor was a widow with two small children and I suppose it made sense for Daddy to marry her and combine the farms, except it had a big mortgage. My new stepmother hated me from the start and hated for anyone to know that Daddy had an Indian wife. She told everyone that I was only a servant girl and tried to keep me at home. 'Why does an Indian need school?' she said. Fortunately, Daddy put his foot down."

"How old were you when your father remarried? Surely you already knew how to read?" Mildred interjected.

"I was ten and reading was my favorite thing. Our farm was isolated and that was all I had to do, except of course keep house for my new stepfamily. The teacher at school was kind to me and lent me books, lots of books. When she found out how my stepmother treated me, she talked to the priest at church and he brought me to Bishop Whipple. They weren't much nicer to me at Saint Mary's, but at least I had all the books I wanted."

"Was that the teacher who wrote to me about you?" Karen asked.

"Yes. When I graduated from Saint Mary's, Stepmother was delighted to have me back as housekeeper, but that wasn't for me. Being a Babel Girl was the best thing that ever happened; lots of work but lots of fun and such wonderful friends from all over. And then I came here."

Obadiah had been quietly sucking on his pipe throughout this discussion, his eyes going from speaker to speaker so that he seemed to be an active participant. Perhaps he was only silent because he felt he had nothing of value to add. He removed his pipe, "I have several books about the Sioux uprising that I would be glad to lend, if you're interested. The descriptions of the attacks by the Indians against the settlers is violent and may not be to your liking, but there's also a collection of Whipple's writings that tell of the government's failure to live up to the treaties before the rebellion." He replaced his pipe and again silence reigned.

Much as Karen hated to tear away from the stimulating company, it was time for them to leave. Armed with Obadiah's books and everyone's well wishes, she and Inger climbed into the buggy. Without asking, Inger took the reins and they left for home.

Karen sighed and closed her eyes. *Minnehaha's in good hands. If only I can do as well for all the girls.*

10
Words of Wisdom

Listen to the words of wisdom,
Listen to the words of warning
From the lips of the Great Spirit,
From the Master of Life, who made you:
"I have given you streams to fish in,
I have given you bear and bison,
I have given you roe and reindeer,
I have given you brant and beaver,
Filled the marshes full of wild fowl,
Filled the rivers full of fishes;
Why then are you not contented?"

The Song of Hiawatha
Henry Wordsworth Longfellow (1807-1882)

Peter and Karen's study was the heart of the rambling Larsen farmhouse. Over the years as they had added on, they had modified the kitchen-living room of the original shack to this quiet sanctuary away from the constant bustle of the rest of the house, and the fireplace had become a favorite gathering place for the family in winter evenings.

Karen sat at her desk intending to work on her next column. All week she and Inger had told and retold their experience of last Sunday at the Benson soddy and Peter had encouraged her to write about them, saying it would get it off her chest. But the story just wouldn't come. It should be different from her usual 'Meet your Neighbors' column. I have to do something other than leave it all to Mildred. Peter just tells me not to worry so much about others. "We have so much, why can't you just be content?" he said. Like Jesse had preached. *But we need to share this bounty. Can telling a sad story help? If only Jesse were here to give me his words of wisdom. He would know what to say.*

She owed him a letter. Perhaps she should write that first and tackle the column some other day. There was time. The interview with Inger's parents was ready and would do for next week's paper. She lit the oil lamp on the desk and pulled out a piece of paper.

Babel Farm
Saturday, September 2, 1890

Dear Sarah and Jesse,
Thank you for Jesse's kind note. It is such a treat to see him that we never want to let him go. He gave such a wonderful sermon that everyone at Danebod still talks about. As you can see from the above, we have taken his message to heart and named our farm. May our babble unite us with one language, one country, the common good.

We were interested to hear about your plans to move to St. Paul. I was a little surprised that you would want to live in a big city knowing how much you disliked New York, but I suppose St. Paul is much nicer. Part of me protests that I don't want any of you to go— it is too far away and I will miss our visits, infrequent as they might be— but I do understand. I know you are concerned for the future of your boys and want to be part of a larger Jewish community.

For us, it is such a comfort to know that teaching the children Danish culture is not just up to us. It is with good reason we all voted to call our church and folkschool "Danebod—the help of the Danes." Although people have accused Peter and me of turning away from the community and becoming American, all our neighbors have been a source of strength and made it possible for us to help immigrants, wherever they might be from. We have also been criticized for letting John go to winter school here in Lincoln and only sending him to Danebod in the summer, but Tyler is too far for him to go everyday and he is too young to live away from home. Besides, this is his country and he needs to learn American ways too, especially if he decides to go to University. I sometimes envy your clarity and the definite line between Jewish religious law and secular life. I suppose that after nearly 2000 years, you have learned how to live in one world while belonging to another. I know it is not easy for you, but at least it is clear. I see so many young people who reject the ways of their elders, dismissing customs as 'old fashioned,' and then drift into a superficial 'modern' life with no purpose.

The Johansens decided to move to Nebraska and we have bought their homestead. It has been hard to work three farms, but the neighbors are being very helpful. It is like the old days in Sønderho when we all worked together and took it for granted that was how it should be. It is difficult here in Minnesota, where everything is so spread out and everyone has different ways, but I think we are demonstrating that co-operative farming can be made to work.

When I come to Marshall at the end of the month for our fall 'outfitting' I will tell you more about our grand plans for the Johansen farm and for young Fred's future and of the budding romance between him and our Danish girl, Elsbeth. We suspect that they will soon want to do more than whisper in a corner and will want to have a place of their own.

Meanwhile the Johansen house stands empty. Peter and I are hoping that you and the boys will visit us for the Succoth holidays and stay there. It is only a two-room shack, but you could have it to yourselves for the week and not worry how to keep kosher. Perhaps it does not qualify as a Succoth booth though the roof leaks and you can almost see the stars, but you could build one in the yard in which to eat your meals. Hanna and Saul are, of course, also welcome—if you do not mind close quarters and she is up to it.

Inger and I drove up to visit the Bullards last week and Minnehaha seems very happy to be there. On the way, we called on some new settlers from Sweden. It was very depressing to see their poverty and I'm worried that they will not survive the winter. Mildred and Obadiah will do what they can but Mr. Benson is a proud man and not likely to accept help. I wish there were more we could do.

Kristina Stavanger arrived just today to take Minnehaha's place. Her eyes are as deep and blue as the Norwegian fjord where she was born. She so longs for the water and mountains of home that her family fears for her health. At seventeen she is younger than I usually allow, but her parents are so worried about her that the other girls and I decided to let her come anyway. We can only hope that the company of other 'displaced' young girls will be a support to her.

It is late Saturday afternoon and the Babel Barn Ladies have left. It continues to go well. This fall, the men will chink the walls and add a stove so we can continue to meet there, at least until winter. Everyone is excited at the idea of your store selling our fancywork; I will bring the first batch when I come. If it sells well, we can also ship to you in St. Paul, when the time comes.

Affectionately,
Karen

P.S. My love to Hanna and Saul. Peter would also send his, except he is off somewhere lecturing on corn silos and other modern miracles of farming and won't be back until late tonight. I still spend my life waiting for him to come home, but at least now he is not gone for years or months at a time. Sarah, maybe someday our men will stop wandering the Prairie Sea and settle down to the joys of home and family!

Karen blew out the lamp and enjoyed the glow of the late afternoon sun. She was about to get up when Lil-Anne came into the study with Kristina in tow; evidently, she was giving a tour to the new girl. Neither of them saw her sitting in the corner.

"This is Papa's study," Lil-Anne explained. "We're not allowed in here without my parents, but it's all right, 'cause I'm just showing it to you. I like to look at all the lovely things they brought back from China and Africa and other places far, far from Minnesota.

She moved to stand in front of the old painting of a ship at sea which hung on the center wall over Peter's easy chair. "This is the painting of my Great-grandpa's ship, the *White Karen*. Isn't she beautiful, just like Mama? But Papa doesn't like Mama to wear white; he likes lavender 'cause that's the color of her eyes. The sea is beautiful too, isn't it? I've never seen anything bigger than Benton Lake and it doesn't ever get big waves like that."

"Is that ship you sail to America?" Kristina asked, showing more interest than she had since her arrival.

"Nah, I was born here. My parents came in a steam ship, also the *White Karen*. Papa was captain."

"If your Papa was captain of beautiful ship to travel around the world, why come to this flat place?"

"Well, Silly, then they wouldn't have found me, would

they? The stork left me under the pine trees out back, that's why they're called the Anne-Trees. It was cold so he couldn't come down the chimney because of the fire in the stove."

Karen sat very still until the two left the room. Lil-Anne was such a sweet child that everyone adored her. Acting as if she were one of them, she bloomed under the sun of everyone's love. She was a little *nisse*, one of those mischievous gremlins of Danish folklore, but with a heart of gold. *How kind of her to notice that Kristina feels homesick. Maybe it was a mistake taking that one. She's so miserable and I don't have the energy. But I need to talk to Lil-Anne about the stork and babies. Not today. Soon. Maybe when Peter gets home.*

One afternoon some days later, Karen was back at her desk. Peter had come home early from the paper with a thick packet of mail from Fanø that had arrived that morning. She smiled, watching her husband go through his familiar mail reading ritual as he sorted the letters by postmark and went through them one by one in order, shifting them from one side of his chair to the other as he finished. Then he passed on to the months-old Danish newspapers piled on the floor, going through them systematically. Her father was a devoted reader of the news and periodically bundled up an accumulation to mail them across the Atlantic and half the American continent to share the news from home.

Peter glanced at his wife, sitting at her desk working on her column. She had devoured and exclaimed over the long letters from Sister Anne and Aunt Kirsten and the customarily shorter note from her mother, Lars-Anne; they were now lying on the side of her desk to be reread over and over, at leisure. Karen was chewing on her pen, a frown between her eyes. He took that to mean that the writing was not going well—an article about the need to help new settlers like the Bensons, she had told him at dinner.

"What's the good of talking about 'love thy neighbor' on Sunday morning, if everyone then goes his selfish way without doing anything," she muttered. "Big-Anne, used to scorn those who dress in their best for church, but are mean the rest of the week. 'Sunday People' she called them. I don't want to be like them but help my neighbors like her."

"You do, you do," Peter argued, trying to get back to his reading. *There she goes again,* he thought. *Worrying about ev-*

eryone. As busy as her grandmother with everyone's business. He had been very fond of Big-Anne. Though tiny, she had had a heart as big as her name, a woman of amazing strength and practical determination, even if she had been too pious for his taste. Left destitute when her husband was lost at sea with their ship and family fortune, she had gone to the mainland to study midwifery. Taking Kirsten with her, then but an infant, she had to leave then thirteen-year-old Lars-Anne with her grandparents at the mill—a desertion that Karen's mother never quite forgave. Although Lars-Anne was in many ways like Big-Anne, the family tragedy that made the grandmother turn to religion left her daughter embittered and over-protective of her children. Karen inherited the best of them both, leavened by her father's intelligence and sense of humor. But there were times, like now, when the family's darker side surfaced and overwhelmed her. Peter dreaded what was ahead, feared that Karen's reaction to the Benson's misery was but the beginning of her spiral into a pit where he could not reach her. Like last time...and the time before....

An article caught Peter's eye. "Listen to this," he exclaimed, relieved to find a distraction from his black mood. "Aakjær is inviting trouble again, this time from both sides of the religious fence: *From living men's dead speech I learned nothing; From dead men's living works I learned all. Long live the dead.*"

Jeppe Aakjær was a popular modern romantic poet of whom they were both fond. Some of his lyrical poems about Danish farm life had been set to music and were favorites at Danebod songfests.

His diversion worked and Karen laughed. "At Askov Folkschool, Dr. Schrøder used to thunder at us students, 'put those pens down and listen to The Living Word,' as if only lectures had value and we could learn nothing from reading. Yet we were expected to consume wagonloads of learned books. Then in church Pastor would preach 'The Living Word' of the Bible. I could never figure out what they meant."

"I guess Aakjær agrees with you. He certainly alienates the Establishment; they accuse him of being an atheistic socialist. Yet now he seems to be going after the Grundtvigians and the 'folkschool poets'. I thought he was supposed to be one of them."

"Aunt Kirsten says that Denmark has solved the country's problem with liberal socialists by sending them all to America."

Amused, Peter remarked, "That seems too cynical for Kirsten."

"She was probably quoting Uncle Paul," Karen admitted. "Maybe we should invite Aakjær to join us here in Lincoln and solve his problems with the Establishment."

Peter laughed and reburied his nose in the newspaper, and Karen bent over the desk, crumbled-up papers heaped at her elbow. With a sigh he finally folded *Berlinske Tidende* and laid it on the side of his chair that was reserved for the already-read. He rose mumbling something about going to talk to Svend about a colicky horse, when he noticed that a tear had dripped onto the page in front of Karen and puddled in the middle of the page. Oh dear, he thought. What now?

In two bounds he was at Karen's side, lifting her almost bodily to sit beside him on the settee, "Whatever is the matter? The article can't be as bad as all that!" he chided.

"Don't scold me," she sobbed. Don't cry, she reminded herself pushing him away to sit upright. He can't stand that; he'll just leave again so he doesn't have to deal with my outbursts.

"I'm having trouble hitting the right note, and it just sounds preachy. It's too hard, I can't do it."

Peter wouldn't understand, she hardly understood herself. Usually she enjoyed writing even when struggling through many drafts. Usually she was as cheerful and optimistic as he. Yet at times like these there was a wall between them. He denied their grief, wouldn't let her talk about it. As if that would help her forget. *Twelve years ago this month. My sweet boy. I can't think about that now. I'll just tell him that I'm upset because of the Bensons.*

Peter took her hand, murmuring comforting noises. "Write your stories and leave the Bensons in Mildred's capable hands. You need to take care of yourself for the next few months."

There he was, scolding her again. "Oh that has nothing to do with it. I'm just fine," She jerked her hand away and dried her eyes. She wasn't fine, but it was better if she pretended. "Just go see about your stupid horse." *Sweet smiles are what he wants. And sweet stories.*

With an angry shrug, he rose and stalked out of the room, picking his way around the scattered mail on the floor like a stork through the reeds. The door closed firmly behind him. Too firmly.

11
Young Love

*Anna's sweet on Anders,
but coy even so.
She meets her love by the rye field's edge,
sits in the grass, and begins to sew.*

*The sun dances joyfully on Anna's thimble,
Brown moths cluster on the buttercups,
the lark trills, and the air drips with scent of blooming rye.
Anna lightly crosses her ankle-slim legs.*

*Anders mutely fingers his pipe.
Watching the rye stroke Anna's sun-browned neck,
he hears their luring silver laugh,
sees them sneaking little kisses where they will.*

*Anders knocks his pipe against his boot,
looks at it with a critic's eye and cleans it with a straw.
Suddenly he throws all down and sliding danger-near,
whispers about the sun-browned neck and the beauty of the day.*

*Anna's nimble needle pauses in mid-air,
the fine round of her arm buried in white.
He grabs neck and stalks together,
kisses Anna's cheek and mouth, a rival of the rye.*

*At first kiss, needle and thread fall among the buttercups.
Anna's new thimble rolls into the grass.
The drossweeds stare, stretching long necks.*

Tiny ladybugs run over Anna's shoes.

Shielded by the rising cupid moths,
gold ring is promised in place of lost thimble.
The rye stalks broadcast news of love and kisses;
What is heard by smallest grain, is known across the field.

By the Rye Field
Jeppe Aakjær (1866–1930)
English translation by Anne Ipsen

The door flew open and Lil-Anne bounded into the study. "Elsbeth's sweet on Fred," she chanted with five-year-old glee. "He's upstairs though I told him it ain't allowed."

"Isn't," Karen corrected automatically. "And don't tattle, it's unbecoming."

"Well, they're kissing in the sewing room, if you want to know." She scampered off to the kitchen to find Bridget and spread the gossip.

The two young people in question came down the stairs and squeezed through the study door side-by-side. Elsbeth was rosy-cheeked and Fred wouldn't take his eyes off his shoes.

"Do you want to talk to us?" Peter asked kindly in Danish.

"Did you mean what you said—about my taking over the Johansen farm? Next spring when I'm twenty-one?" young Fred finally managed to stammer.

"Of course," Peter said. "We always meant for you to keep your parents' farm, we only took care of it for a few years while you were growing up. But the Johansen's place would be a fresh start for you and we would help you rebuild the house. If swapping's all right with you, that is."

"And we'd like to get married," Fred blurted, the words stumbling over each other. Elsbeth said nothing but her blush had now spread down her neck and up to the tip of her ears.

Karen jumped up and embraced the two young people, smiling. "I'm not exactly surprised. You certainly have our blessing, but Elsbeth's papa might have something to say about it."

Elsbeth stammered, "We hope you'll talk to them. Remind them that Frederik is from a nice Danish family and…" "…and a fine upstanding fellow," Fred added, his usual confidence rebounding in a grin.

"Peter and I can call on the Rolfs after church on Sunday," Karen said.

Peter nodded. He searched through a stack of papers and unrolled a map. "Look at this plat. The reason Johansen couldn't make a go of his farm was that it really is not suited for wheat," he explained.

As if Elsbeth and Karen were not in the room, Peter pointed. "Here's a shallow lake, I think we should drain it and plant grass for...."

Fred pulled the map towards himself and enthusiastically picked up the argument, "...grazing a dairy herd. The better land, here, can be planted with corn, sorghum, and fruit trees."

Peter bent over the map again, "If we put apple trees here and here, bordering our new orchard, we could build more bee hives. Jesse tells me that he can sell all the honey we can produce."

"Elsbeth is good with bees."

"Let's walk the land. Soon, in case it snows. And take Svend with us. He can help you plan for the horses and he's even pretty good with cows. He's full of ideas on enlarging the herds and we could shift all the animal husbandry over to the two of you."

"Yeah, but Svend would never work for me. He's so devoted to Karen."

"We'll just make it clear that it is to be a joint effort. Next summer you can take on calves from the neighbor farms to graze on the lake bottom and then feed them out in the fall."

Peter rolled up the map and gave Fred a congratulatory slap on the back, looking as proud as if this fine young man they had taken under their wings were truly his son. "Bring the plat on Sunday and you can impress the Rolfs with your plans."

Seeing that Elsbeth was pouting at being ignored, Karen affectionately pushed her out the door. "We better leave the men to talk farming and go upstairs. I'll help you finish that shirtwaist you started. When I go to Marshall next week, I'll get some extra dress lengths for you. You'll also need more nightgowns and to finish those sheets you've been hemstitching."

As they went up the stairs, she continued babbling, "It's too bad Minnehaha isn't here, she's much better at the sewing machine than I. They taught her at school to hold the material like the reins of a horse, with just a little tension. To make a turn, you pull slightly on that side...."

Now two more girls are headed for safe harbor, Karen thought, feeling more cheerful than she had for weeks.

At the end of church the following Sunday, Karen casually asked the Rolfs if she and Peter might call that afternoon. They would hardly be surprised, having known Fred since he was a child, and seeing his covert glances across the isle during services.

The Rolfs' suspicions were confirmed when Karen, Peter, and Fred drove up in the carriage, driven by Svend himself. The coats of the fine black Larsen horses gleamed, and their silky manes were braided with the last fall wildflowers as if for a wedding. Svend was responsible for this fine display, for he counted the young couple part of his own family and their proper betrothal serious business.

"*Go'daw,*" the indomitable driver boomed in greeting, raising his tall black hat. The hat had seen better days, dating from the time he was a coachman back in Ribe, but he was wearing his Sunday suit, as befitted the occasion. Dispelling any possible lingering doubts as to their errand, he added, "A brings the groom for inspection."

The whole Rolf family was waiting in front of their modest house and had raised the Danish flag in welcome. Elsbeth, having had dinner at home, was hiding in back of her parents. When Fred jumped down from the carriage she could restrain herself no longer and ran to seek the reassurance of his arm around her shoulder. Her two younger sisters giggled behind their mother and her older brother gave Fred a hearty slap on the back before helping Svend with the horses.

Soon the company was settled at a table already conspicuously laden with white linen, the best china cups, cakes, cookies, and a steaming pot of coffee. The amenities having been observed, the discussion turned to the business at hand. It was quickly settled with little discussion except to fix the date of the main event and count backward for the reading of the banns. The end of April seemed propitious: late enough for good weather and for Karen to have recovered from her confinement, while early enough so as not to interfere with the planting season. The engagement would be announced at services next Sunday with a collation on the church lawn afterwards.

The wedding plans settled, Peter prompted Fred to bring out the map. While the women cleared the dishes, the men bent over the table, discussing drainage ditches, apple trees, and milk cows. "Peter took me to an Extension Service lecture on feeding out yearlings," Fred explained eagerly. "If you grind up corn cobs and mix in extra minerals, they get sleek and fat for shipping to market by October. And Svend here will be my partner. He knows about horses."

Thus introduced, Svend proudly launched into an ambitious plan for the brood mares, more loquacious than was his wont.

The women retreated into the parlor for a discussion of laces, linens, and bridal dresses. Gitte said, "My dress may be a little short." Pointing to the Rolf's fading wedding portrait on the side table, she added, "My mother was very small, though we lengthened the dress a little for my wedding, but Elsbeth is a head taller than me and much skinnier."

"We ought to be able to do something beautiful with a piece of lace," Karen suggested.

"Perhaps you would like something more modern," Gitte wondered, turning to her daughter.

"No, no," the girl protested, blushing at all the attention. "Grandma's is beautiful. I would love to wear it. Just like in the picture."

"Take good care of it, I wanna wear it too," her younger sister blurted.

"Me too, me too," added the youngest.

All too soon, the approaching sunset prompted their departure. Fred lifted Elsbeth onto the backseat of the carriage as if she were a precious parcel and climbed in beside her, the two of them taking up hardly more room than one person. Karen settled in across from them and Peter sat next to Svend up front.

"*Go' Javten*," Svend said in farewell, once again formally raising his hat. Peter and Karen waved good-bye, but the two young people were absorbed in their whisperings.

Karen leaned against the side and closed her eyes, content with the day though a little irritated that the whole world seemed to know about her condition—she really wasn't ready to share the news with everyone yet. *Suppose something goes wrong? Like before?*

She dozed to the swaying of the carriage and Peter's rumbling voice. She would have protested if she had realized they were talking about her and not horses and apples.

"I'm afraid that this year the trip to Marshall will tire her too much. It's fifty miles roundtrip," Peter said.

Svend agreed. "Ja, you knows how she gets."

"I have a plan," Peter answered mysteriously.

Peter's plan was put in motion that night, beginning when Svend came into the kitchen after supper and announced in Danish, "A's driving Mistress Moon to Marshall." He mimed driving a carriage so that even Bridget-madmor could not fail to understand his meaning.

"Certainly not," Karen said immediately, bristling. "My fall shopping trip is my special time with Lil-Anne. The two of us can manage just fine by ourselves."

Peter poked Elsbeth and, as if on cue, she asked, "Please, may I come? Papa has given me money to buy yard goods—for my trousseau."

At this point, Lil-Anne played right into the plotters' hands. "Let's take the train," she pleaded. "Please can we? I always wanted to take the train." She galloped around the table whistling stridently, an engine at full steam.

John, as if he too were in on the plot, exclaimed, "You lucky dog, to get to ride the train. It can take you anywhere in the world! My teacher came all the way from Minneapolis by train!"

Karen capitulated. She knew that she was being manipulated but was helpless against Lil-Anne and Elsbeth's pleading eyes. If truth be told, she had been dreading the long drive, afraid that the horse would balk or her that her might stomach betray her again. For form's sake she protested, "But how will we get to the station with all our boxes? And we would have to change in Tracy."

Peter swept argument aside. "Svend will bring the three of you to Lincoln in time for the 9 AM train and pick you up at 5:30. The boxes will go in the luggage car and be transferred in Tracy. That way you can just enjoy your day without worries."

12
Marshall

[Father] said that we would wait at the railroad until the train passed. The railroad ran along the east shore of Lake Marshall. Father described the engine and cars as best he might to one who had never seen such wonders. Then we waited. We first heard a distant whistle. We stood as close to the track as father thought prudent; he held me tightly by the hand. We heard a tingling in the rails, which rose rapidly to a fearsome pitch; we saw the vast black engine sweeping down upon us; it passed in a cloud of dust and steam; it rounded the curve and sped away across the bridge; a trailing cloud of black smoke was blown rudely down upon the snow by the winter wind; many cars swayed and rattled after; last of all came the red caboose.

...

The things that were to be seen in Marshall were hardly short of spectacular. The red–front store was a wonder in itself. Nobody would think so many fine things could be got together. There were shelvesful of rich cloths—enough to make dresses for all the ladies in the world. Of boots and shoes there was no end. Many of the boots designed for boys had copper toes. Men's boots were big; ladies' shoes were small. Apples were there by the barrel. Sugar and crackers filled other barrels. Vari-colored candies, artfully moulded in sticks that looked like augurs, were displayed in glass jars. There were tank-like kegs of fish. The store was an exposition, no less."

A Human Life, Memories of a Pioneer by his "Oldest Boy."
Willard Dillman (1872-1949)

October 1890

Svend had the wagon ready early on Tuesday morning, the back loaded with straw-lined boxes of apples, honey, cheese, and eggs as well as packages of knitting and fancywork from the Babel Barn women, all for delivery to Jesse's store in Marshall. Elsbeth and Lil-Anne, wearing their Sunday bonnets, white gloves and excited grins, climbed on board as soon as they could escape from breakfast cleanup. Karen followed, armed with everyone's wish list of purchases to be made in town. In her good dress and a large hat with a trailing veil covering her face, she felt svelte and fashionable. *No one will suspect,* she thought. Svend flicked his whip and everyone waved good-bye as if they were to be gone months instead of hours.

Arriving a few minutes later in the center of Lincoln, Svend pulled up smartly in front of the small station. Importantly, he boomed instructions to the stationmaster to signal the train to stop, completely ignoring that the good man spoke no Danish and needed no prompting to carry out his job. While Karen purchased the tickets, Svend commandeered a baggage cart and, refusing all help, piled it high with the boxes from the wagon. Within minutes the fire-breathing dragon came to a halt by the platform and enveloped all in steam. After checking that the conductor was helping his women on board, Svend supervised the loading of his cargo, repeating "Marshall" and "Larsen" several times so there would be no mistake about the destination and the owners.

"See you at five-thirty," Karen called out the window over the sound of the whistle. Jerked to her seat, she unwrapped her hat. "I don't think Svend really wanted to come—he hates Marshall. Besides he would have been more of a hindrance than a help."

Lil-Anne appropriated the seat by the window and eagerly watched the fields and prairie whizzing by. "Why do the houses along the road move so fast but the cows in the fields in back of them hardly move at all?" she wanted to know but paid no attention to the explanation. When the train came to a rumbling halt in a few minutes, she sighed in disappointment, "Aw, are we there already?"

She was about to jump up from her seat and dash down the aisle but Karen restrained her. "We're only in Tyler. Soon we'll be in Tracy, and then it'll take another half hour. It's twenty miles from there to Marshall."

All too soon they arrived. A boy from Jesse's store met them with a delivery wagon and took care of the boxes. "I'm Tom," he announced. "And who are you, little girl?" he asked Lil-Anne as he lifted her onto the seat next to him, leaving the women to fend for themselves.

"Only Mama is 'lowed to call me 'Lil', 'cause I'm five," she retorted angrily. "But you can call me 'Anne'."

"Well, Anne, since you're five, would you like to help hold the reins?" And with that they rode the few blocks to the store.

Jesse's wife was waiting on the steps with her brother-in-law Saul, who immediately started to unload the boxes.

"Sarah, may I present Elsbeth, Elsbeth this is Mrs. Schneider." Karen introduced formally in English, knowing that Sarah spoke no Danish. "Elsbeth and Fred are engaged to wed in the spring, so she came along to get some fabrics for her hope chest."

"Congratulations and welcome, Elsbeth, but please call me Sarah." Giving Lil-Anne a hug, she added, "Hanna is waiting for you upstairs with a pastry. The steps are a little hard for her right now, but she's eager to see you right away. Mama and Elsbeth will come up soon."

Lil-Anne gave Sarah a kiss on the cheek and asked, "Where are Jonathan and David? Will David sing me a song?" Scampering up the stairs without waiting for the answer, she yelled, "Guess what, Aunt Hanna? We rode the train all the way from Lincoln!"

Shaking her head and smiling at the child's eagerness, Sarah said, "There's a wonderful new yard-goods store down the street that I'll take you to after lunch. I imagine both of you have long lists."

"We're having tea with Birthe at three, but the train doesn't leave until five, so we have plenty of time," Karen pointed out.

Lunch was a lively affair. Jesse's sons, Jonathan and David, came home from school and kept Lil-Anne entertained, leaving the adults to talk. Jonathan was a serious nine-year old, a smaller edition of his father with dark hair and eyes and a yarmulke that continually threatened to slide off the back of his curls, to be rescued in the nick of time. David was a year and a half older than Lil-Anne with the same sparkle in his eyes as his mother. He was very proud of being in first grade and was teasing Lil-Anne about not being able to read.

"I can write my name," Lil-Anne argued stoutly. "Mama is learning me to read Danish and you can't even speak it."

"Yeah, but I speak Yiddish and read Hebrew, and they doesn't even have the same alphabet as English," David pointed out.

"You've only finished your first section of *Torah*, so don't brag," Jonathan admonished. "Anne's pretty smart, especially for a girl." He was a peacemaker like Jesse and didn't appear to understand why the little girl, whom he adored as if she were his younger sister, looked daggers at him. Finally they both settled down when he promised to read them a story after lunch.

Jesse sat at the head of the table, beaming at the assembly of his favorite people. Sarah was a skillful hostess, managing to keep an eye on the needs of her guests and a restraining arm on her youngest son, while regaling everyone with a funny story. One of the leading ladies in town had bustled into the store and demanded instant service and ridiculously low prices. "And then she had the nerve to complain about the quality of a blouse that she had bought elsewhere and stalked out of the store, forgetting her loaf of bread!" she finished.

Jesse's sister, Hanna, was large and uncomfortable but her pleasure at the coming event shone in her eyes. Karen had known Hanna in Ribe since she was a school friend of her cousin's, and she was very glad to see her so happy. Saul, unusually attentive, was fussing over his wife, bringing a pillow for her back and a stool for her feet. Finally, he sat down at the other end of the table, his usual hearty self. *I'm glad to see that he's so considerate of her. But, she doesn't not look well. I'm worried about her.*

Even Elsbeth, encouraged by a friendly question from Sarah, overcame her shyness and told everyone about Fred's ambitious plans for the old Johansen farm. "He's already started repairing the roof on the old shack so the snow won't ruin the floors. That is, the floors that he'll put in as soon as the roof is finished. I want red gingham curtains in the kitchen and Mrs. Bullard, I mean Mildred Bullard, has promised to help me and the other girls make a wedding-ring quilt for our bed." Then she blushed prettily at her daring reference to the bed.

Karen started to explain about Mildred, but Jesse had already read them her story in the *Pioneer* and told them about the wonderful quilts, so she changed the subject by asking, "Are you really moving to Saint Paul?"

"Yes, but not until next year," Jesse answered.

Sarah added, "But we'll miss your big event."

Karen should have blushed also, but she had no patience with such pretence and merely changed the subject, "You'll all have to come and visit us. Riding the train is so easy, I think we'll do that every time we come to Marshall. I looked up the schedule for St. Paul and I think you only have to change once. By spring, Hanna's baby boy will be old enough to travel."

"What baby?" Lil-Anne interrupted. "Where is he? I wanna see him."

Now it was Karen's turn to be embarrassed. She had still not told Lil-Anne the facts of life, so she mumbled, "Later— he'll be here later." Sarah intervened by suggesting that David and Jonathan take Lil-Anne outside to give Bessie some carrots.

Diverted, Lil-Anne took Jonathan's hand and pulled him through the door, protesting, "Bessie's just a horse. We have plenty of those, but you promised us a story."

The children safely out of the way, everyone started talking at once. "Hanna might have a girl, you know," Sarah said.

"If Karen says it's a boy, I'm sure that's what it will be," Saul, the eager father, bragged.

"And she and Peter are calling their daughter 'Rachel'," Hanna announced.

Karen interrupted, "Tell us about your move to Saint Paul."

"I just returned from a visit," Jesse explained. "It's a very clean city, not at all like New York, and with plenty of opportunity. There's a brand new synagogue, not far from the center of town, with an active Jewish community. The boys can go to the Hebrew school and Saul and I've found a good place for a store. Instead of general merchandise we'll sell only clothing and specialize in handmade items. We've already found a good tailor to do alterations."

"I'm sure the Saturday women would like to make mittens, socks, and sweaters for you to sell," Karen said enthusiastically.

"Karen's Knits!" Hanna exclaimed.

"No, 'The Babel Barn Cooperative'!" she and Jesse chorused to general amusement.

Finally, Karen reluctantly announced, "I'm afraid we have to go. Elsbeth needs to get her lace and gingham, and I must buy shoes and winter boots for John and Lil-Anne. How that boy grows — his feet are almost as big as Peter's. 'Big-foot' and 'Bigger-foot' I call them."

As they were saying goodbye Karen gave Hanna a hug and whispered in Danish, "Take care of yourself."

"You too," Hanna whispered back.

"Oh, I'm fine."

Saul came downstairs to the store and helped Karen find some sturdy Red Wing work boots for Peter and John and Sunday shoes for Lil-Anne. He promised that they would be wrapped and placed in the wagon. "Tom will bring everything to the station."

Sarah walked them down the street to the new yard goods store. It was a great success. Soon flannels for winter nightgowns and nightshirts, dress-lengths of calico, and even red gingham for curtains were piled high on the counter. Best of all were the yards of lace for Elsbeth's gown that she insisted be wrapped separately.

"Let me take all these bundles back to the store while you go have tea with Birthe," Sarah offered, but Elsbeth clung to her package of lace and would not relinquish her treasure.

They walked down a side street the short distance to Birthe's house. Birthe was the first of Karen's 'girls,' having come to the farm before Lil-Anne was born. Her stay had been such a success that soon word had spread. Her successor had come a few months after the birth and then the others, in turn. Birthe now lived in Marshall with her lawyer husband and their two children, ages three, and five months.

Karen felt like a mother-in-law when she visited any of her 'graduates.' They always insisted on showing her all their accomplishments, waiting anxiously for her praise. She sometimes wondered if they thought her too critical. Yet, her mother used to worry about the same thing, and all the Fanø 'girls' had obviously worshiped Lars-Anne. If truth be told, they had never resented her the way Karen had—that is, until she had been separated from her mother by two seas and half a continent and realized how much she had learned. *If only Mam were here*, Karen thought. *She would understand.*

Birthe met them at the door, little Karen hiding behind her skirts, one finger in her mouth. Baby Tobias was lying on a blanket, solemnly chewing on his big toe. Lil-Anne, delighted to finally get to see a baby, bounded over and scared the infant by sticking her face right up to him.

"Gently, gently," the mother admonished, but, after settling the little girl in a big chair, she allowed her to hold the squirming baby on her lap.

Lil-Anne was entranced. "Let's buy one to bring home," she said. When everyone laughed she insisted crossly, "What's wrong with that? I need a little sister. A baby boy would be all right too, if the girls are sold out, but a sister would be more fun."

"I'll see what I can do," Karen promised, thinking that it was definitely time to have that talk with both children. *On second thought, maybe I'll leave John to Peter.*

After tea, they had to admire all the additions to Birthe's lovely home and garden. "Are you all right?" Birthe whispered so Lil-Anne wouldn't hear. To no avail because Miss Sharp-ears immediately wanted to know what the secret was.

"Birthe thinks I look tired, but it's been a long day and I can rest on the train," Karen explained, surprised and a little irritated that Birthe too seemed to know her secret.

Finally, Birthe drove them to the train, where the boxes waited. Elsbeth sat with her package in her arms, stroking the brown paper and dreaming of her future home. Lil-Anne slept with her head in her mother's lap while Karen half-dozed, grateful not to have to drive the wagon home. *I wish people wouldn't fuss so. I'd like to forget, to stay happy for a little while longer.*

13
Karen's Folkschool

Most of the readers of this newspaper know of Danebod Folkschool, our neighbor in Tyler, but may not know about the inspiration for its development. It was built by the first Danish settlers in accordance with the educational principles of the remarkable Bishop Grundtvig, who was instrumental in establishing many such schools in Denmark during the middle of this century. The first was in Rødding, Schlesvig then the southern-most part of Denmark. It was to be a school for the people, a 'Folkeskole' for young adults of the rural areas who had no opportunity for learning anything other than what rigid schoolmasters could cram into their heads until they were fourteen. Grundtvig's goal was to teach students to appreciate Denmark's ancient culture and history and thus counterbalance the German influence in Schlesvig.

After the fateful war between Germany and Denmark in 1864, the border was moved and Rødding became part of Germany. The school was no longer allowed to teach in Danish. Consequently the year after the war's end, three of the teachers: the theologians Rector Ludvig Schrøder and Heinrich Nutzhorn and veterinarian Rasmus Fenger founded a new school in Askov, a small village just north of the new border. The railroad had just been completed through that part of the country and the Vejen train station was only a few miles away. Just as important as the railroad was for the development of Minnesota, it was crucial for the physical and spiritual reconstruction of Denmark after the war. Students were able to come to the new school from all over Jylland without spending days in a stagecoach, and it was hoped that other young people, living in the south under

German domination, would also come and learn about their Danish heritage.

Until the development of the folkschools, the only opportunity for higher education was the University in Copenhagen, and to be admitted students first had to matriculate from an exclusive Latin School. Grundtvig himself had gone to University and was a classics scholar as well as a pastor, but he had hated his years at Aarhus Latin school, hated the rigid discipline and narrow conventional thinking. He felt that in order to become free citizens, young people from the rural areas need a more relevant liberating education. He also held that the education of women as well as men was important for the development of both the individual and society. This spirit then became Askov in 1865. Our Danebod School was established less than thirty years later for the Danes of rural Minnesota according to these same ideals.

Karen Andersdatter
The Lincoln Pioneer
October 15, 1890

On a dreary fall day, cloudy and with a biting wind from the southwest, the girls were in the kitchen for their afternoon reading. Inger had left for the Bullards as Maia's time was near, but the other three had spent the morning doing household chores. As usual, after the midday meal was cleared away, the girls were spending the afternoon on their mutual intellectual education. Often one of them read aloud in English or retold the story if it was in some other language. After each chapter they would stop to discuss the material. They could sew or knit while they talked, but the reigning madmor, Bridget now that Minnehaha had left, was supposed to keep the conversation from deteriorating into gossip.

Karen was letting down the hem of a dress for Lil-Anne who was supposed to be practicing knitting. Frustrated with dropped stitches and bored by the adult conversation, Lil-Anne jumped up, abandoning her grubby facecloth-to-be on her stool. "It looks like rain," she mumbled and ran out to see if she could talk Svend into picking up her brother at school. John usually walked the mile-and-a-half, but sometimes she and Svend would pick him up in the wagon when it rained. It didn't really look like rain, but Lil-Anne could be very persuasive.

Kristina was reading aloud from *A Dollhouse* by Henrik Ibsen. Karen had been searching for some way to reach the still-homesick Norwegian girl and had managed to find a newly translated copy of the play. She had two motives; Kristina might appreciate knowing that her famous *landsmand* was respected in her new country, and reading aloud would help her English.

The fine plan was not working. Kristina had never heard of Ibsen and had never seen any play, much less one by the controversial playwright. The translation was awkward, the English difficult, and Kristina frequently had to stop for help in pronouncing the unfamiliar words. Even for the rest of the girls, the play was too sophisticated; the concept of a wife leaving her home and children was shocking.

Karen finally threw up her hands and put a stop to everyone's misery. "Let's try this a different way. At Askov when we ran into trouble with a difficult assignment, we each read the book and then discussed it later. I'll find a copy of *Dukkehuset* in Norwegian for Kristina and Elsbeth while Bridget can read it in English. Then we'll each take a part and read a scene aloud. You'll see, that'll be much more fun. It's really a wonderful play and will teach us modern thinking about women and marriage." *It may even do me some good*, Karen thought morosely.

Kristina, looking sullen, whispered to Elsbeth, "What's this Askov that Karen always talks on? Some other dreary flat-land town?"

"Yeah, it's a town in flat-land Denmark," Elsbeth whispered back, just loudly enough for Karen to hear. "It has a school, something like Danebod. She went there once, a long time ago."

Karen was about to protest that Askov might be flat, but it wasn't dreary when Bridget-madmor came to the rescue, her sweet brogue exaggerated. "C'n you no tell us a story from your school days?"

A chorus of enthusiastic 'please' followed. Karen was reluctant, protesting that she was too tired. She suspected that they were trying to divert her from discussing modern literature, but she loved telling stories and was quickly persuaded.

"You're so smart, Karen. Couldn't you have gone to Latin School and University?" Bridget asked, knowing the answer.

"Well, my brother, Christian, did and he's now a classics scholar at the University, but I was a girl and Danish girls only go to school until they're fourteen. One of Bishop Grundtvig's new ideas was that girls too should be educated. He felt that even if women can't vote, the future of the country is in the hands of mothers."

"Did you go to Askov when the school first opened?" Elsbeth asked.

"I was only eight then! I didn't go until I was sixteen, and even so I had to get special permission because I was supposed to be at least eighteen or twenty. Or maybe no one told them my age. I was never sure and I certainly wasn't going to bring it up."

"Were there lots of neat boys there? Was that where you met Peter?" Kristina suddenly seemed interested.

Aha. Maybe that's Kristina's secret. Maybe that's why she's so unhappy—she left a beau back in Norway! Now who might be right for her...? Aloud, Karen answered, "They were very old-fashioned. The girls' program was during the summer while the boys went in the winter, so there was no chance of any funny business. The summer teachers were all married men—or their wives. We were supposed to concentrate on our studies! But it was really marvelous to be exposed to great ideas and be taken seriously for a change. That's why I make you girls study as well as work. I can't give you Askov, but we can at least learn something. Even if you never have the chance to go to university, you can hold your own in any conversation."

"Yeah, but does it have to be boring Ibsen?" Kristina mumbled. Then, returning to what was foremost on her mind, she became more animated. "Weren't you homesick? Wasn't it boring without boys?"

"Some of the girls had never been away from home before and they were homesick. One girl was from a wealthy merchant family in Randers and wasn't used to sharing a room and she grumbled a lot. We made our own fun on Sundays, and the rest of the week they kept us too busy listening to lectures, writing, reading and doing gymnastics for us to be bored—they were big on gymnastics, that and singing. No dancing though. For some reason they thought dancing was indecent. Anyway, there wasn't anyone to dance with; the teachers were too married and too old!"

"I'm glad they let us dance at Danebod, the Saturday night dances there are the most fun," Elsbeth burst out. "But I like the singing too!"

"Weren't there any boys in the town?" Kristina asked; she couldn't seem to get away from the subject.

"We weren't allowed to talk to the local farm boys, besides, the town was very small. There were ways though…." Karen had a gleam in her eyes and the girls settled in for the story.

"Soon after I arrived in Askov, I received a letter from my aunt in Ribe that she and my two older cousins were visiting her brother, my Uncle Mathias. Since his farm was only about five miles from Askov, the whole family was driving up to the school and taking me out to Sunday dinner in the nearby town of Vejen. Of course, I had no trouble getting permission for something so respectable. I was still wearing traditional Fanø clothes then, scarves and all, but since Aunt Ingrid had sent me a lovely summer dress as a present, I decided to wear that. I shared a room with three other girls—and did we have fun dressing me up and piling my hair on top of my head!

"Soon after church, two carriages drove up filled with ten cousins, three aunts, and two uncles—a noisy group! Imagine my surprise when I discovered that Svend was driving one of the carriages. 'Go-daw Mistress Moon' he said, tipping his hat."

"Is that how you met Svend?" Elsbeth interrupted.

"No, we met the winter before in Ribe where he was a carter and sometimes carriage driver. Already then he had decided to be my guardian angel and began calling me by my nickname. That summer, he had driven the family up from Ribe. When Uncle Mathias saw his skill with horses, he was so impressed that he hired him as groom.

"Even more surprising was that my friend Michel Mogens from Ribe was driving the other carriage. I thought at first that he was just one of my uncle's hands until he echoed, 'Go-daw Mistress Moon'. He had somehow wrangled an invitation to come along to the farm and then to stay for the rest of the summer. He could be very persuasive. This is where the story really begins because Michel was a poet with romantic ideas about me."

By this time, all eyes were fixed on Karen's face. No one was sewing anymore. The girls were so absorbed in the tale, hardly believing that their proper mistress had ever had a romance — other than with Peter, of course.

"We had a lovely respectable dinner at Vejen Inn, and they dropped me at Askov on the way back to the farm. I thought that was the end of the adventure, but the next Sunday Svend drove up with the carriage again, only this time it was empty. 'Go-daw Mistress Moon' he said as before, and handed me a note.

Everyone, including me, assumed that it was an invitation to my uncle's farm, and I didn't tell them otherwise.

"The brief note was in English. 'The carriage will bring you to my magic kingdom deep in the vast forest. Come *in cognito*.' I recognized Michel's style. He knew that I could not resist an adventure."

"Did you wear your beautiful dress?" Elsbeth asked, her mind on wedding dresses.

"No, because *in cognito* means in disguise, and that dress was as conspicuous as my Fanø clothes. I wore my everyday apron and a plain bonnet instead of my scarf, and looked like any farm girl from the area. Soon Svend and I took off. Around the bend in the road, there stood Michel with a big grin and a picnic basket.

"We had a great afternoon. Then for the rest of the summer, but only every few weeks so as not to raise suspicion, Svend would show up and take me to Michel, and we would go somewhere for a picnic. One time we even brought the other three girls from my room, sworn to secrecy, of course. In the fall, Michel was to teach at Askov, and he would immediately have been fired if anyone had suspected that he was meeting students. And the rest of us would have been sent home."

But if Svend was your guardian, why did he agree to help you?" Kristina asked.

I hope I'm not giving anyone ideas, Karen thought, but continued her tale. "I suppose he wanted to make sure Michel behaved. And without a chaperone, I would not have agreed to go. Michel was very handsome and romantic, but I didn't really trust him."

"So did ye fall in love with him?" Bridget asked. "What about Peter, I thought he was your beau?"

"I was young, very young, and it was fun to be courted, though I didn't realize until later that that's what Michel was doing. Besides, Peter was sailing in the Pacific and had not asked me yet. Michel did propose, but not until the fall. I had just received Peter's letter suggesting we become engaged when Michel suddenly showed up on Fanø and asked if he could speak to my father. He planned that we could get permission to be married in the spring when I became seventeen and that I return with him to Askov and become a teacher too. My mother was all for my marrying Michel instead of Peter, but my mind was made up."

"But when did you and Peter finally get married?" Elsbeth asked, her mind still on weddings.

"That's a story for another day," Karen replied. "Besides, here come the children." She was glad to distract the girls from what had turned out to be a more risqué story than she had intended. Fortunately, she too was distracted and felt much cheerier.

Not only had John returned from school but right behind the Larsen wagon came the Bullards' buckboard with Minnehaha at the reins, Inger next to her with the youngest Benson child on her lap, and the three older children in the back.

Mildred said we should have a treat," Minnehaha declared. "She stayed home to visit with Mrs. Benson."

The three children scampered off to the orchard to play hide-and-seek with Lil-Anne. Karen told John to help Svend with the horses and Kristina and Bridget to take the youngest out to the kitchen for cookies. Pulling the two visiting girls off to the study, she asked about the Bensons.

"Mildred thinks it might be today," Minnehaha said. "She wanted us to get the children out of the way."

"We'll take them back to the Bullards' house tonight," Inger added.

They reported that with Oskar working at the Bullards' place and spending more time at home, things were a little better for the family. Every day, Mildred thought up more improvements for which she needed Oskar's cabinetmaker skills, and Obadiah was very pleased with his work. His English was not very good, but if Mildred drew a sketch of what she needed, he would get busy with ruler, saw and hammer until a masterpiece emerged. Often it was not exactly what Mildred had envisioned, but Oskar's grin as he lovingly ran his hands over the satin-smooth wood was irresistible. At home he was still impatient and rough with the boys, but with more food on the table, the hollow cheeks of the four children were filling in and they were starting to smile more. Maia was a little better but still too thin, and the doctor had been brought in. He was very concerned about the imminent delivery and had ordered her to be off her feet as much as possible.

Inger and Minnehaha were working at both houses, going to the soddy in the mornings while Oscar worked at the Bullards. He still resisted their help and became furious if Maia didn't have his dinner ready on his return, but most of the time the girls managed to have him think that Maia had prepared it herself and was merely lying down afterwards.

"I'll probably be able to come home here in a few weeks," Inger predicted.

"I'll miss you," Minnehaha said fondly. "Mildred is so full of plans, she keeps us all busy. We've made a stack of squares for Elsbeth's wedding-ring quilt, and in a few more weeks we'll be ready to piece it together. It's going to be *so* beautiful. I can't wait to start one for myself."

"Have you picked out the groom too?" Karen teased. "Isn't there a certain Hans that has his eyes on you?"

"Let him keep his eyes to himself. Who said anything about getting married? I just like the pattern," Minnehaha retorted, tossing her braids. "If you're all going to jump to conclusions, I'll make a Dresden Plate quilt instead! Then we can make one with wedding rings for Inger here."

"Hoho, is Karl Johnson from the newspaper still hanging around?" Karen asked, but Inger only blushed and wouldn't look at her.

Minnehaha had more news. The rector of her church in Tyler had offered to write a letter to the clergyman in charge of Saint Cornelia Episcopal Church in Norton to find out more about her parents.

"St. Cornelia is Chief Good Thunder's church, being built on the land he donated to Bishop Whipple and named for the bishop's first wife," Minnehaha explained. "I'm grateful to Rector for his kindness, but I'm afraid of what the answer will be. If Papa won't talk about it, it must be a dreadful story. Mildred says that if Papa's family came from Redwood Falls, they may have been in one of the massacres in the Sioux uprising. Or what if he killed one of my mother's relatives and feels guilty, even after all this time?"

"Don't you think you will be better off knowing the truth than imagining a thousand possibilities?" Karen asked. She knew what havoc burying the past had done to her mother's spirit.

"That's just what Mildred says. But what if they were all killed in their beds, or …?"

A loud clap of thunder followed by a torrential shower interrupted them. The laughing children returned from the orchard with their clothes drenched and Karen scurried to find something dry for them all to wear. Then John came inside and also needed a change of clothes. Soon all settled in the kitchen with hot cider and cookies, surrounded by dripping shirts and wet socks draped in front of the stove.

14
Longing for Home

A memorable year in Finmarken, in the spring, so many brave fishermen were lost in a terrible day and night of storm. When it was all over, women were in mourning all along the coast [of Norway]. Wives never saw their husbands again; mothers had one or two fewer sons. Many a strong women was broken when the young man to whom she had given her life's hope did not return. The mighty sea had risen and taken more than its tithe. During the summer that followed ... during white nights, many eyes looked from the top of the hills and cliffs with a view to the north. They sought the boats that were expected but never came. The eyes stared and stared. They teared, were dried, and stared again. Wasn't that a boat, — that speck out there? — Dear God, could that be a boat?

> *Længselens Baat—The Boat of Longing*
> Ole Edvart Rølvaag (1876-1931)

That same evening, Maia Benson had her baby. The birth didn't help Karen feel any better, for Maia was still very weak, and it would be several weeks before Inger would be able to come home. The Benson family was constantly on Karen's mind. Leaving them in Mildred's hands was fine in theory, but worries kept her up half the night and she lost her temper over the slightest problem. To make matters worse, this week's column for the paper was only half finished, and they had had no word from Jesse about Hanna's baby. Karen had a feeling that something dreadful was about to happen—it always did when she was pregnant.

Kristina continued to try her patience, but this morning she had been furious. "How could you forget?"

The girl seemed less homesick now that the young men of Lincoln had discovered her and swarmed about her rosy cheeks and blonde braids as if they were bees and she the honeysuckle by the apple orchard. But Karen often found herself saying "certainly not," that hated phase of her mother's. Just last week it had been, "Certainly not. You may not go riding alone with Olaf Johnson."

"You went out with your poet, why can I not?" Kristina protested. Her English had improved, but Karen suspected she reverted to old habits when she wanted pity.

"You may go anywhere during free-time—if Svend is willing to be your chaperone," Karen replied with a smile. She had feared that telling the girls about her Askov escapades was a mistake, and here the story was, back to haunt her!

This argument was only one of innumerable others that she had had with Kristina: about going to the Methodist Church instead of with her Lutheran parents, skipping church altogether, shirking her work, or dressing improperly. Last night, she had caught herself saying, "Certainly not. You may not go to the Harvest Dance at Danebod with Jakob Hansen."

"But everyone go, even if not Danish."

"It has nothing to do with your not being Danish. You know that your church doesn't allow dancing and I promised your parents. You talk to *them*."

Today Kristina was still sulking, and now she had 'forgotten' to do the milking. Elsbeth had done it for her and never complained, but Bridget-madmor had told Karen about this latest problem. She sighed. *I don't have the energy for arguments.*

She sighed again and went looking for Kristina. The moody girl was on Lil-Anne's swing by the springhouse, looking for all the world as if she had nothing to do but while away the morning. That was when Karen lost her temper and shouted, "How could you forget the milking?"

"I yust did," Kristina sulked.

"Nevertheless, it's your responsibility to remember. We all have our chores, and Elsbeth shouldn't have to do yours, especially when we're shorthanded with Inger away."

"You no understand. I yust forgot," Kristina repeated stalking off and muttering in Norwegian, *"Det var jo ikke jeg som ville reise til dette kjipe stedet*—It wasn't me that wanted to come to this dull place." They had heard the word *kjipe* frequently lately, until Karen was ready to scream.

Peter was mounting his horse to go off somewhere for the day. He understood the Norwegian only too well. "What's all the shouting?" he asked Karen as he pecked her cheek good-bye. "You sound just like your Mam scolding you."

"That was different. Mam was impossible."

Peter laughed. "Maybe Kristina thinks you're impossible."

"You can laugh," Karen said. "But I'm the one who promised her parents that I'd watch out for her. I knew it was a mistake to take someone that young." Then she too had to admit that it *was* funny and started to giggle. Here she was in Mam's shoes and was even using the very same words.

"But what am I going to do about Kristina?" She smiled wryly. "Maybe she'll just go away like I did, and then I don't have to worry about her any more."

"I'm afraid she doesn't have as much sense as you and might do something more stupid than become a folkschool student," Peter said soberly. "If Kristina doesn't like it here, perhaps you should talk to the Stavangers about her going home."

Karen squinted fondly up at her husband. *He looks more like a western cowboy than Kaptajn Storkeben.* "But with Inger away, how would we manage? And if Kristina leaves now, how will we fit a new girl into our rotation schedule?"

"You'll figure something out; you always do."

"That's easy enough for you to say," she retorted remembering when he had proposed in a letter from the other side of the world but she was the one who had to face Mam. Although Kristina was not her daughter, she didn't want to relive such a battle.

"Maybe you've learned a little something since then. Besides, you need to practice handling seventeen-year-old girls," Peter chuckled. "Anne will be that age only too soon. I'm not looking forward to the boys swarming around that honey-pot!" He spurred the horse and cantered off. At least he would be home tonight, only going to Tracy to see a man about a hog.

Karen decided that maybe she *had* learned something over the years and would try one more time to have a talk with Kristina. First she would ask Bridget-madmor for advice.

"I don't think Kristina's that unhappy here," Bridget surprised her by saying. "She's certainly not as homesick for Norway. It's hard for her to be responsible for herself, the way you're trying to teach us; she finds it difficult to balance freedom and responsibility. Let Elsbeth and me talk to her and explain that we all felt the same way at first."

"That's a good idea, but let me talk to her first. I wish Inger were here. She's got a good head on her shoulders, and Elsbeth won't be much help to you, she's so wrapped up in her Fred."

"We'll manage."

That afternoon, Karen worked at the desk in the study and Lil-Anne was on the floor with paper and colored pencils, whining about being bored. To distract the child, she said brightly, "In a bit, you and I'll go into Lincoln to see if there's a letter from Jesse. And we can visit Papa at the newspaper, if he's back. Now please be good and find Kristina; I need to talk to her. Then ask Svend to hitch up the buggy."

"Oh-oh, Kristina's in trouble again," Lil-Anne exclaimed and scampered away.

While Karen waited, she debated whether to confront Kristina from behind the desk. *It'll be friendlier if I sit on the couch.*

Her eyes wandered around the familiar room, looking at each of her treasures and finally come to rest on the photographs. The pictures had been last winter's Christmas present from Fanø and usually made her smile because the photographer had managed to catch the personality of each member of the family despite the formal poses.

Next to her parents' picture was one of Sister Anne, her husband Karl, and their two small children. She still resembled the 'Lil-Anne' of her childhood, a sunbeam on a dull day, like her American niece. Husband Karl looked dependable, baby Klaus impish like his mother, and little Karen the spitting image of her father. Anne, who had long since abandoned traditional dress, was elegant in her simple skirt and jacket, the long peplum extending well over generous hips. Her blonde hair was a frizzy halo around her face while a bristle of hairpins failed to control the thick bun at the nape of her neck. Her lips were pressed together to keep from laughing at the restless boy on her lap. The child's pudgy hand held a wilting flower, which had probably been given to him in a vain attempt to keep him still. Karen had met neither her sister's husband nor their two children, but the contentment of that next generation of Sønderho millers shone from the picture as it did in Anne's occasional letters.

Contentment. Gratitude for all that we have, that's the message of Jesse's sermon. Kristina is old enough to solve her own problems. She just needs to know that she can.

In the picture of her parents, Papa looked sturdy, Mam aloof. She was standing behind and slightly to the side of Papa's chair, dressed in her best apron, blouse, and Fanø scarves. The apron had knife-edge pleats, the silk so stiff it showed on both sides of the chair. The silver buttons on her overblouse had been polished until they reflected the light from the flash-powder, and the silk headscarf had been perfectly tied so the ends fairly bristled with pride. Papa, sitting down so as not to tower over his wife, had buried his right hand in the folds of Mam's skirt. The other thumb was hooked into the west pocket over the watch chain that was looped across his massive chest. Good humor radiated from his eyes and he half-smiled.

Today Karen didn't feel like smiling back, troubled over what to say to Kristina. Her mother must have had conversations like this with her many girls over the years, but all being from Fanø they at least hadn't been homesick, had gone home to their own mothers each evening. How to be wise like Mam? How to say the right thing? She thought of the many times Mam had lectured her about lack of responsibility, shirking chores, wandering off, dreaming. Had the lectures ever done any good? Had they only stirred resentment? Or had the lessons buried deep, made her strong and able to face the hard times? *Or did she only teach me to push the hard times out of the way, like a storm swell out at sea that is hardly noticed until it comes crashing onto the shore?*

Could they have avoided our monumental fights over Peter? Probably not, given how stubborn they both were. *But if each of us had bent a little, the hard times might have been easier, the distance between us less.*

I wish you were here now, telling me to stand tall. I wish Papa were here to lift me up with his strong hands and to make me smile.

Karen's thoughts were interrupted by Kristina's quiet knock on the door. "Enter," she called. Patting the couch next to her, she watched the girl slump into the far corner as if she feared another scolding.

Speaking slowly and in Danish so Kristina would feel free to answer in Norwegian, she asked, "*Hvordan kan vi gøre dit liv mindre kedeligt?*—How can we make your life less boring?"

Correcting the last word so the girl would understand, she repeated, "*mindre kjipe.*"

Kristina looked stunned as if no one had ever asked her opinion before, then a torrent of singsong Norwegian poured forth. Karen only half understood, but it didn't matter, and she let the words flow over her without interrupting. Kristina *hated* her parents for dragging her away from home and friends where she'd been *happy*. She missed the sea and the mountains; she *hated* the endless corn and wheat fields of Minnesota.

Finally, the litany of complaints wound down. "Why do you think your parents wanted to come to America?" Karen asked.

"I don't know. Something about opportunity. But they could've used the passage money for a bigger fishing boat or a better house in Norway, instead of the awful shack we have now."

"Did they emigrate to make a better life for you and your brothers?" Karen felt she was voicing the obvious.

"I suppose so," Kristina mumbled. "But it's lonely and boring. The food is boring and the lake fish taste as flat as the Prairie."

"It will be hard work for a few years, but here your brothers don't have to go to sea, and when you marry you won't have to worry whether your husband will make it through the next storm. Can you understand that?" *I do sound just like Mam. Next I'll be saying, 'Wed a sailor and weep at his grave'!*

She handed the girl a handkerchief and watched her wipe her eyes.

"Oh, I don't mind hard work—I'm used to it from home, but there I knew everyone—they were all my friends and they understood me."

Karen remembered how homesick she had been when she first came to America and how frustrating the language barrier was. She had seen the same with many of the immigrants: the young children adjusted quickly while the parents struggled to find their place between the old world and the new; but the adolescents had the hardest time. On the scattered farms they had little opportunity to make friends or to improve their English. They had not chosen to be torn away from their old life and now felt alienated both from their family and new home. She was convinced that the more quickly they learned to fit in the better and that the company of others their age made the adjustment easier. How best to convince Kristina? Well, she could but keep trying, and the other girls would help.

"I know how difficult a new country is at first, everyone feels that. I promise it will get easier, especially now that your English is so much better. You'll find that people are the same everywhere, and not so different from your old friends—you just have to get to know them."

Kristina looked doubtful, protested that she wasn't the same as everyone else, no one had ever been as miserable as she, no one understood how difficult it all was.

Now for the test. "Would you rather go home?" Karen said, as if the idea had just occurred to her. "There's an Icelandic girl who is anxious to come. We can write her and see if she wants to take your place."

Kristina started to answer that she wanted more than anything to go home but it was impossible; *ever*. Then she realized that Karen wasn't talking about returning to Norway. "Please don't send me back to my parents and that dreadful shack on the dreadful Prairie," she wailed and started to cry again. "They never let me have any fun. There's no one to talk to except my dumb brothers. At least here there are girls my age." Her expression added a silent "and boys."

"Would it help if I explained to your parents about the Harvest Dance? I can point out that you're old enough to make some decisions for yourself. They might agree if I tell them how important it is to you and that it's well chaperoned and quite innocent."

"Oh yes, please, and I promise to do better about the chores," Kristina brightened, straightening her back.

Papa's right, Karen thought. *Let people talk and they'll eventually convince themselves to do the right thing.* "You'll still have to settle with Bridget and Elsbeth. They've had to do your share of the work and should have a say."

"I'll do whatever they want. Don't give away my place, *please*. I'll even read Ibsen."

Karen suppressed a smile. "That won't be necessary. Just stand tall and be proud of who you are—the rest will follow." There she was, quoting Mam again.

Later that afternoon, while Lil-Anne and Karen did errands, the three girls met. Apparently matters were settled to everyone's satisfaction, for at supper that night, the table was ringed with smiles and cheerful conversation. Lil-Anne sensing that Kristina needed special attention, sat next to her, making sure that food was passed their way and providing a running translation of the conversation. Would wonders never cease?

The next day was Saturday and all morning, despite the threat of thunderstorms, the Babel women arrived with their children. This might be the last time until spring that all could come and that they could meet in the barn. Kristina's family came early, and her mother was climbing off the wagon when Karen spoke to her about the dance. The Stavangers seemed truly concerned about their daughter and agreed that if it would help to allow her to go to a harmless dance, so be it.

"But don't you boys get any ideas," Mr. Stavanger said sternly in Norwegian to his sons sitting in back of the wagon. He cracked the whip over the backs of the oxen and the wagon lumbered off towards Lincoln and Saturday errands while his wife carried her workbasket and food dish into the barn.

Bridget and Elsbeth went down to the orchard to arrange games for the younger children, but it was Kristina's turn to be in the barn. Lil-Anne was still treating her as her special charge and was gravely supervising as she helped the women arrange their lunch baskets on a long trestle table. When Mrs. Stavanger came in with a pot of *fruktsoppa*—fruit soup, Kristina's happy greeting gave no hint that she 'hated' her mother. On hearing that she would be allowed to go to the party after all, she broke into an even wider grin.

"We're going to the dance!" Lil-Anne shouted gleefully, jumping up and down and clapping her hands.

Karen quietly explained that Kristina was going, but Lil-Anne was too young.

"Oh, I *know* that," the child said impatiently. "I'm *always* too young. But I'll dream about being there. And Kristina will tell me all about it; won't you?" She looked up at her new friend, her blonde curls forming a halo around her face.

15
Covenant

And I will give unto thee, and to thy seed after thee, the land wherein thou art a stranger, all the land of Canaan, for an everlasting possession; and I will be their God. And God said unto Abraham, Thou shalt keep my covenant therefore, thou, and thy seed after thee in their generations. This is my covenant, which ye shall keep, between me and you and thy seed after thee; Every man child among you shall be circumcised. And ye shall circumcise the flesh of your foreskin; and it shall be a token of the covenant betwixt me and you. And he that is eight days old shall be circumcised among you, every man child.

Genesis 17: 8-12.

Now these be the last words of David. David the son of Jesse said, and the man who was raised up on high, the anointed of the God of Jacob, and the sweet psalmist of Israel, said, The Spirit of the LORD spake by me, and his word was in my tongue. The God of Israel said, the Rock of Israel spake to me, He that ruleth over men must be just, ruling in the fear of God. And he shall be as the light of the morning, when the sun riseth, even a morning without clouds; as the tender grass springing out of the earth by clear shining after rain.

2 Samuel 23: 1-4

By the end of October, the weather turned colder. It was too early for snow, but each dawn there was frost on the ground and by day, black storm clouds scudded across the prairie. Monday morning Karen and the girls raced to get the laundry out on the line and then had to rush the still-damp sheets into in the barn ahead of a driving rain. On Tuesday they were still wet, so the girls lugged them back outside to take advantage of a brief period of sun and a brisk wind. By noon they were dry, but the girls had barely folded them and brought them inside before it started again.

That's me these days, Karen thought. *Every day is colder and the sun hardly has a chance to warm us when it time for another storm.*

After the dishes were cleared, a knock on the door announced the arrival of a soaked Karl Johnson carrying an envelope. "This telegram came to the *Pioneer* office," he said. "Peter went to Lake Benton for a meeting. I thought it might be important so I brought it right out."

Karl stood rooted to the entrance, vainly searching the room for Inger so intently that Karen had to wrest the telegram from his hand. With shaking hands, she tore open the envelope—news from Marshall, but to her relief, good news. Hanna's baby had arrived during the night, the boy that Karen had predicted but had hardly dared hope for. "Bris on Thursday STOP Please come STOP Jesse," the telegram concluded.

"Hallelujah," Karen exclaimed. "Peter and I are both free Thursday. We'll take the train in the morning and be home right after dinner."

She grabbed a piece of paper and said to the dripping boy, "Inger isn't here, but Bridget-madmor will find you a dry shirt and pants. Fred's might fit you. Then go right to the telegraph office and have them send this reply. Peter will pay for it tomorrow."

"Why're you laughing?" Lil-Anne interrupted. "What's going on?"

Karen read the telegram aloud but had trouble explaining why Lil-Anne couldn't come to the *bris* if it was like a Jewish baptism. "You have to be older," she said lamely.

"That's what you always say when you don't want me to do something."

"You got to go to Marshall last time. Now it's John's turn to ride the train—besides Friday is his birthday." *Let Peter explain what a circumcision is*, she thought gleefully. *Serves him right for not telling me he was out of town today. The sneak probably thought I wouldn't know he was gone as long as he was he was back in time for dinner.*

Karen leaned back in her chair, a wave of contentment

chasing away the depression of the past week. She finally rose and went outside. The storm clouds had melted away, and the orchard trees were yellow silhouettes against the blue October sky.

That evening, Peter offered to brush Karen's hair, as he often did before they went to bed. He let the soft strands glide through his hands and watched her breath slow to a dreamy purr as he slowly counted the strokes.

"Your eyes are narrow slits, like a cat's," he murmured.

She bolted upright and sent dagger glances at his image in the mirror. "Oh no you don't," she growled. "You don't get around me that easily! I'm still mad at you for leaving town. You promised!"

"It was just a short meeting five miles down the road," he protested. "Lake Benton Town Council was discussing how to attract tourists to the area, and I needed to take notes for the paper. I can't tell you every time I'm gone for a couple of hours."

"But suppose something happened and I needed you?"

"You're turning into such a worrywart. Nothing is going to happen, and someone will always know where to find me."

She continued to grouse until Peter said firmly, "I'm in too good a mood to let you spoil it by your whining." That would stop her. *She knows I can't stand whiny women. She isn't being fair. I'm always there when she really needs me. Except for that one time. And I couldn't help that. Could I?*

Peter felt too happy to let Karen's moodiness ruin it. Hoping to lift her up with him, he waxed eloquent about what a good week it had been. Even though it was still October, the threshing was done for the season, even at the outlying farms on the fringe of the cooperative.

He never talked about his concern about finishing the threshing in time, but in town they still recalled the dreadful year when many farmers were ruined by a mid-October snowstorm. Back in 1880 that was, the fall before he and Karen came to Minnesota. The stacks of wheat of all the surrounding farms had been caught in the early hard freeze. The winter that followed had not been particularly bad, but it had been long and the cold had stayed in the ground. Come spring, the thaw revealed mounds of rotted grain under the melting snow. Ever since then the region prepared early for the Minnesota winter.

"The bank draft for our share of the *MS Karen*'s season came today," he said. "The mortgage is nearly paid off, all but a bit of the loan for the Johansen farm. The cold weather can come when it will. We'll be snug."

"Mmmm," Karen purred, as he plaited her hair in a loose braid. No sign of her earlier anger, but she was so volatile these days—like the October weather.

"Your column this week was especially fine," he said, knowing that she had fussed over it a long time. "Several people stopped me on the way home and said how much they liked it."

She nodded, looking pleased. But then she must have realized that he was flattering her and glared at him suspiciously in the mirror.

Persuasively, he continued, "By the way, I want to talk to you about Thursday...."

"I sent them a telegram that we're coming to the circumcision. I thought we could take the train. Isn't that all right?"

"It turns out that I have to give a talk in Red Wing the next day."

"Not another trip!"

Peter ignored the interruption. "So why don't we go together, take a little holiday at the Saint James Hotel? It's right on the Mississippi River and quite luxurious."

"I can't just take off and leave everyone like that! Red Wing's so far!" Karen stood up to open the window.

"Is this the daring woman who sailed all over the Pacific with me on the *Lady Roselil*? Red Wing's only a few hours by train, and you'll be home the next evening. Anne can stay with Helga, and John can bunk with the men. Surely, the girls can look after themselves for a day."

"I told John he could come with us to Marshall. He's looking forward to skipping school and being alone with us."

"We can put him on the train Thursday afternoon and then we go on to Red Wing. Svend can pick him up at the station. Don't look like that, he's almost as old as your brother when he ran away to sea!" Peter pointed out.

"He's only ten and Christian was twelve. Besides it's his birthday on Friday, and I promised him a special treat."

Peter grabbed Karen about the waist with one arm and tilted her chin up with his other hand. "You're getting to be a nice armful," he murmured as he kissed her.

"You're terrible. You know I can't resist you," Karen said, fighting to catch her breath. "All right, All right. But we'll just stay at the hotel in Marshall and I'll come home with John the next day while you go on to Red Wing."

"Having a ten year old with us at the hotel was not quite what I had in mind," Peter protested ruefully.

"Jesse will let John sleep with their boys," she said, sliding into bed. "They'll all like that."

"Mmm," Peter agreed, well content with the compromise, his goal all along. At least he had averted a fight about traveling. "Tell me again what they do to the poor kid at a *bris*."

"Come here, cowboy, and I'll show you. Then *you* can explain it to John."

Peter recoiled in mock horror. "Please don't hurt me."

"I promise, you idiot," Karen laughed, pulling him under the covers by his nightshirt.

Thursday morning Svend and Lil-Anne drove the three travelers to the station and saw them onto the train. Karen sat next to Peter while John was across the aisle, pretending he was traveling alone. He looked out the window and exclaimed whenever they passed October-brilliant trees.

Peter stood up and took a Bible out of his valise. After a few minutes of searching, he found what he wanted. "Here, Son," he said, leaning across the aisle and pointing to the page. "Here's the passage I was telling you about. I expect Hanna and Saul are calling the baby Abraham so he will have 'all the land of Canaan, for an everlasting possession'."

"Don't fill his head with stories," Karen reprimanded. "Saul's father's name was Abraham, and he had very few possessions. He passed away last year, so they're naming the baby for him."

"I like my version better."

She examined the open page in Peter's lap and asked in surprise, "Why the English Bible study?"

"I wanted to read about the *bris* from the source so I don't say something foolish to Jesse. He's such a scholar. Besides, John wanted to know where it comes from."

"But why in English? Don't you want John to learn the Danish Bible?" she teased. "Fru Skov told me that she makes her children say their prayers in Danish because she doesn't want them to speak to God in a language she doesn't understand."

Peter laughed. "Well we don't have to worry. Our children can talk to God in any language they want, and we'll figure it out. I like reading the Bible in English because it always seems so much fresher that way; you know, less familiar, more thought provoking. Take the beautiful word 'covenant'. The Danish '*Pakt*' doesn't have the same ring to it."

Peter babbled on, continuing by savoring the word 'sojourner' until he noticed that he'd lost his audience, both of them having closed their eyes to stop his lecture. He gently moved Karen's head from where it was bouncing on the windowpane and placed it against his shoulder. With his other hand he reached over to lightly stroke the blessed mound in her lap. Across the aisle, John briefly opened his eyes then quickly scrunched them closed and blushed.

"He's growing up," Peter mumbled in Karen's ear. "It's time to talk to him about another kind of covenant—the covenant between man and wife."

"You don't spend enough time alone with him."

"Perhaps next week I can take the boy with me when I go to the dairy farms in Anoka. He'll enjoy the trip and we can walk around Minneapolis between trains and have a chance to talk, man-to-man."

"Not another trip! You're hopeless!" Karen protested. "What about school?"

"Some things are more important than school."

And more important than your wife, she thought resentfully. *Any excuse to get away.*

Karen must have dozed because next she knew, Peter was immersed in the second book of Samuel. Seeing that she was awake, he whispered, "I think we should call our little one David. I like the idea of a son being a 'sweet psalmist' and 'as the light of the morning'.

"But she'll be Rachel. I told you," Karen said adamantly, almost forgetting to whisper.

"You can't know for sure."

"I do know. She has to be a girl."

"'Rachel' is a fine name and Jesse likes the idea, but let's think about 'David' just in case."

She closed her eyes again and mumbled, "If we ever have

another boy, he should be 'Lars' for my Grandfather since 'John' was for your father."

Peter started to protest, but the door at the end of the car opened. "Marshall. Marshall next," the conductor called, and the train slid into the station.

16

Minneapolis

"On June 11, 1888, [four railroad lines] were unified to form the Minneapolis St. Paul & Sault Ste. Marie Railway Company, the 'Soo Line,' with operations in five states and headquarters in Minneapolis....

"Within the Twin Cities, the railroads cooperatively formed the Minnesota Transfer Railway Company in 1883. The large transfer yard was laid out in the Midway area, and the MT was designed to handle interchange among the various Twin City railroads through this yard....

"Electrification of the street railways in Minnesota was launched during the year 1886, and the horsecar lines of the Twin Cities and Duluth were entirely converted by 1892. Dobbin, having had his day, bowed to the system of wires, power stations, and traction motors. There was one exception, at Mankato, where the Mankato Street Railway Company experimented with a horsecar operation as late as 1886."

Rails to the Northstar
Richard S. Prosser

In early November, John was allowed to take several days off from school to accompany Peter on his trip to Anoka. They would have plenty of time to talk as it would take most of a day to get there; two days touring the several modern farms, and then a day for the return trip.

Accordingly, about a week after Peter's trip to Red Wing, Svend once again brought the Larsen family to the train station in Lincoln, this time to say farewell to Peter and John. Karen and Anne made a big fuss about them leaving, but it seemed more for form's sake than a prelude to an argument.

John, one trip under his belt, talked about riding the train as if it were an ordinary occurrence, but he was so excited that he barely waited for the buckboard to stop before he jumped down and ran to the platform looking down the track for the approaching engine.

Peter had to grab him firmly by the elbow to prevent him from jumping on board the still moving car. Even when they climbed up the steps and found a place to sit, John wriggled restlessly in his seat and not until the conductor cried "all a 'board" and they chugged out of Lincoln did he settle down. Peter pulled the window closed, but even through the glass he could tell that Anne was calling after them, "Don't forget the trees."

"I won't," he mouthed back.

John, forehead pressed against the window so he would miss none of the sights, chanted a litany of the towns en route, adding each new station as they alternately whistled through or came to a jerking halt. "Lincoln, Tyler, Tracy, Lamberton, Sleepy Eye, ... " Finally, the conductor announced, "Mankato next. Mankato."

"While we wait for our train, we'll order the Christmas trees," Peter said.

"Don't forget the Anne-tree," John reminded him.

"I wouldn't dare."

They carried their valises down the block to an empty lot. Peter had to tell John to stay on the sidewalk so he wouldn't be run down by the horsecar that came lumbering by.

"Can we take one? Can we?"

"We're already there!" Peter answered, pointing to a man wearing a bushy beard and a bulky sweater. He carefully wrote their order in a big black book: "Two dozen cut firs, to be shipped to the Lincoln station in late December; one pine roots wrapped in burlap; shipped tomorrow—just like last year."

Peter settled the bill, and they walked back to have lunch at the station restaurant while waiting for the train to Minneapolis. This was John's first experience in a restaurant—he didn't count the familiar cafe in Lincoln where everyone called him by name and he was treated as one of the family. His eyes became as round as the chicken potpie that was placed before him with a tall ice cream soda that was evidently to be consumed through a hollow straw, but he had no trouble stowing the novel fare. Back on the train, he could not suppress a large burp as his eyes closed, a contented smile on his face.

Peter watched the sleeping boy and thought about how best to explain the facts of life to his son. It was good to bring John on this trip so they could talk. Fred had badly wanted to come since they were to visit several dairy farms, but Peter was firm in wanting to spend some time with his younger son.

As a farm boy, John would be familiar with the basic biology, but the idea of parents behaving like animals might be another story. His own father had been lost at sea off the coast of Africa when he was twelve. He had only figured out the way of a man with a maid when he was much older, and sailors on board his first ship had teased the naïve cabin boy without mercy. Peter wanted his son to find out in a more civilized way.

Also, he needed to warn John about Karen's moods. Even if they could avoid a repetition of the illness that had assaulted her before Anne was born, she was already showing signs of a sad withdrawal. He wished he could comfort her, but it was as if his very presence brought back the memories of when they lost Lars; then she would cry until her health suffered. Even when John was born she was very sick, but at least then they were on Fanø and she had her mother. They had both warned him—her mother and grandmother—it was better not to talk about Lars so Karen could forget.

She might complain about his traveling, but she seemed to cope better when he wasn't there, and everything was fine when he returned. *For a while anyway. Why troll for tragedy and worry about everyone? Why not just cherish the good times when the three of us sailed the Pacific and forget the bad?*

The train tracks that had been following the east bank of the Minnesota River crossed over a wide swampy area on a long bridge and the city lay before them. John woke up in time to stare out the window at all the marvels. Tall buildings whizzed by while horses hitched to loaded wagons, carriages filled with people, and waving pedestrians stopped on the busy streets to let them pass. They pulled into the depot tunnel and the conductor helped them down the steps onto a cement platform, one of many that ran in parallel lines under the huge bow of the ceiling. Passengers scurried to and fro as they were disgorged or swallowed by trains going to all points of the compass. Even

Peter had to stop to ask for directions to the stairs that would take them underground so they could catch the local train to Anoka.

Again they settled on a seat, this time a bench of hard wood. "We're on the Stone Arch Bridge. Below is the mighty Mississippi," Peter announced to the awed boy. "At the Transfer Yard, where all the railroad lines meet, we'll swing north and follow the east bank of the river for the twenty-mile ride to Anoka. Upstream of the Saint Anthony falls it will be not much wider than the Minnesota."

A buckboard was waiting for them at the train station to take them to the Reidel farm, right along the east bank of the Mississippi River. Mr. and Mrs. Reidel welcomed them graciously from the wide steps of a white clapboard house.

Peter and John picked up their valises and followed their host up a curving staircase to the second floor. "What a beautiful house," Peter said, impressed.

"Thank you," Mr. Reidel said, opening the door to the guestroom. "We built it eight years ago when we first settled here. Mrs. Reidel knew exactly what she wanted, had dreamt of owning such a house since she was a young girl. There's a pitcher of hot water and towels over there for you to clean up. Dinner will be in fifteen minutes."

Hands and faces clean, hair water-slicked, Peter and John went down to a beautifully appointed table where Mr. and Mrs. Reidel graced either end. Overawed by all the finery, John sat down in the chair next to his father. Tired after the long trip, but never too tired to eat, he sampled each of the strange dishes that were put before him, gratefully accepting a second helping of fried chicken and never mentioning that he had already had chicken once that day. He said 'please' and 'thank you' and, after stowing a generous slice of chocolate cake, even mumbled *tak for mad*. Papa explained that this was a Danish custom that also meant 'thank you'.

"Why, how lovely," Mrs. Reidel exclaimed. "What a polite young man."

In the morning, they inspected the bright and airy dairy barn, each cow contentedly chewing her mash in a separate stall. They admired the big grinder where corncobs were chopped into small pieces and mixed with minerals and studied the mechanism that delivered hay and mash to the mangers. Then they rode in a buggy out to the fields where calves were being fatted up to be shipped off to the slaughter house in St. Paul and even as far as Chicago. The next day, they visited other dairy farms in the area, going as far as Blaine; but none was as impressive as the Reidels'.

Their last day, they rose before sunrise to take the train to Minneapolis. There they walked down to the river from Union Station and visited the Washburn Mill, part of the industrial complex that was powered by the Saint Anthony Falls.

The friendly foreman offered to show them around. "Minneapolis is called 'Mill City'," he said. "The trains pull right up here to the platform where we're standing and unload grain from western Minnesota and the Dakotas. The elevators carry the grain up to the mill where it is ground into white flour and filled into sacks. Over there the bags are stacked on box cars to be shipped to eastern states."

"Is that what all the trains that we saw at the Transfer Yard are for?" John asked. "All for wheat and flour?"

"And corn and hogs from Iowa; lumber from the north; apples, milk, bricks from all over—all are shipped here. That which isn't consumed in the Twin Cities goes on to Chicago and further east."

They learned about the difference between stone grinding and steel cutting. "The steel cutting process is what makes it possible to use spring wheat from the colder northern states where winter wheat cannot be grown. That invention is what opened up the Dakota Territory to settlers, that and the extension of the railroad within the last 10 years."

"My grandfather owns the gristmill on Fanø back in Denmark," John bragged. "He says stoneground makes good bread."

"But the modern process makes a finer white bread and the flour keeps longer without turning rancid," Mr. Barker explained.

After they left the mill, boy and father walked along the mighty Mississippi. Seeing two huge towers in the distance, John pulled Papa along the street closer to the wondrous sight of two side-by-side bridges crossing the river. The older bridge, where they stood, was suspended from long cables between four stone towers, one pair on either bank. Beyond it, tandem steel arches spanned the river in two graceful loops, and the roadway already reached halfway across.

The older bridge had connected Nicollet Island to the west

bank of the river since 1876, but was to be torn down as soon as the new one was finished. The traffic rushed in both directions on this 'Gateway to the West'. John dragged his father to join the milling pedestrians, and, stopping halfway across, they stared down at the turbulent rapids of the Saint Anthony waterfalls. Below that, the water flowed downstream in a wide ribbon hemmed in on either side by wooded banks as far as the eye could see.

Even Peter was in awe of the fifty-six-foot wide wooden roadway that was flanked by two twelve-foot sidewalks. "This was the site of the first bridge to cross any part of the Mississippi," he bragged. "The first for two-thousand miles—all the way to New Orleans."

Downstream from where they stood, the Stone Arch railroad bridge made a diagonal curve across the river. Further down was another bridge filled with more traffic.

Peter pointed to the imposing limestone buildings on the bank to the left. "That's the University. If you do well at school, perhaps you can go there someday. Become a lawyer or a teacher or a doctor—whatever you wish."

John was more impressed by a car filled with passengers. "Where's the horse?" he asked.

"It's one of the new street trains coming from St. Paul."

"But there's no engine."

"It's powered by electricity. See the wires hanging overhead and the pole from the car up to the wire?"

A train chugged across Stone Arch bridge and the rumbling of the wheels reminded John that he was hungry.

"I saw a restaurant where we can buy some sandwiches. Back there on Hennepin Avenue," Peter said.

When they returned home, the boy was fast asleep in the carriage, replete with adventure. Peter carried him up to bed and then went to give a full report to Karen. It was close to midnight, and all she wanted to do was go back to sleep, but Peter made her listen.

On the return trip, he had finally had his father-son talk of how the love between a man and a woman resulted in blessings, like the one they were expecting. John was so embarrassed that, as soon as he figured out what his papa was talking about, he blushed and closed his eyes, pretending he was asleep. From the rigidity of his shoulders, Peter had sensed that the lad was listening and so he continued his awkward monologue.

At one point the boy's eyes had flown open in surprise, but then he mumbled, in English, "I know all that, Dad."

"I figured that with his 'Dad' he was rejecting Danish as the language of childhood, not suited for man-to-man talk," Peter chuckled. "But I also took it as a sign that he had heard me."

At this point, Karen could no longer keep her eyes open. "Mmph," she acknowledged and turned on her side away from Peter's droning voice.

At breakfast the next morning, Lil-Anne cross-examined her brother. "I want to hear *everything*," she insisted, unsatisfied with his sparse description of his great adventure.

"You wouldn't understand," John said grandly. "The running of dairy farms is a very complex grown-up business and the city is too big for little girls." But the rest of the day, he couldn't keep from showing off, dropping little tidbits of newfound knowledge.

"Just imagine, we crossed the mighty Mississippi!" John exclaimed that evening at dinner. "Teacher says that it's one of the world's mighty rivers. It goes two thousand miles to New Orleans on the Caribbean. When I grow up, I'm going to take a steamboat all the way down. All two thousand miles!"

At that point, Peter picked up the story. "We stayed at the Reidel Farm, right on the Mississippi. Mr. Reidel has one of the biggest and most modern dairy farms in the state. Their milk and butter go to people all over Minneapolis, every day."

Lil-Anne, bored by all these descriptions of places beyond her comprehension, growled impatiently, "Argh. Did you remember the trees?"

Peter solemnly reported that the trees had been ordered in Mankato and would be shipped in December, all except the potted one.

"The Anne-tree is in the wagon," Peter said. "We'll plant it Saturday morning."

17

The Anne-Tree

"Oh, to be as big a tree as the others!" sighed the little tree. "Then I could spread my branches all about and see the wide world from the top!"...

"Be joyful along with us!" said the air and the sunshine. "Enjoy the freshness of your youth in the open!"

But the tree wasn't at all happy. It grew and grew; it was green summer and winter—dark green. People who saw it said, "What a beautiful tree!" And at Christmas time it was the first to be chopped down. The ax bit deep to the core, the tree fell to the ground with a sigh. It was faint with pain and thought no longer of happiness, it was so sad to part from home, from the place it had grown up; for it knew that never again would it see old friends, the little bushes and flowers all around, perhaps not even the birds. Leaving was not at all pleasant.

The tree only awoke when it was unpacked in the square and heard a man say: "That one is magnificent! That's the one we want!"

The Spruce Tree
Hans Christian Andersen (1805–1875)

Christmas at Babel Farm was a very special time, and preparations started long before December because boxes for Denmark and letters for friends around the world had to be mailed in October. Throughout the summer, Karen collected presents to send home, and John and Anne made things for distant relatives. Already in September, they laid out the boxes and gradually filled them with gaily-wrapped packages.

The Christmas of 1890 was no exception, and, despite her waning energy, Karen too was caught up in all the preparations and traditions. "There's no point in sending them things they can buy as easily over there," she explained to her troops as she tucked hay around jars of honey. "But what we've made with our own hands or gathered from the fields is always appreciated."

When Lil-Anne helped her place fragrant sachets of lavender from the garden on top of each box that was to be sent home and sprinkle cinnamon and cloves over everything for that proper Christmas smell, the child pleaded, "Tell me again how it will be when they open the box."

Karen described how the Fanø part of the family would gather in the Southroom of Millfarm on Christmas Eve. "Grandpa Anders will cut the string and open the box. The room will fill with wonderful smells of cinnamon, cloves, and lavender. Then Grandpa will distribute the packages, and everyone will exclaim over each new treasure as it's brought out."

"And what'll Cousin Karen and Cousin Klaus say?" Lil-Anne prompted.

"Cousin Karen will be amazed. 'Did Cousin Anne really knit this facecloth all by herself?' But Cousin Klaus is too young to say anything but 'Ba', which is what he calls everything that he likes."

"What'll they think of the bags of Indian wild rice?" Lil-Anne herself was not overly fond of that strange food, complaining that it tasted like a mouthful of hay.

"Grandma Anne will wonder, 'What am I supposed to do with this hay?' but Aunt Anne will reach for her notebook on top of the beam in the kitchen and say, 'Karen's recipe's right here,'" Karen said, stretching one arm up towards the beams overhead to show how books were kept at Millfarm. "Of course, on Fanø the ceiling is much lower than in our Minnesota barn, so the top of the beam is easy to reach."

"'I never use recipes,' Grandma will grumble, but she'll tell everyone in town about the delicacies from America." Lil-Anne giggled and then put her hand over her mouth to keep still while her mother continued her story, "Grandma will have to sneak it into the conversation because she isn't one to brag; nevertheless, she'll find some excuse. Her after-Christmas letter will thank us very nicely, but the one from Aunt Anne will have a good story about Grandma running all over town to spread the word about the package from *A-mer-ika*. They each have their own way of showing that they really appreciate the presents."

"But what about Uncle Christian?"

"My brother and his family get that package in the corner. We have to send it to Copenhagen because that's where they live, and they spend Christmas with Aunt Amelia's parents."

"I think it's a shame that Cousin Anders and Cousin Niels don't get to spend Christmas on Fanø," the little girl argued. "If I lived in Copenhagen, I'd go even if it took all day to get there."

"Help me wrap this jar for Ribe," Karen said to change the subject away from her sister-in-law's snobbish rejection of her brother's family. "Great-aunt Ingrid really likes our apple blossom honey."

By mid-October the boxes were ready to be brought to the post office for the train trip across the continent, the brown paper-wrapped parcels securely tied with string. In New York they would be loaded aboard the special steamship, called the 'Christmas Ship' because it carried presents from all over the USA to Danish relatives. Eventually arriving in Copenhagen, the boxes would be unloaded and placed on trains for delivery to families all over the country.

Over the next few weeks Peter and Karen wrote and mailed long letters, addressed to exotic places like San Francisco, Holland, India, and Hawaii where they had sailed the first years of their marriage. Peter had introduced his bride to all the people he had met on his previous voyage, and together they had made new friends wherever they went. Karen usually loved to receive news from all over the world during the cold and dark Minnesota winter, but this year, she found it increasingly hard to write the same cheerful letter over and over to each of them announcing the coming event. By the time she mailed the letter to Hawaii, she was tired.

In early November, while Peter and John were away, she wrote to Elizabeth and William Bendixen in San Francisco with relief. This was the last letter because it would need the least traveling time. Only to Elizabeth was she able to confide her growing sadness, a sadness that had overwhelmed her with each pregnancy. She had hoped that with their increasing prosperity and contentment on the farm she wouldn't suffer this time, but she felt more anxious each day. *I fear something terrible is going to happen*, she wrote.

She put down her pen and thought about Peter. He was growing more distant. Although cheerful as always on the surface, he increasingly avoided talking to her about anything more personal than the newspaper or the corn harvest.

When she complained he put her off. When she tried to talk to him about problems with the girls or difficulties of the neighbors, he said, "You worry too much about everyone. Don't take on the burdens of others. It'll just upset you and make you ill."

What if the unthinkable happened? *What if he and John get caught in a snowstorm on the way home and never make it back?* She looked out the window to check the weather. The low afternoon sun shone from a brilliant November sky. *How unreal can you get*, she scolded herself. *Peter will be home tonight and laugh at you again. Well, I won't give him the satisfaction. Anyway, they'll be late, so I can just pretend to be asleep.*

She dried her tears and sealed the letter to Elizabeth.

Sure enough, Peter and John returned safe and sound from Anoka. The following Saturday, the whole household walked to the end of the row of pines to the west of the house. They clustered about a small tree, standing in a bushel basket with its roots wrapped in burlap.

Anne explained to Kristina, "When I was little, I used to think that the trees were named for me, but now that I'm five I remember. Last year, John teased me because I forgot that they are named for Aunt Anne back in Sønderho where they plant their Christmas tree every year. We can't wait until Christmas to plant our tree because the ground will freeze."

When the men had dug the hole and lifted the bare-rooted tree in place, each member of the farm contributed a shovel full of dirt. Patting the soil around the little trunk and brushing the dirt from her hands, Anne added importantly, "Now we have ten, one for each year we've been in Minnesota."

"You haven't been here that long," John scorned. "You're only five, but I'm ten, so I have."

Anne ignored her brother and looked critically at the spindly tree. "It sure looks puny. Will it be all right out here in the cold all winter?" She turned to Kristina. "It gets awful cold here, you know."

"It's from up north, like me," Kristina reassured her. "Like Norwegians, it's used to the cold. It'll have time to grow roots before winter."

"The others were just as puny when we first planted them," Peter said. Lifting Anne up on his shoulder he walked to a bigger tree in the middle of the row, "See, the one we planted the year you were born is now taller than both of us together."

That evening, Lil-Anne asked her mother to tell the story of her namesake trees. "Because the girls haven't heard it before," she explained.

"Bridget and I were here last Christmas," Inger protested. "But do tell the story again—it's wonderful."

Karen gathered her thoughts while everyone settled in to listen. "My brother Christian brought the first Anne-tree to Millfarm for Christmas of 1875," she began.

"Grandpa Andersen's Millfarm is on Fanø," Lil-Anne whispered to Kristina. "That's an island in Denmark."

"Shh, I know that," Kristina whispered back.

Karen gave that look that said clearly: be quiet while I tell the story. "It all really started the year before, the first year Christian went away to school. He brought home a little fir tree, the first Christmas tree on the island. We decorated it with paper garlands and candles, and we all loved it, especially my sister, who was still called Lil-Anne then. The whole town came to see it, but they were not sure that they liked this new idea—Christmas trees weren't *traditional*.

"But, when we read Hans Christian Andersen's fairy tale *The Spruce Tree*, Lil-Anne became very upset that the tree would die and be ignominiously discarded on the trash heap, just like in the story. She insisted no dead trees would ever again be allowed in the house. "Even Uncle Hans doesn't approve," she said. She always called Hans Christian Andersen 'uncle' because we had the same last name, even though she knew we weren't related.

"The following fall, Peter and I were engaged. Everything was a flurry of activity, because the wedding was to take place at the end of February, so we had those preparations as well as for Christmas."

Karen paused, not wanting to explain about her scandalous trip to Holland to meet Peter at landfall when he returned from sailing around the world. She had only been seventeen. Her mother hadn't wanted her to marry so young and disapproved of Peter because he was a seaman. They had a monumental fight until Aunt Kirsten brokered an agreement to postpone the wedding for a few months. Therefore, instead of eloping, as planned, they became engaged in Holland and had a traditional Fanø wedding at Millfarm.

"As usual, everything was a flurry of preparations for Christmas," she repeated, avoiding the touchy subject. "Whereas the previous winter had been dreadful, in 1875 the weather cooperated fully, and Christian made the sail from Ribe in good time for the celebrations. He was then thirteen and all gangly arms and legs. His voice was a changeable bass punctuated by embarrassing squeaks. Just as he had the year before, Christian brought a tree, but this time it was a living tree, planted in a tin bucket.

"Lil-Anne was furious. 'I told you, no dead trees!' she yelled.

"'If we take good care to water this tree,' Christian reassured her, 'We can plant it outside as soon as the ground thaws. It's not very big but very much alive.'

"'OK, but only for Queen Antoinette's sake—so she won't feel homesick,' Lil-Anne declared. Queen Antoinette was a French doll that had once belonged to Cousin Margrethe on the mainland. When Margrethe was too old to play with dolls, she sent her to Fanø with the message, 'Antoinette wants to visit Lil-Anne for a while, she feels lonely and wants to travel.' Lil-Anne always called her 'Queen Antoinette'."

"I'm not too old to play with dolls," the American Lil-Anne hinted, but was once again shushed. Her mother picked up her tale:

"My mother objected, not liking the idea of a tree cluttering up her Southroom and dripping needles on her floor for several months until the ground was frost-free. Finally a compromise was reached and the tree was to be enjoyed indoors in all its splendor until the Feast of the Three Kings—what Americans call Epiphany—then it would be placed in the barn until it could be planted outside.

"Otherwise the usual traditions were carefully followed, and by the morning of Christmas Eve the preparations were declared complete; even the birds had begun their feast by flocking around the sheaf of wheat mounted on a pole in the courtyard and the dog was contentedly chewing on a succulent bone.

"During the holidays, the Sønderhonings called, inspected and approved the decorated tree. Lil-Anne showed off both the tree and Antoinette to every guest when they came into the house and made sure that everyone had a cookie before leaving. 'If they don't eat at least one cookie, they'll carry the Christmas spirit away,' she explained solemnly to Antoinette. The doll was wearing her best taffeta dress and caused quite a stir among the visitors. They were used to Christmas trees from the year before. However, all agreed that one that could later be planted outside was much less wasteful, and if a French Queen approved, it must be all right.

"Grandpa Anders suggested they plant the tree between the house and the Nordby Road. "Every year since then, an Anne-tree has been planted at Millfarm, and now there's a whole windbreak," Karen finished. "And when Peter, John, and I came to Minnesota, we started the same tradition."

"Only we plant the Anne-tree in November, so we can have a big regular Christmas tree in the house," John felt obliged to explain.

"A dead tree," Lil-Anne added, having the last word.

18

Queen Antoinette's Christmas

Welcome again, God's smallest angels,
From heaven's lofty halls,
To earth's shadowy valleys
Wearing beauteous sunshine garments!
A good year ye foretell for bird and dormant seed
Despite ringing frost!

Under open sky at midnight,
Well-met on the snowy path to church!
Ye will not seek to carry Christmas off,
On that we can depend.
Do not pass by our door,
Oh, do not disappoint!

Danish Christmas Carol
N.F.S. Grundtvig (1783-1872)

The planting of the Anne-tree in early November always marked the end of mailing to distant points and the beginning of Christmas preparations for the farm itself. Even those took time, and the month passed with much whispering behind closed doors as the two children and four girls whittled, glued, knitted, and sewed presents for their families and to be exchanged with each other.

Lil-Anne was by this time thoroughly tired of making facecloths, potholders, sachets, and rice bags. "I'll have to start again right after New Year's to get ready for next Christmas," she sighed.

But all the drudgery was forgotten by the time the last of

the Thanksgiving turkey bones had been put in the soup pot when boxes and letters began to come from all corners of the globe. Every day, Peter went to town in the buckboard, in case something had arrived at the post office. At night on his return he would drive right up to the door with a mysterious smile on his face and carry the day's haul up the stairs to be locked in the sewing room. Lil-Anne knew where the key was kept, but beyond peeking through the keyhole she knew better than to go any further.

One evening in December, Anne ran from one person to another announcing the news. "The Christmas trees are here," she said to Elsbeth-madmor. "Papa and I are going to the station tomorrow to pick them up," she told Kristina. Then she pulled on her coat, hat, and mittens and ran across the road to tell the Iversons.

Bright and early the next morning, she was over there again repeating her announcement to be sure everyone had heard. Gudrun came into Helga's kitchen with a bucket of water. This Icelander was the latest of the girls, having come at the beginning of the month when Bridget left to take a housekeeping job in Minneapolis. Anne liked to say her full name: "Guðrun Eriksdottir, intrigued by the old-fashioned sound of the last name. She had quickly learned to pronounce the 'ð' as 'th' and roll her r's in the proper Icelandic manner. Papa said she sounded like she was declaiming *Nials Saga*, but she didn't know what that was.

At church on the Sunday after Gudrun arrived, Anne had introduced the latest member of the family to each member of the congregation. "She's from Min-ne-o-ta—the town that sounds like our state but without an s," she added, relishing the taste on her tongue of the town that lay some thirty miles north of Lincoln.

This morning, when she came with the water she grumbled "I had to break the ice in the cistern. What will we do if it freezes?" But no one listened—the trees were more important, so she asked, "What trees?"

"The Christmas trees Papa and John ordered last month."

"I've heard of them, but never seen one," Gudrun exclaimed, as excited as the little girl. "There aren't many trees on Iceland so we don't have them in Minneota."

"There aren't any trees on Fanø either, so Mama and Aunt Anne didn't have one when they were little as me. Neither did Papa. We always have two, one for each of the parlors, but we aren't allowed to see them decorated until Christmas Eve. They're just beautiful. Papa and John ordered trees in Mankato for us, and for school, and Danebod Church, and Danebod School, and lots more. They ordered so many that they're selling the rest at Danebod to raise money for the new church. And we're delivering them today in the big hay wagon."

Then turning to Helga, Lil-Anne ordered, "Don't you dare bake cookies until we get back." Then turning to Gudrun, she explained that they had to bake a lot of cookies because no one who visited the farm during the holidays was allowed to leave without at least one. "Otherwise they'll carry Christmas out of the house, like the Christmas carol says."

Helga lifted the little girl up in the air and swung her about, "You can turn the grinder crank for *vanilliekranse* and show Gudrun how they're made," she promised. "Come right over when you get home. Now run along and don't keep Papa waiting." She set the child down on the table, rebuttoned her coat, and wound a long scarf around her neck until only the two sparkling blue eyes showed.

Anne was out the door as soon as her feet hit the ground. "Svend, Papa said to harness the team to the hay wagon. We have a big load of trees coming. He said to ask nice and not bossy."

Svend chuckled and lifted the child onto his sturdy shoulders for the ride back to the main house. "A'll tell *Kaptajn Storkeben* you asked nice," he assured her. "Now don't knock off my cap that my mama made special. She told me it's red so's A won't disappear in the snow."

The next couple of weeks passed in a whirlwind of preparations according to ancient traditions. Back in Denmark, Karen's mother had always insisted on a spotless house and stable and baked enough cookies so that if the whole town decided to visit, each person could be given a treat. Karen claimed that her mother was such a traditionalist because of her unhappy childhood, but Peter pointed out that Karen was just as bad, that she changed the farm into Little-Denmark so that their children could have a 'proper Christmas'.

Since each of the girls came from a farm that was nearby, they were all to go home over the holidays to be with their families. Even Gudrun would go back to Minneota on the Sunday before Christmas. Her father would drive down the day before and spend the night in the sewing room, weather permitting.

At this time of year, all plans were "weather permitting," and this year was no exception. By mid-December a snowstorm threatened, and everyone worried that the roads would become impassable by Christmas. A real blizzard could last three days with snow driven across the prairie by biting winds. Even when it wasn't actually coming down from the clouds, the winds would whirl the snow already on the ground up into the air and pile huge drifts against every obstacle. Guide ropes had long since been strung between the house and barn, up to the springhouse, and even to the house across the road; there would be no stories of anyone from the Larsen farms freezing to death within yards of the front door.

Wednesday morning a week before Christmas, Anne looked at the swirling flakes clattering against her bedroom window. "The snow is falling up!" she announced from the middle of the stairs.

Out in the hall, Peter stomped his boots and then came into the kitchen in his stocking feet looking for his breakfast. "It's a complete white-out. John can't go to school and Inger and Gudrun should not go to the Iversons. Svend has already milked the cows, and he'll just stay over there until the storm passes."

"Does that mean we can't go home?" Gudrun asked; she was turning out to be the worrier of the group.

"Staying here wouldn't be so bad," Kristina pointed out. "It's much cozier than at home and definitely warmer."

"Yes, but its Christmas!" Elsbeth-madmor wailed. "Fred was going to come with me and everything."

"We have almost a week. There'll be plenty of time to clear the roads," Peter reassured them, hoping that they could all leave so Karen could have a restful holiday with him and the children.

That evening everyone gathered in the study in front of the open fire, each working frantically on some last-minute present. The snow had stopped, and the wind was dying down. If it didn't start again tomorrow they could quickly shovel the few inches of accumulation and any drifts that had piled in inconvenient places. The girls would be able to go home after all, and Christmas was assured.

"How will you manage all the chores while everyone is gone?" Gudrun fussed and had to be reassured that the only essentials were feeding animals and people.

"The *nisser* will help," Lil-Anne told Gudrun and then had to explain about the invisible gnomes that had come with the family from Denmark. "They can play dreadful tricks on people if they aren't treated nice," she said solemnly. "But we're very good to ours and always leave porridge in the barn for them so they will be nice to us all year. That's why our farm is so lucky—just like Millfarm back in Denmark."

"In Iceland we have trrrolls," Gudrun said, raising her eyebrows and rolling her r's, as only she could. "But the *jólasveinarrr* are terrrrible and steal children for mother Grrr'yla's stew pot. We don't give them any of our food, because they would just steal it all."

Anne burst out crying and ran to hide under the knitting in her mother's lap. Gudrun hastened to add, "But there aren't any *jólasveinar* here in Minnesota; they only live in Icelandic mountains."

"We have *nissen* in Norway too, "Kristina said. "They come down from the cold mountains and help out on the farms and fishing boats in return for being allowed to live in houses and barns. Do you suppose some of them came with us to Minnesota?"

Inger looked puzzled, "I wonder if *nisser* are what we call *tomten* in Sweden. I'll tell Mama to put out Christmas porridge, in case some live at our house. We could use some better luck."

Lil-Anne nodded, "We *always* put out Christmas porridge, it's tradishon. As long as they have their porridge, the *nisse* clean all the animals extra speshul in time for the smallest angels to enspect them at midnight!"

Forgetting her fear, she climbed into Gudrun's lap and confided, "Svend is really a *nisse* that got visible. Maybe he can ask one of his friends to go home with you to make sure the terrible *jólasveinar* don't come to Min-ne-ota."

Karen laughed. "Svend does look like a *nisse* in his red hat. Be careful Lil-Anne, don't let him know you found out his secret. He might get annoyed and play tricks on you!"

Suddenly, Elsbeth-madmor threw down her half-knitted

sock and exclaimed, "I can't stand to wait any longer! We can't wait until we all get back." She looked at each of the other girls for permission and then dashed out of the room.

When Anne figured out what was going to happen she exclaimed proudly, "I didn't tell nobody!"

A few minutes later Elsbeth returned with a book and ceremoniously placed it in front of Karen. Anne pointed to the beautiful letters on the cover and spelled out the title:

Karen's Recipes
by
The Babel-Farm Girls

"We collected all the recipes you've taught us and all the ones we know from home," Elsbeth explained. "Kristina did the writing because she has the nicest hand."

"But Elsbeth-madmor found the blank book in Marshall when she was there with you," Kristina added. "It was Inger's idea to fill it with recipes."

"Helga helped find out where the old girls live now," Inger said. "Bridget wrote and asked them to send us their special dishes."

"I copied out my mother's fish stew," Gudrun contributed. "Though I don't know where you're going to find *torsk* so far from the ocean."

Anne was not to be left out, "And I didn't tell nobody the secret."

"You did too, you told me," John piped up. "But I only told Papa, and he would never tell anyone."

Karen was nonplussed. She leafed through the notebook admiring each page and the beautiful script. Kristina had hidden talents! She read the list of names of all the girls that had passed through the farm over the last five years. Eighteen names from half that many countries; perhaps, after all, the Babelfarm seed corn would bring an abundant harvest. Imagine them all working together like this. She reached for Peter's hand that was draped over her shoulder. Unable to speak for the lump in her throat, she croaked her thanks.

"She likes it," Anne declared.

"I'll treasure it always," Karen finally managed to say.

"And there's plenty of room to add more recipes," Inger pointed out.

The weather held, and all four girls departed for their homes, leaving the house strangely quiet. The day before Christmas Eve, Anne wandered around the house looking for someone to talk to, but everyone was too busy. "When can we start eating the cookies?" she asked Helga.

"Tomorrow night," was the patient reply.

"When are we putting up the tree?" she asked Papa.

"Tomorrow, but John and I will do it while the women cook."

"When are the presents?" she asked her mother, but answered herself, "I know, I know — tomorrow night. I wish it was tomorrow *now*."

Even helping deliver baskets of food to the list of poor families and plates of cookies to the neighbors, didn't take long enough to distract her. "Why do the neighbors all get cookies, when we can't eat any?" she complained. "I know—tomorrow."

Finally after supper that night, even Karen couldn't stand the wait any more. "I already had my special present, so I think the children should each be allowed one. There's a large box from Ribe addressed to: 'Master John and Mistress Anne Larsen.' Cousin Margrethe usually only sends a card, so I'm dying to find out what it is."

She fished the key out of her pocket and sent Peter up to the sewing room. He returned with the mysterious box with 'fragile' stamped all over it. Two parcels and a note were inside. John ripped open the one addressed to him and exclaimed as the paper fell away, revealing an elaborately painted toy ship with 'Lady Roselil' at her bow and stern. Karen restrained Lil-Anne and helped her carefully unwrap hers. Inside lay an old-fashioned porcelain doll wearing a red velvet dress.

"Antoinette," Karen breathed and read the note aloud:

Christmas, 1890

Dear Family,

The other day, I found Antoinette up in the attic. She has lived there ever since she returned from visiting Karen and Anne on Fanø all those years ago. She was propped up against my brother's old model ship and looking longingly out the window to the west. "I want to visit Lil-Anne in America," her highness whispered. I guess she was tired of waiting for me to have a daughter. I made her a new velvet dress for I fear the striped taffeta dress was badly soiled and the rest of her wardrobe was missing.

I hope John will enjoy the ship that belonged to my brother when he was a boy. Jens repainted it with the flower garlands and new name when we returned from your wedding. When he came to visit this fall, he agreed that it would be a fitting conveyance for Queen Antoinette on her progress to the New World.

Mother and Father send their regards, as well as my dear Persil and our two boys. We all wish you and yours a very Merry Christmas and wonderful New Year.
Affectionately,
Margrethe

"This is the best Christmas ever," Lil-Anne exclaimed.

"But it hasn't even started yet," John protested, though he could hardly take his eyes off his treasure. "Besides, you're too young to remember last year."

"Nevertheless...."Lil-Anne retorted. Hugging Antoinette she whispered in her ear, "Tomorrow, weather permitting, we'll visit the Anne-trees. You can borrow my coat that got too small for me. It'll be big on you, so you won't need mittens. It gets awful cold here, you know. After dark is Christmas Eve. When we bring the porridge out to the barn for the *nisse,* I'll help you hide in the stable so you can see them and the smallest angels. At midnight the animals kneel in their stalls to honor the baby Jesus. Humans aren't allowed, so you have to be brave by yourself and tell me about it later. But you're a queen, and queens know how to be brave."

Everyone left on the farm spent Christmas Eve at the Iversons so Karen wouldn't have to cook dinner. Although they were eight around the table, all the hands and the girls had gone home, so it was blessedly peaceful—yet empty, as if someone were missing. As soon as they had danced around the tree and waded through the abundance of presents, Lil-Anne and Karen went home to bed, both exhausted with the excitement of the day.

The next morning, Peter served Karen breakfast in bed. It was very thoughtful of him, but she was so tired that she could hardly eat a bite. "Why don't you just sleep in," he said. "I'll take the children to church, and you can have a quiet morning."

Gratefully, Karen turned over in bed. She barely heard him shooing the children out the door and closing it behind him.

19
Minnehaha

Before the Europeans came, the Dakota Indians lived and hunted in the land of lakes. Even before Minnesota became a state in 1858, the Indians had been pushed west in a series of abrogated treaties that allotted them payments of gold and food in exchange for their hunting grounds. The Minnesota River Valley was set aside for their use and the Upper and Lower Sioux Agencies were founded to distribute the allotments.

In August of 1862, government attention being focused on the Civil War, the gold shipments were delayed and food distribution withheld despite repeated pleas to the unsympathetic Agents. When a hunting party of young hotheads massacred a family of white settlers, the Dakota went on the warpath, contrary to the counsel of wiser chiefs. Several Christian leaders, including Good Thunder, helped settlers to escape and negotiated the release of 270 white captives being held near Chippewa Falls. By the time the conflict ended in late September, it had claimed over 500 Whites and 60 Dakota. More than 300 warriors were convicted in hastily convened courts and were to be executed. Thanks to the intervention of President Lincoln, only 38 were hanged. The rest remained in prison until, three years later, they were finally allowed to join their exiled families.

Meanwhile, 1700 Indian women, children, and elderly were forced to walk 150 miles along the Minnesota River up to Fort Snelling on the Mississippi. White settlers lined the road in every town and village, throwing garbage and rocks at the four-mile long procession. Uncounted numbers died along the way and throughout that miserable winter. The following May, the survivors were transported like cattle downriver to St. Louis and then up the Missouri to Crow Creek in South Dakota. A desolate place, this reservation was so devoid of resources that after three years of disease and starvation the Dakota were sent a hundred miles downriver to the Santee Reservation in what is now the State of Nebraska.

Even recent settlers in southwestern Minnesota have heard of the terror the Dakota inflicted and understand the desire for revenge and justice. But revenge on innocent women and children is not just. Lest we feel that this is all ancient history, we need only remember the massacre of Indians that took place at Wounded Knee in South Dakota less than two months ago. In the last few years Chief Good Thunder has led a return of a few Christian Santee to the Minnesota Valley. Let us welcome these returning neighbors.

The Lincoln Pioneer
January 13, 1891
Karen Andersdatter

January 1891

During the winter months, the Babel Barn Cooperative met in the parlor. It was too cold to work in the barn despite new insulation and the pot bellied stove. On Saturdays after Christmas, only a few sleighs jingled into the courtyard to deposit neighborhood women and their workbaskets at the front door, there to be met by whichever of the girls was assigned to help with the wraps. Peter joked that he could tell the temperature by the number of boots by the door: the fewer, the colder.

Although they lived farther away than most of the other ladies, Mildred Bullard's boots were usually there next to Minnehaha's fur-lined moccasins. Minnehaha was very proud of the moccasins; a present from Mildred and Obadiah that they had ordered from the Indian community in Faribault. Mildred's corn chowder was a welcome addition to the lunch fare, appreciated as much as her advice on piecing scraps of fabric into attractive quilt tops. The ladies did the quilting together, and the large frame was a permanent installation in the parlor. The first effort had been to complete Elsbeth's wedding-ring pattern, a stunning covering much admired by one and all. In fact this quilt inspired other projects and soon several log-cabin quilts were bundled for shipment to Jesse's new store in St. Paul. The profits from the first sale were returned in the form of bolts of fabric to supplement the leftover scraps for the next quilts and skeins of yarn to be knit into socks, hats, and mittens. Eventually, they hoped to reap a profit and, after deducting for the expense of materials, the money was to be apportioned among the women according to a complicated scheme that Karen was to administer. The women were grateful for this supplement to their budgets, however small it might be, but mostly they appreciated the fellowship.

While they worked, they told stories. Most of the women were immigrants from Scandinavia where the winter days were even shorter than in Minnesota and, in some places, even colder. Those from the mountains of Norway and Gudrun from Iceland had harrowing tales to tell of much deeper snow and cold more penetrating than the others could imagine. They told of houses buried to their second stories and of families isolated for days and even weeks by impassible mountain roads where the only form of transportation was by ski.

"What did you do all winter?" Karen asked.

"Much like here, we would sit and talk. Sometimes we would just sit," Gudrun answered. Mrs. Johnson, who was from Finland, and the Norwegian Kristina nodded agreement.

Gudrun went on, "But there are hot springs. Even in the middle of winter, we would go and sit in warm pools of water. It was awesome to sit there, surrounded by glaciers, hear the howling of the wind, and watch the snow coming down all around and yet be quite warm. I miss that most of all about being in America."

"My husband has built a Finnish sauna in back of our barn," Mrs. Johnson said. "You're welcome to come and join us on a Saturday night. When our faces are red from the heat, we go outside and roll in the snow."

"Don't your clothes get all wet? "Lil-Anne asked.

"We don't wear clothes," Mrs. Johnson confessed.

Lil-Anne was amazed. "No clothes at all?" she repeated. She had a half-pieced doll quilt top in her lap. The project, intended for Queen Antoinette, was really beyond her skill although Mildred had suggested that a simple six-square in scraps from her old dresses would be the easiest. She had started with great ambition, but now used any excuse to put it down.

Karen imagined Lil-Anne describing this amazing Finnish custom to everyone they met and quickly changed the subject. "It's much darker in Finland, isn't it?" she asked.

"Much darker...and colder." Mrs. Johnson explained. "In Lapland, above the polar circle, the sun doesn't rise at all in winter."

"Then how can anyone ever get out of bed in the morning?" Lil-Anne asked distracted by this new idea. "I hate getting up in the dark."

"If it's very cold, some people stay in bed and tell stories in the dark."

The conversation turned from geography to Elsbeth's favorite topic of weddings. Each woman had a different story to tell of marriage customs in her hometown and Mildred contributed a description of the ceremony that had joined her to Obadiah at the Society of Friends Meeting in Providence. The ladies were surprised to learn that Quakers had no clergy, so the congregation served as witnesses, as the two had joined hands in front of the facing bench of Elders.

"Is that why your ring is on your left hand?" Lil-Anne asked. "Because you're not really married?"

Karen, much embarrassed, tried to explain but was drowned out by Mildred's laughter. At her encouragement, the married ladies all stretched out their hands and showed how some had rings on their left and some on their right, depending on which side of the Atlantic the ceremony had been held. Again, Karen feared that Lil-Anne would insert a comment on wedding rings into every conversation. At least it was a better subject than naked Finns!

The story of Karen and Peter's wedding was a favorite, and she had to tell it over and over again, making sure to skip her trip to Holland and Peter's romantic proposal lest she shock American ears.

"We were married in late February," she began her story. "Many weddings were held then, just before the ships sailed in the spring." She went on to describe the preparations from the scrubbing of the house from end to end to the verbal invitations, delivered by her little sister a week before the ceremony, all according to tradition.

"The morning of the ceremony," she went on, "my bridesmaids came to Millfarm to get dressed. Mother helping me and Aunt Kirsten, the other girls."

"Couldn't you dress yourselves?" Lil-Anne wanted to know. "I can do everything myself except my hair and the buttons on the back."

"My skirt and blouse were not a problem, and over that I wore a starched white apron and white shawl. But my mother had to sew the bridal crown into my hair. The bridesmaids wore similar but less elaborate crowns of dried flowers, and they helped each other while Aunt Kirsten told them what to do. Lil-Anne, please run into the study and get the photograph of Papa and me, so everyone can see."

When the picture was passed around, Elsbeth studied it carefully. She was particularly taken with the bridal crown. "That's so beautiful. Could you make one for me?" she asked.

"April is a little early for fresh flowers—I don't think you want a crown of catkins and pussy willows! Perhaps Jesse can find some silk flowers in the city for us to sew on your veil. At home, because the usual wedding was held in late winter, we used heather and "everlasting" statice flowers saved from the summer, but sometimes they were of silk."

One Saturday in late January, Mildred and Minnehaha came earlier than anyone else. Minnehaha was so excited that she hardly waited for the sleigh to come to a jingling stop before she jumped out and ran in the door. Barely taking the time to remove her moccasins, she ran through the kitchen and into the parlor, shouting to anyone who would listen, "We had a letter from the Lower Indian Agency with the most romantic story about my parents."

She pulled the letter from between the buttons at the front of her shirtwaist and handed it to Karen, her hand shaking with excitement. It was still warm from having rested next to her heart. "I cry every time I look at it, so please, you read out loud to everyone. It's so sad and yet so beautiful."

"Let us wait to see if anyone else comes," Karen said.

To pass the time, Minnehaha went out in the kitchen to gossip with Inger and Elsbeth. Eventually, two more women arrived with a couple of their children. They sat down in the parlor with their knitting while Elsbeth and Mildred went to the frame to put the last stitches on the latest quilt, and Kristina took the youngsters outside to build a snow fort.

When everyone was settled, Karen picked up the letter and announced that Minnehaha had asked her to share it.

Dear Miss Samuelson,

The priest at the Lower Agency Mission asked me to write you because he knows that I grew up on the Santee Reservation in Nebraska where you were born and I want to tell you about your family. You may not remember, but we also met a few years ago at a social at St. Mary's Hall. I'm David Birch, that awkward Shattuck Senior who asked you to dance. You were fourteen and already much too grand to speak to me.

Minnehaha interrupted, saying, "I do remember and he was truly awkward. I was even worse and very shy because I was new and didn't have a proper dress for such a fancy affair. I didn't know how to dance and didn't know how to refuse without confessing my ignorance. No wonder he thought I was a snob. You can skip the rest of that page because it just explains how he put together my family's story and how the Sioux uprising began. The stuff about my father really begins on the next page."

When the Civil War started, your grandparents had a farm just south of the Minnesota River near the Lower Sioux Agency. In 1861, when Ralph was ten, Mr. Samuelson left with the First Minnesota Regiment to fight against the South.

"Ralph is my father and Grandfather died at Gettysburg," Minnehaha explained.

The Dakota of the Minnesota Valley went on the warpath in mid-August and Chief Good Thunder sent a warning to the settlers to seek shelter at Fort Ridgeley. Ralph's mother was expecting another baby and could not travel. Instead, a nearby Dakota family hid them and the boy made friends with their six-year-old daughter, whom he called Lulu. Ralph's mother died in childbirth and Lulu's father was killed in one of the battles that followed.

Minnehaha sniffed loudly and wiped her eyes with the edge of her apron. "I'm sorry," she apologized, "but it's so sad how everyone was killed. Please read on. I'll try to behave."

Ralph stayed with his new family throughout the harrowing walk to Fort Snelling, the soldiers all thinking him a Dakota. Although the boy was only eleven, he did what he could to protect them from the settlers' stones and insults. Mary, Lulu's mother, told me once that if it had not been for his help and the food he managed to find, they would have perished. Not until they arrived at the fort did the Reverend Hinman from the Lower Agency find out who Ralph was. He finally persuaded the army officers that one of the captives was a white boy and arranged for him to live with his aunt and uncle in St. Peter.

After that Mary and Lulu lost track of Ralph until 1870

when he suddenly showed up at the Santee Reservation. During all those years, he had tried to find out what happened to them and had finally traced the Reverend Hinman to the reservation, through Bishop Whipple. Ralph was in the army and, by God's grace, was stationed at Fort Randall, only thirty miles upriver from the reservation. The two young people were reunited and Hinman married them a few months later.

"Isn't that incredibly romantic? My father was such a hero!" Minnehaha burst out. "All this time, I thought him a coward. I began to believe my stepmother when she said my mother wasn't really his wife and that I was illegitimate."

Ralph left the army to work for the trading post at the Santee agency. You were born the following spring, when I was four. I remember coming to the store with my father when you were but a papoose on your mother's back and later a toddler running around underfoot. And I remember your mother's funeral at the church when I was nine because I was a new acolyte and it was my first funeral. There were many deaths that winter because of an influenza epidemic; your mother's was but the first.

Reverend Hinman's widow, who is a half-blood Santee like yourself, tells me that soon after that, you and your father returned to Minnesota. He took over the homestead in St. Peter where he had been raised and his aunt looked after you—you know the rest better than I. Imagine my surprise to learn that the beautiful young lady at St. Mary's Hall was the toddler I had known back home on the reservation.

Mr. and Mrs. Hinman moved back to the Minnesota Valley in 1887 where he taught at the Birch Coulee School until he died last spring. Mrs. Hinman was delighted to hear that you and your father are both well and asked me to send you her greetings.

I have only told you the bare facts, but I do remember your mother as a gentle Christian woman who always had a kind word for me. If you would like, I will write you again and tell you stories about her and some of your Dakota relatives. Or if you and your friends visit Faribault sometime, I would be delighted to meet with you.

"The letter is signed, David Birch," Karen finished, stunned.

"Hoho," Mrs. Johnson interjected. "That young man is interested in you!"

"Nah," Minnehaha replied, her blush contradicting her denial. "He only said I'm beautiful because he's polite."

"I wouldn't be so sure," Mildred chuckled. "Didn't he say

that he is now a student at Seabury Divinity School? We'll have to go to Faribault and see what he's like."

That night, Karen told Peter about Minnehaha's excitement at learning about her family.
"I've been reading about the Sioux war in some books that Obadiah had lent me, but hearing the impact of the war on individuals made it seem that much more terrible. "Why don't we know about the treatment of the Dakota?" she asked. "We need to do something. Can't you write an article for the paper?"
"I don't think that would do any good," Peter said in his 'now be reasonable' voice. "Those that lived here in '62 or had relatives that were murdered will hardly listen to a foreigner saying it wasn't all the Indians' fault, and the new settlers really don't care what happened before they came."
"But they need to know that there was fault on both sides!" Karen protested.
"Calm down. You worry too much about ancient history."
"It's not ancient history. It happened again at Wounded Knee just last month!"
"But that was in South Dakota, hundreds of miles from here." Peter was still using that calming, placating voice that Karen couldn't stand. "You shouldn't read about wars and battles. It just upsets you for nothing."
"Maybe I'll write about it myself. Except, they certainly won't listen to a woman. They just want me to tell homey little stories about their nice neighbors. No one paid any attention to that piece I wrote about how we need to help those less fortunate than ourselves, like the Bensons."
"Now don't get hysterical. You'll make yourself sick."
Silently she yelled at him. *You too; you only want me to write about our nice, homey now. I need to talk about what happened back then, before someone dies.* She didn't say it out loud because she knew she wasn't making much sense. Even more than tears, Peter hated her to be illogical.

20

The Wind Does Blow

Over the river and through the wood
To Grandfather's house we go.
The horse knows the way
To carry the sleigh
Through white and drifted snow.

Over the river and through the wood —
Oh how the wind does blow!
It stings the toes
And bites the nose,
As over the ground we go.

Lydia Maria Child (1802-1880)

February 1891

As January ended, the weather became worse. Karen usually looked forward to the coming of February as there were often bright sunny days that make her forget the winter cold, but that year, not even the sun could lighten her heavy heart. Both Svend and Peter discouraged her from venturing out, and soon she even stopped going to interview neighbors for her column.

On Saturdays, only the most stalwart women from the immediate neighborhood made it to the Babel Barn get-togethers, and sometimes it was only a gathering of the girls. The conversation often turned to talk of Elsbeth's wedding and then drifted to other gossip. The only topic of conversation that was never broached was the growing evidence of Karen's pregnancy. Even Lil-Anne knew that this subject was taboo; though she was usually quick to pick up on any veiled comments of the Babel Ladies, she never mentioned the coming event either. Each Saturday on arrival, the women would covertly inspect Karen's face and figure for signs of progress, but less and less quilting was done as they all pointedly switched to knitting little white garments. When they departed and she cheerily invited them back the following week, they would seek reassurance that she was 'up to it.'

"I'm glad for the company," she always answered, although sometimes her smile was forced.

Peter was less inhibited and often teased her about her growing girth, as if he thought that joking would cheer her up, but even he confined his comments to the privacy of their bedroom. The girls all knew, of course, but frank as Karen usually was with them, the expected baby was seldom mentioned. John obviously knew more than he wanted because even if Peter was the one who broached the subject, the boy turned red and found an excuse to go elsewhere. Karen kept expecting Lil-Anne to ask about the growing pile of soakers and saques in the sewing room, but the usually unreserved and curious child remained quiet, and Karen was reticent to broach the subject.

One Saturday in February, Mildred was the only neighbor to brave the elements, pulling up in her sleigh about midmorning. The roan's coat gently steamed in the frigid air, and Mildred's cheeks glowed as she jumped down and tossed the reigns to Svend.

"*Go' morn, Fru Bullard*" Svend greeted, touching the edge of his red knit cap respectfully.

"Good morning, Svend," she responded and then smiled. "Call me 'Mildred', please." She was about to explain when she saw from his closed face that he would not hear.

Mildred found Karen at her desk in the study, staring at the front page of last week's *Pioneer*.

"No one is coming today," she said morosely. "Peter put an announcement in the paper last week that the Babel get–togethers are cancelled until further notice. He didn't even tell me, and I only noticed it today."

"I saw it," Mildred said. "I came anyway to cheer us both up. It's a beautiful day, sunshine and no wind. Elsbeth told me that Kristina took Anne for a ski lesson out in the orchard. By your looks, you too need fresh air. Let's go for a drive after lunch and leave the girls to their own devices."

"Peter doesn't like me to go out," Karen hesitated with a longing glance out the window.

Mildred, blunt as usual, made a dismissing noise, "You'll get the megrims closeted away in this gloom. Besides Elsbeth told me Peter is in town today, so what he doesn't know won't bother us. Men don't understand what their womenfolk need. They panic too easily."

"But Svend won't let me...."

"You sound like a child dependent on the whims of others. You usually have a mind of your own. Svend can drive us if he wishes, while we have a nice girl-talk. Where shall we go?"

Karen suggested that Elsbeth's parents' farm would make a perfect outing as she needed to talk to Gitte Rolf. "Elsbeth-madmor is leaving at the end of this month, and the daughter next door to Gitte would like to become a Babel girl."

After a quick lunch of hot soup and fresh bread, Svend bundled his charges under buffalo robes and started the sleigh down the road. He had unhitched the roan to give it a chance to rest before Mildred's return trip and substituted one of the Larsen blacks.

"Did Peter put you up to this?" Karen suddenly asked suspiciously. "Why would you want to drive all the way to my house and back, and then suggest another trip in addition?"

"Not at all." Mildred returned her gaze without guile. "I needed a change from worrying about the Bensons. Now that we don't have enough work for Oscar around the house, he's started taking jobs away from home again. Maia spends too much time alone with the children and looks very poorly. Minnehaha and I help them as much as we can, but there seems little we can do."

"I needed a change also, so I'm happy you came," Karen said squeezing her friend's arm.

"Inger told me when I came in that you seemed upset."

"I'm so glad that she'll be madmor next month," Karen sighed. "Elsbeth is sometimes a trial, and right now she's next to useless!"

"Inger'll be good with the baby."

Karen ignored mention of the baby. "I'm very fond of Elsbeth. Fred has almost finished fixing their little house, but I'm not sure that she's ready for a household of her own."

Mildred nodded sympathetically. "Sometimes we're mother hens clucking over our chicks!"

Karen cheered up once they were underway and told the story of Lil-Anne's birthday party, which had been the previous week. "The next morning, she appeared at breakfast dressed to go out. We asked where she was going. 'To school, of course', she said. 'Now that I'm six, I need to go.' We had a terrible time explaining that she would have to wait until fall. She was upset, but finally settled down when we promised that she could go to the girls' summer school at Danebod."

They rode in silence for a time, Mildred wondering how to get Karen to talk. There was obviously much on her mind. "When is your time?" she finally blurted.

"Not until end of next month. I feel like a sack of wet wheat, about to burst!"

"So, one in February and now an almost-spring baby. My two were both born in the summer and the others in the fall. How about John? Was he born in Minnesota?"

"He was a September child, born in Denmark. Then the following March, when he was old enough to travel, we left Fanø and came here—ten years ago, next month."

"Didn't you live in California before you came here?"

Karen looked as if she could barely remember, as if California were a long time ago. "For a while," she said, coldly.

If Mildred had any faults it was curiosity about other people, but she knew when not to pry. Changing the subject, she hummed the tune to "Over the river and through the wood...." When Karen recognized the song, she joined in.

"I know it's for Thanksgiving," Mildred said. "But the wind *is* biting my nose."

"At least our toes are warm."

"The author of that poem, Maria Child, came to talk to us at school. She was a famous abolitionist, but also a wonderfully imaginative New England writer. I just gave Minnehaha her novel, 'Hobomok' about a colonial girl that lived with an Indian and bore his son. I thought she would enjoy reading a more sympathetic view of her people than tales of massacres in the Wild West."

"That sounds pretty shocking for a New England writer."

"Boston didn't quite know what to make of such a radical feminist. Yet she wrote lovely stories for children and a very entertaining book on how to be a frugal housewife."

"Might that be a good book for the girls to read?"

"Excellent idea, I'll bring it down sometime. And I'll write to my son in Boston to send a copy as a wedding present for Elsbeth. That reminds me, you've never told us the story of how Peter and you became engaged."

Apparently that was a safe topic, for Karen laughed. "It's a romantic tale, but you have to promise not to be too shocked. That's why I don't usually tell anyone."

Mildred giggled like a gossiping schoolgirl. "I'm all ears and promise it will go no further."

"Peter first proposed from the middle of the Pacific on his trip around the world as First Mate of the *Marianne*. My mother and I had a huge battle, and I ended up living at my grandmother's house. Then my timid Aunt Kirsten asked me to go with her on the train to Rotterdam. She was anxious to see her husband—he was *Marianne's* captain and had never seen his son—but she was afraid to go by herself. The brig had left twenty months earlier and Rotterdam was to be their first landfall in Europe. Thus I would be respectably chaperoned, and Mam reluctantly agreed to let me go. It turned out that Aunt Kirsten had pointed out that she really had no choice since I would probably run away if she didn't give me permission. Svend, my self-appointed guardian even then, insisted that he come too, and the three of us, plus little Frederick, took the train to Rotterdam where we stayed at the Rembrandt Inn."

"I knew you were keeping a good story from us!" Mildred exclaimed. *No wonder she didn't want the girls to hear this. Might give them ideas!*

"It gets even better. When the *Marianne* arrived, Peter took me down to his cabin. He had filled the tiny space with willow branches and hung them with bangles and proposed again, this time properly in person. The next day we had a riotous Yes-party on board—that's a traditional Fanø engagement party."

"How romantic. What happened then?"

"Uncle Paul refused to be separated from his wife and son, so he brought them home on the train. I stopped in Ribe on the way to visit my Aunt Ingrid. Meanwhile, Peter took over the *Marianne's* bridge and sailed her and the remaining cargo to Esbjerg, the big harbor on the mainland next to Fanø."

There's more to the story, Mildred thought suspiciously. *Something that she's not telling.* "So you took the train back with your aunt and uncle?"

Karen laughed. "I was hoping you wouldn't notice. No,

I stayed with Peter at the Rembrandt Inn while the *Marianne* had minor repairs. Peter had wanted the Captain to marry us before he left and I had secretly planned for us to elope, but Aunt Kirsten talked me out of it."

"Didn't your aunt object to leaving you and Peter in Holland un-chaperoned?" Mildred asked, more surprised than censorious.

"Uncle Paul persuaded her. 'After all they're engaged,' he said and pointed out that the only difference between my tight-bed at home and the Inn, was that at the Rembrandt Peter had room for his legs."

Mildred raised her eyebrows.

"On Fanø, the prospective groom often moves into the bride's home after the engagement party. Pastor Engel scolds the whole town every December when most of the engagements take place, but his heart isn't in it and his sermon on the subject is now just one of the traditions."

Mildred chuckled. "In the country back home, some parents still allow their daughters to 'bundle' with their sweethearts." Then with a gleam in her eye, she added, "Some of us managed to dispense with the bundling-board."

Karen looked puzzled. "What's a bundling-board?" Then she burst out laughing. "Oh, I get it. But Peter's long legs would never have fit in my bed and Mam's presence in the next room would have been more inhibiting than any bundling-board!"

"What did your mother say when you came home?"

"She knew the minute she saw me, but by then there was little she could do. The reason I stopped in Ribe on the way home was so everyone could talk, but no one would really know for sure—except Mam. There was never any hope of keeping secrets from her. As it was, Peter went to his home in the northern town of Nordby and only came to Sønderho for the reading of the banns."

She paused a moment. "And then we were married—fifteen years ago tomorrow."

There was no time for more, for they had arrived at the Rolf Farm. Gitte Rolf brought them down the road to meet Neighbor Hansen and be treated to the inevitable coffee. Soon final arrangements had been made for Katinka Hansen to come to Babel Farm in two weeks. They declined second cups.

"I want to get home before dark," Mildred explained. Svend tucked them back into the sleigh and flicked the reins lightly.

"I'm dying to hear more," Mildred blurted. "So Peter became Captain of the *Lady-ship Marianne* and you sailed with him?"

"Yes, but not until later, and Peter renamed the *Marianne*. He rounded up a crew and sailed her to Sønderho the day of the wedding, bringing what seemed like most of Nordby for the celebration! He and I spent our First-night on board."

"I imagine bedding on a ship is...?" Mildred said but delicately did not finish the sentence.

Karen blushed and smiled but went on with her story, "During the *fest*, the crew painted the new name on the bow. Before we were even properly dressed the next morning, Peter took me out to see that she was now the *Lady Roselil*—for an old Danish song. He said it was my morning gift."

Mildred raised her eyebrows in question and Karen explained that it was a Danish tradition for a man to present his bride with a gift the next morning to show that she had pleased him. "Usually it's jewelry and, of course, he couldn't give me the *ship*, just the name. But that was pretty wonderful. The painters had been a little the worse for drink and some of the letters were crooked so Peter made them re-paint it during the day. Then we had a ship christening before dinner."

"Where was your honeymoon?"

"Just a few nights on board ship. Then, until we sailed for the Orient at the end of summer, we moved to Peter's mother's house in Nordby—that's about seven miles north of Sønderho. We had a lovely large room on the second floor. There was plenty of talk in town for the bride and groom are expected to move in with her parents, not his. Our excuse was that Peter was studying to get his captain's papers at the Navigation School in Nordby and I needed to be near the office in Esbjerg where I worked managing the family shipping business."

"Did they also think it strange that you were a business woman?"

"It was very common for a Sønderho woman to sell shares for her husband while he was at sea, so they were used to that, but were a little surprised at my actually having an *office* and in *Esbjerg*, at that. We went to Sønderho almost every Sunday.

Everyone was very nice to us—very nosey, but very nice. Peter gave me piles of fabric: silks and velvets from China and cotton from India. By summer, I had a whole modern wardrobe."

"Did that mean you stopped wearing traditional dress? What did your mother say to that?"

"I always dressed properly when I was on Fanø—even at Peter's mother's— so no one would criticize. But she knew, as she knew everything. On board ship, Peter liked me to look fashionable. I often dreamt that I forgot to change and appeared someplace dressed wrong and everyone thought I was a stranger! And then we went to sea."

"*Vi er hjemme,*" Svend announced as he pulled up at Babel Farm.

"I'm glad you came," Karen said. "I did need to get out. I would offer coffee but know you want to get home before dark."

"I had a lovely time too. I hope you will let me come again—just the two of us." She gave Karen a hug and whispered, "Happy Anniversary." Karen looked like she was about to cry but gave a wan smile. *Has everyone forgotten?* Mildred thought. *Should I go in with her and say something? Surely Peter wouldn't forget? Doesn't he know that she needs him?*

Svend helped Karen down from the sleigh. Carefully but without fuss he held her arm until she was safely in the house. He opened the door and called out loudly that Mistress Moon was home and required hot coffee. The meaning of his Danish was unmistakable.

While hitching the Bullard roan to the sleigh, he said what sounded like, "Is goot dee kom, Mistress Mildred."

She wasn't sure whether he had spoken in English or Danish and wondered if Svend understood more English than he let on. Acknowledging the new form of address, she smiled. *He's added me to his flock.*

21
Snowbound

Unwarmed by any sunset light
The gray day darkened into night,
A night made hoary with the swarm
And whirl-dance of the blinding storm,
As zigzag, wavering to and fro,
Crossed and recrossed the winged snow;
And ere the early bedtime came
The white drift piled the window-frame,
And through the glass the clothes-line posts
Looked in like tall and sheeted ghosts.

So all night long the storm roared on;
The morning broke without a sun;
In tiny spherule traced with lines
Of nature's geometric signs,
In starry flake, and pellicle,
All day the hoary meteor fell;

And, when the second morning shone,
We looked upon a world unknown,
On nothing we could call our own.
Around the glistening wonder bent
The blue walls of the firmament,
No cloud above, no earth below,—

Anne Ipsen

A universe of sky and snow!
The old familiar sights of ours
Took marvelous shapes;
Strange domes and towers.

Snow-bound
John Greenleaf Whittier (1807-1892)

Every weekend since New Year, John had helped Svend and Fred to fix up the old Johansen shack to welcome Fred's bride in April. The roof had been repaired, the floor laid, and cracks in the walls stuffed with felted wool. The kitchen, the main room of the house, had been enlarged and a small bedroom for Svend added to the back. The old stove could barely heat the original two rooms and loft but would be replaced by a new modern stove with four nested cook rings and a baking oven. Svend had already transferred his few belongings to his room and often spent the night there to keep an eye on everything.

The outbuildings and barn had been repaired and fencing added to make a sheepfold and hog pen. The sheep had been installed late last month in time for the lamming, and the ewes seemed content with their new accommodations. Come spring, they would fence the new-drained meadows with barbed wire and by planting time, only Babel Farm fields would be seeded with corn and grain. The Johansen farm would have the grazing meadows and, if all went according to plan, they would take in animal boarders for at least this first summer.

One Saturday afternoon at the end of February, John, Fred, and Svend were preparing to move the horses to their new stalls. Eventually, all the animals would be transferred, but the cows and chickens would have to wait until after the wedding when the new mistress would be in residence.

That morning the skies closed in and the air smelled like snow. "A three-day blizzard," Svend predicted gloomily.

"Batten down the hatches," Karen commanded her troops. That's what Peter would have said, but he was in North Dakota at a Grange meeting.

When it started to snow, John was in the kitchen scrounging a snack before leaving and excited by an adventure with the men.

"You have to stay here," his mother said. "By the time you finish bedding the animals down, the snow will be too deep for you to come home."

"Aw, Mom. It's just down the road. They need my help—one of the mares is due to foal and I have to be with her."

"A'll take good care of the boy, Mistress Moon," Svend promised, in that way he had that made it a command.

At this point Fred came into the kitchen carrying a bucket of snow that he put on the stove to melt. "Helga packed us a big pail of pea soup and a loaf of bread."

"And there are plenty of canned beans at the house," the boy added, his mind on his next meal rather than the weather.

By the time they were packed up, the wind was howling around the barn. Enveloped in a shawl, Karen followed them out the door and watched the three of them walking down the road single file, each sheltered between the broad haunches of a horse on either side. Soon the swirling snow swallowed them. *Svend will keep my boys safe*, she reassured herself.

She peered through the white-out at the windmill barely visible at the top of the rise, the creaking not audible over the howling of the wind. What would they do if it stopped and the cistern froze? How would they water the animals?

She shook out her snow-covered shawl and stamped her feet in the hallway between the back door and the kitchen. Peter had taken the train for North Dakota early that morning, planning to return by evening. Now that would not be possible. Would he stay at some farm there and ride out the storm? Or freeze on the way home like the windmill?

That afternoon, Peter was to speak. "The Great Plains were made for grain and corn," he would say.

He was convinced that with the adoption of modern machinery and chemical fertilizer, a revolution in farming was on its way. The days of the small field, no larger than could be plowed or harvested by one man in a day, were of the past. The immigrant farmer needed to forget the traditional methods of European subsistence farming and think on a larger scale to suit the spacious New World. No longer was it necessary to grow all that the family needed on their own land, but farms should specialize, sell their products, and buy the rest of their supplies. To prevent depletion of the land, the modern farmer must use three-crop rotations and chemical fertilizers to supplement manure from the animals.

"I envision a sea of billowing tassels reaching over the horizon," he would preach. "The navy of harvesting machines will be more numerous than steamboats coursing the Mississippi, and the iron horse will carry the work of our farms to the mills of Minneapolis! As we move into the twentieth century, we must learn new methods. We must build silos on every farm and grain elevators at every railroad crossing."

Karen knew his speech well as he had been rehearsing it about the house all week, but she was more concerned about her sailor husband turned farmer than about modern farming and visions of the twentieth century. These days it seemed he was home less than when he had captained their steamship between Fanø and England.

She wiped the frost off the hall window with her apron and watched the gray clouds closing in from the west. "You need to leave soon or you'll not find your way home, much less the way to the twentieth century," she muttered with more humor than she felt.

Going back to the kitchen and slamming the door behind her, she announced, "I'll make the rolls."

Ordinarily bread baking was Madmor's responsibility, but today she and Katinka, the latest addition to the household, were busy moving a three-day supply of firewood from the woodshed into the hall off the kitchen. Dough was usually put up in the morning, and there was enough bread to last through the weekend, but Karen wanted fresh rolls for the Sabbath. She would let the dough slow-rise overnight, ready to form into rolls and pop into the oven first thing on Sunday morning. Besides she was in a mood to punch someone or at least something.

"Flour shouldn't travel," she said to no one in particular as she pushed around the sticky mass. "This flimsy stuff just doesn't have it. Everyone says how white and fluffy it is, but it has no substance, no taste. My Papa knows how to make flour. But then back home there's a proper windmill, not the flimsy contraption we have—all it does is pump water! Mam says she can feel the difference between fresh from our mill and boughten flour even as she scoops it out of the barrel. Papa says flour was never meant to sail, and it certainly wasn't meant to ride a train!" With that she gave the mound a final resentful punch and flattened it with the heels of her hands. She folded the dough over as if she were slamming the lid of the wood box and all but threw the ball into a bowl.

"There," she growled, covering it with a towel. "See that you behave and rise to the occasion!"

Katinka, being new to the ways of her mistress, gave Ingermadmor a frightened look. "Why is Mistress so angry at the bread?" she whispered.

"Don't pay her no mind. She's just worried because of the storm," Inger whispered back. "John's at the Johansen farm and Peter's in South Dakota. She's afraid for them."

"Peter never did have the sense to heave to in a storm," Karen continued her diatribe, pretending not to have heard the whispering girls. "He always wants to head into the wind and sail right through. He'll be just stupid enough to try to get home. John is a chip off the old block, but at least he has Svend to keep him safe."

By Sunday morning they were closed in, and it was still snowing. The roads were obliterated and the farm hands were kept busy clearing a path between the two houses and to the stables so the cows could be milked. John and Fred made their way home by lunchtime when the snow lulled briefly. It started again and the hands had to shovel twice more to keep the paths open.

Fred was worried about his mare, and Kristina volunteered to ski with him to bring Svend more food.

"This is nothing," she said. "If we keep the wind on our left going out and on our right coming back, it'll take only a few minutes."

The two young people set out right after lunch. Elsbeth gave Kristina a jaundiced look as they went out the door, but was not about to brave the snow herself even for her beloved Fred. Kristina returned alone well before nightfall. They heard her knocking the snow off her hickory skis and stomping her boots in the hallway.

"All iz vell," she announced, her accent accentuated by stiff lips. But she was none the worse for wear, seeming to thrive on cold and exercise.

Still it snowed, and still Peter was missing. Karen tossed

and turned all night and by Monday morning she was a wreck, having dreamt about disaster. She fussed at everyone and tried to write, but couldn't sit still. Pacing up and down in the study, she imagined digging a frozen Peter out of a snow bank. *What if this is the end? What if Peter...* but she couldn't finish the thought.

At dinner she tried a cheerful face for Lil-Anne's sake, but the child was not fooled and would not eat. She just slumped tearfully on the bench, clutching Queen Antoinette.

Peter finally returned later that evening, exhausted and complaining of a sore throat. During the storm, the front of the train engine had been buried in a snowdrift and he had spent a cold, uncomfortable night. Eventually, the male passengers had dug the engine out and they managed to clear enough of the track so the train could inch along. Finally a plow engine from Lake Benton had met them and they had crept east.

On arriving in Lincoln late Sunday, Peter had decided to stay the night at the newspaper office. He and Sam had spent the morning delivering Saturday's edition to the stores while Karl took care of home deliveries to the subscribers. Since no one had ventured out during the storm everyone was hungry for even stale news, and the stores did a brisk business. Peter set out for home early in the afternoon. Even so, it took him several hours to work his horse through the drifting snow, and darkness fell before he arrived, chilled to the bone.

Karen grumbled while dishing up a large bowl of pea soup. "Serves you right for leaving when I asked you not to," she muttered, just loudly enough for him to hear.

"This soup is so thick the spoon will stand by itself," Peter joked, ignoring her scolding. Lil-Anne was perched on one knee and John sat as close as possible on his other side.

"What do you expect? It's been on the stove for two days waiting for you. You're lucky it hasn't all stuck to the bottom of the pot."

With that, Karen emptied the rest of the soup into the pig-bucket and slammed the pot onto the counter. She filled it with hot water from the kettle and banged it back on the stove to soak until morning. When she turned around, Peter was asleep, head resting on his daughter's head, spoon limp in his hand.

She woke him enough to hustle him off to bed, tucking him in with a hot brick. "You should have stayed in South Dakota," she scolded.

"Then you'd still be worried that I was floundering in a drift somewhere."

"You could at least have come home this morning."

Peter ignored her grumble. "Come here and warm me up," he said, lifting a corner of the covers invitingly. "Mmm, much better than a brick," he mumbled, half asleep. He turned on his side and Karen snuggled up with the curve of her belly up against the cold skin of his back. The baby stirred but Peter woke only enough to mumble "Mmph" and turn to face her. She turned also, spooning her backside into him. His arm went around her and he pulled her into the curve of his lap. "Quiet, Rachel. Papa's home," he whispered. With his hand resting on the baby's bottom they all drifted off to sleep.

22
Maia's Retribution

Frank had had an exciting day. Since noon he had been drinking too much, and he was in a bad temper. He talked bitterly to himself while he put his own horse away, and as he went up the path and saw that the house was dark he felt an added sense of injury. He approached quietly and listened on the doorstep. Hearing nothing, he opened the kitchen door and went softly from one room to another. Then he went through the house again, upstairs and down, with no better result. He sat down on the bottom step of the box stairway and tried to get his wits together. In that unnatural quiet there was no sound but his own heavy breathing. Suddenly an owl began to hoot out in the fields. Frank lifted his head. An idea flashed into his mind, and his sense of injury and outrage grew. He went into his bedroom and took his murderous 405 Winchester from the closet.

...

His unhappy temperament was like a cage; he could never get out of it; and he felt that other people, his wife in particular, must have put him there.

O Pioneers
Willa Cather (1873-1947)

The next morning when Karen came down stairs, everyone was finishing breakfast. Katinka, the new girl, was at the sink doing the dishes, and Peter was putting on his boots.

"You can't really mean to go to town today?" Karen exclaimed.

"I have to," Peter said, only it came out "A hab do." Pulling out an already soggy handkerchief, he blew his nose resoundingly and added more clearly, "It's already Tuesday, and we've barely begun to get the Saturday edition put together."

"Well, don't blame me if you end up with pneumonia," she grumbled, slopping hot oatmeal into a bowl. "That's all I need, a house full of sick people."

Lil-Anne leaned down to Antoinette, next to her on the bench and whispered, "Don't mind her, Your Highness. She's not mad at us." Hurriedly finishing her oatmeal, she scooped up the doll and beat a hasty retreat before the fallout could reach their end of the table.

"It's just a cold," Peter said. "Besides, it's a beautiful wonder world outside. Go take a walk; that will make you feel better."

Karen slammed the empty bowl down next to Katinka and sniffed. "And just where am I to go in this mess." She gestured out the window, half covered by a snow bank.

As she walked by his chair, Peter grabbed her and pulled her down on his lap. Putting his arms about her and spreading his hands over her bulging waist, he murmured, "It won't be much longer now."

Karen wasn't sure whether he meant the winter or the baby. Resentfully, she struggled to get out of his grasp, but succumbed to the security of his arms. She leaned her head back on his shoulder, savoring the warmth.

"Good thing too," he joked. "Soon I won't be able to reach around you." Turning to Gudrun, he added, "When you go to Helga's this morning, take Mistress-Full-Moon with you. Karen needs to get out, but if she falls in the snow, she'll be as helpless as a snapping turtle on its back, so don't let her go alone."

Winking at a scandalized Katinka, he gently pushed Karen off his knee, blew his nose again and was out the door.

Karen's spirits were sufficiently restored by fresh air and a coffee-chat with Helga Iverson for her to work on the newspaper accounts. When Peter came home later in the afternoon, he came to her in the study. He was white in the face and looked even more tired than yesterday as he slumped on the couch.

Believing that his cold was worse, she said crossly, "I told you not to go out."

"Come over here, I need to tell you some bad news," he said, patting the space next to himself. Karen heaved herself out of the chair and ponderously waddled across the room. Reassured that Peter's forehead felt cool to the back of her hand, she steeled herself for the news while he blew his nose.

"Is it Papa?" she squeaked in sudden panic.

He grasped her hands, as if to keep her from flying to pieces. "No, no everyone at home is fine, but there's been a tragedy at the Benson's. I was at the sheriff's office when Obadiah rode up and asked him and Doc Patterson to come right away. I went too, and the four of us rode out to the homestead." His voice was calm, as if he were merely reporting news for the paper, but his eyes were full, his face ashen.

"We found a wild-eyed Maia clutching her limp baby, a butcher knife at her feet. Oskar was on the floor of the bedroom in a pool of blood."

Karen started to shake before Peter had half finished. Then she screamed and the household came running. Folding his arms about her, Peter gestured with one hand that they should all go away.

"You have to listen," he said. "You have to hear all of it. When we got there, Mildred was sitting on the bench next to Maia, huddled in the corner with a limp baby in her arms. Mildred's hands were folded in her lap, but her eyes never left Maia's face. 'Minnehaha's with the children at the house,' she said. When the doctor went towards the bedroom to check Oskar, she explained that only Maia needed him. 'She's been badly beaten and is out of her mind.'"

Peter and the sheriff pieced together the story from what the eldest boy told. According to Thomas, Oskar had been gone for three days, caught in Marshall by the storm. When he returned late Monday, he was drunk and had beaten Maia, because his dinner was cold. While she was at the stove, he slapped the oldest girl when she couldn't keep the baby quiet and Thomas because he didn't bring his beer quickly enough. The four children had finally eluded his reach and crawled into bed. The next morning, Thomas had awoken to find his father and baby sister dead, mother out of her mind. Screaming for help, he and his three siblings stumbled through the snow to the Bullard farm. Obadiah and Mildred had rushed over and found the baby and Oscar dead, Maia unresponsive.

The doctor said the baby's neck was broken and that Oskar had been dead since about midnight. "We may never know what really happened. Maia is catatonic and will not recover for some time, possibly never. He probably beat the baby when she wouldn't stop crying, then passed out in the bedroom. Maia must have waited until he was asleep and then killed him. The doctor is taking her to the State Hospital in Saint Peter in the morning."

"It's all my fault," Karen sobbed.

"How can it be your fault? Mildred was right there and doing all that anyone could do."

"I knew something bad would happen. Someone always dies."

"Don't cry," Peter pleaded, rocking her back and forth as if she were a baby. "Everything will be all right. Nothing will happen to us. This tragedy has nothing to do with Rachel."

"It's all my fault," Karen sobbed again. *I prayed that death would not take one of mine.* But she couldn't say it out loud.

"Don't cry," Peter begged. "You'll make yourself sick—like last time. Think of little Rachel."

She felt herself lifted and carried up the stairs. "I'm so tired," she mumbled.

"I know, I know. Just rest—the girls will take care of everything."

He pulled her dress over her head and tucked her under the covers.

When she opened her eyes, it was night, but the other side of the bed was empty. "Peter," she called weakly. There was no answer. "Well are you happy now? Is your blood thirst satisfied?" she whispered, not sure whom she was addressing. Finally she slept again, but the memories that she had pushed aside all winter haunted her in repeated nightmares.

When she woke in the morning, she was feverish and had a shattering headache. Her limbs were so heavy she couldn't move, not even her eyelids. She heard voices but could make out no words for the roaring of the darkness. It was easier to hope for oblivion. Gathering her last strength, she turned to the wall, away from Peter's empty side of the bed.

23
Svend's Importunity

And [Jesus] said unto them, Which of you shall have a friend, and shall go unto him at midnight, and say unto him, Friend, lend me three loaves; for a friend of mine in his journey is come to me, and I have nothing to set before him? And he from within shall answer and say, Trouble me not: the door is now shut, and my children are with me in bed; I cannot rise and give thee. I say unto you, Though he will not rise and give him, because he is his friend, yet because of his importunity he will rise and give him as many as he needeth. And I say unto you, Ask, and it shall be given you; seek, and ye shall find; knock, and it shall be opened unto you.

Luke, 11:5-9

March 1891

Following the tragedy, the Bullards and Minnehaha cared for the four surviving Benson children until the county authorities could decide on their fate. Although painfully shy with strangers, they had spent enough time at the house during the last few months for them to feel at home, but Mildred and Minnehaha struggled to cope with the children's nightly terrors and daytime despair. Thomas was the eldest and the only one to have started school. He had some English and felt he should take charge of his younger siblings, yet he barely had the energy to appear at meals and listlessly poke at his food. Olga sought refuge in a rocking chair in the corner of the kitchen, sitting there most of the day crooning a Swedish lullaby to a rag doll that belonged to her younger sister. The two younger could not understand the tragedy that had befallen their family, but knew that their world had changed. They alternated between clinging to Olga's skirts and racing around the house, exploring every cupboard and banging every pot they could reach. Mildred's day was filled trying to limit their wanderings to the safer rooms and dealing with their tantrums when they felt thwarted. At night she was exhausted and fell into bed soon after the children were in theirs.

Obadiah went to Saint Peter with Doc Patterson and Maia. After seeing them safely to the asylum, he walked over to his son-in-law's house to explore the legal ramifications with Judge Brown. He returned that evening, and the three of them discussed the possibilities.

According to their custom, they started with silent meeting, but Mildred was at the end of her energy and in no mood to be silent. After a few minutes, she burst out, "Lord, we know thy will that we be concerned for the plight of orphans, but Thee could have opened a small door of opportunity, not a floodgate!"

Minnehaha lifted her head in surprise. Calmly, Obadiah ended their meeting with the customary handshake. "Do not be shocked at Mildred's way," he advised.

"I never heard anyone scolding God before," Minnehaha replied.

"Do you think the Lord doesn't know how I feel if I keep silent?" Mildred asked. "Voicing my complaints helps me accept His will."

Obadiah, more loquacious than his wont, proposed a plan. He would rent the Benson land for the cost of the mortgage payment and hold it in trust until Thomas became of age. This arrangement was similar to the one Peter had made when the Larsens adopted Fred. "Henry Brown will take care of the legal work."

"What if Maia recovers?" Mildred asked. "What did Henry say about her?"

Obadiah explained that in the remote possibility that Maia were released from the hospital, she would have to stand trial for murder, but would probably be acquitted on a plea of self-defense. They would address this problem when the time came. The more pressing issue was what to do about the children. Daughter Emily would find good homes for the younger girls in Saint Peter. "Instead of adopting children when the Orphan train comes through next month, we will raise Thomas and Olga."

"That means splitting the family."

"But we had never planned to take any children that young—they are too much for thee."

"We'll manage," Minnehaha said. "They can all stay here until Emily Brown finds someone."

"Thank the Lord, He sent thee to us," Mildred exclaimed as she went off to bed, subconsciously slipping into the Quaker speech of her youth.

The snowstorm lion of February became a muddy March lamb as the weather turned warmer and a spring thaw took hold. Long icicles dripped from the edge of the porch roof, and puddles formed in the ruts of the road. By Saturday, travel was next to impossible; sleighs were no longer useable, and wagon wheels crunched through thin night-formed ice only to mire in the mud. Minnehaha and Olga were on their way back from scattering grain and collecting the breakfast eggs in the chicken coop when they were surprised by the sound of slow hoofs coming down the drive to the farm.

Svend Schultz appeared on the back of *Sorte*, the most powerful of the black Larsen geldings. The horse was lifting each hoof with deliberate care, alternately shattering ice and scattering mud. Svend was bent over the spattered mane, whispering encouragement into the horse's ear, his slight body melting into the back of the animal. Only his red hat, red nose, and penetrating eyes hinted at a human passenger.

Horse and rider came to a halt halfway between the stable and house, *Sorte* turning longing eyes towards the stable but waiting patiently for Svend to slide off his back.

Minnehaha assumed that Karen's time had come. "Is it the baby?" she asked, rocking the egg-filled basket as if it contained an infant. "Is Karen all right?"

Svend shook his head in denial. "*Nej, nej. Ingen* baby *endnu. Men A maa straks tale med* Mistress Mildred," he said, all the while leading *Sorte* towards the stable door, the immediate needs of the horse taking precedent over even his obviously urgent errand.

Minnehaha had only learned a smattering of Danish while

she was one of the Babel Girls, but understood enough to explain to Mildred that Karen was not yet in labor.

Mildred called to one of the hands, "Kurt, take care of *Sorte*. Svend, you come inside and tell us what's the matter." She took Svend by the arm and firmly led him towards the house so her meaning would be clear.

Svend refused to go further than the boot bench just inside the kitchen door, gesturing apologetically to the mud puddle forming at his feet. "Mistress Moon *har det daarligt*. Mistress Mildred *maa komme hjem og tale med hende*," he said, warming his hands around the hot mug of coffee that Minnehaha handed him.

"Is it Karen's time?" Mildred asked. "Has the doctor been called?"

"*Nej, nej, ingen* baby, *ingen Doktor*," Svend repeated, shaking his head vigorously. When he could tell that the two women did not understand, he switched to German, "*Nein, kein* baby. *Kein Doktor. Karen ist traurig, sie isst nicht. Sie bleibt den ganzen Tag im Bett.*"

At this point, Obadiah appeared, having been told by Kurt that they had company. He caught Svend's last sentence with the help of a few years of German in school. "Hello, Svend Schultz. *Sprechen Sie deutch? Ich spreche ein bisschen.*"

Gratefully, Svend explained his mission. Having grown up in the border region in Denmark, he spoke a fluent though somewhat rusty German. He wanted Mildred to return with him to Babel farm to help Karen. She was sick in bed, but not in labor. At first they thought she had caught Peter's cold, but though the slight fever was gone, she didn't rally, sleeping most of the day and refusing to eat more than a few sips of soup. *Kaptajn Storkeben* had been out of town since yesterday and was not due to return until late evening.

Svend turned towards Mildred. "Mistress Mildred *kommen Sie. Sprechen Sie mit* Mistress Moon."

"He wants you to come with him and talk to Karen Larsen," Obadiah translated. "But the roads are terrible and I wish you would not go. They have plenty of other people there to help."

"If Karen has need, I must," Mildred answered firmly. "Svend wouldn't ask if he didn't think it necessary, and it's only five miles. Minnehaha, can you manage the children until tomorrow? I'll need to stay the night."

She turned to Svend. "I'll come. Obadiah, explain to him that I'll throw a few things in a bag and then we can leave."

Upstairs, while Mildred changed into a riding skirt, Minnehaha said, "Last fall in Marshall, Birthe told Elsbeth that Karen had the same problem last time. Karen suffered from melancholia before Anne was born, but then was fine afterwards. That's why Peter arranged to have Birthe come as the first Babel Girl. There were problems even when John was born, back in Denmark before the Larsens came to Minnesota. The girls have been wondering why Karen never talks about the baby, and lately her moods go up and down so much."

"I'm surprised that Peter would leave Karen, if she's so unhappy," Mildred said. "I don't know what I can do, but I'm going to try. You're sure you can manage here?"

Arriving at Babel Farm, a muddied Mildred slid off the back of the gray mare and handed the reins to Svend. "We'll figure out something to help Karen," she said to him in as reassuring a tone as she could muster.

Inside, she was greeted by a surprised Inger-madmor who threw herself into the opened arms of the older woman.

"Svend brought me to see Karen," Mildred explained.

"I'm so glad you're here. Everyone is so upset. I don't know what to do! I'm so afraid. First Maia, and now Karen."

Mildred stroked the girl's hair and made comforting noises. "We all feel terrible about Maia," she murmured.

"If I had only stayed with her longer, she might have been all right."

"It isn't your fault. You stayed as long as you could. You were a great help to her last fall—she told me how grateful she was, many times."

Gudrun came into the kitchen. "Helga is sitting with Karen this morning. That seems to quiet her. But she won't eat and she won't talk to anyone."

Mildred nodded to show she understood. "Karen's strong. I'm sure she'll be fine. Let me just change out of these muddy clothes, then I'll go relieve Helga."

24
Letting in the Sun

The days passed. Days in sun. Days in gloomy abandonment, so cold all life froze. There was one who did not heed the light of day, neither when it was gray nor when golden. Beret stared at the dirt floor of the shack and saw only night.

Beret saw only darkness all around. She tried but could not let in the sunshine.

Ever since she had arrived, her conviction had grown that here was the retribution, her meet punishment from the Lord God. He had finally sought her out and now she must drink the cup of his wrath....

Strange how Destiny had arranged everything. Fate had tumbled her about for ten long years, until it finally placed her here. Right here in the big silence where there was nothing to hide behind; here was to be her punishment! Yes, where could she be more easily found than here?

Giants in the Earth
O. E. Rølvaag (1876-1931)

Mildred found Karen in bed. Helga, who was knitting in a chair in a corner of the darkened room, got up and left quietly when Mildred indicated that she would take over the vigil. Mildred pulled the curtains to the side of the window and moved the vacated chair closer. Sitting without speaking, she studied the ailing woman.

Karen was not asleep, but her fingers were restlessly moving over the counterpane, as if her hands were pacing in place of legs too enervated to move. Her head was turning from side to side, eyes focused on a faraway place. "Don't run so fast," she murmured, then sobbed, "He's dead. They're all dead. Someone always dies."

Mildred took her right hand and moved it to lie between both of her own. Karen turned towards her, eyes looking somewhere beyond her shoulder, "Hello, Elizabeth," she said haltingly. "I'm too tired to talk right now." With that she pulled her hand away and turned over on her side, her back to Mildred. Her body relaxed and her breathing drifted into peaceful slumber.

"It's all right, I'm here and we can talk later," Mildred whispered. She cupped her hands loosely in her lap, bowed her head, and closed her eyes. A listening silence crept into the room.

Some time later, Karen awoke and turned towards her. "Oh, it's you," she whispered.

"Who's Elizabeth?" Mildred asked quietly.

"She's a friend from San Francisco," Karen said slowly, as if trying to remember. "I dreamt she came to visit."

"Inger brought us some soup. You need to eat something. Sit up a little and I'll help you." Mildred moved Peter's pillow from the other side of the bed to support Karen's back. She picked up the bowl and coaxed a few spoonfuls. "Tell me about Elizabeth."

Reviving a little, Karen answered, "She's a Quaker like you. Or at least, she was until she married William Bendixen and moved to San Francisco. She helped me when ...," but her voice trailed.

Mildred raised another spoonful of soup and changed the subject. "Tell me about San Francisco."

That seemed to be the right question because Karen found her voice—the impersonal voice of the storyteller.

"Late in the autumn after we were married, *The Lady Roselil* made landfall. Peter had been there the year before and made friends with the Bendixen's, so they were the first people I met. They have a beautiful home on top of a hill, overlooking the Bay—such a magnificent view of the water and the fog rolling in."

Mildred didn't want to interrupt, but her curiosity got the better of her so she asked, "Did you really sail around Africa? Wasn't the weather terrible? Weren't you seasick—and frightened? I used to visit my grandparents on Nantucket during vacation from school in Providence, and I was always seasick the whole way to the island and back."

"I was very lucky and the weather was much better than we had expected. We had a few rough days, but I had my sea legs by then, so I managed most of the time. There were some bad days, and I was two months along ...." Her voice drifted.

Mildred didn't allow surprise to show on her face and hurriedly brought the conversation back to safer ground, "Did you enjoy being *Madame* Captain?"

"It was as thrilling and exciting as I had dreamt. The men were wonderful. Some sailors are superstitious and think that a woman on board is bad luck. But our crew told me that, even with a good captain like Peter, a lady-ship is a much friendlier; more like a family."

"Did you stay in San Francisco?"

"Only for a few days, then we were off to Hawaii and then Japan. When my time was near, we went back...." Again her voice faded and she hesitated.

Mildred held her breath until Karen continued, "Peter made a few short trips to Seattle, and then afterwards we went to sea again."

Again there was a pause while Mildred offered another spoonful of soup. "What was the baby's name?" she asked softly, hardly daring. She waited patiently for the answer.

"We called him Lars after my grandfather." Karen paused but then continued without prodding, voice stronger, "When little Lars was two months old, we left San Francisco, sailing to Hawaii again and then Hong Kong. Oh, how the crew loved the baby and he them! Especially Bosun Kelolo. He was Hawaiian and adored children."

She was warming to her story, revived by the soup and the telling. The afternoon slipped away as she told of sailing to the Orient, luaus on Hawaii, meeting other lady-ships, and of life at sea with an infant. Joyful times.

"Wasn't it difficult to have a child on board?" Mildred blurted. "I can't imagine having an infant crawling about on a heaving deck." She regretted the impulse, knowing that Karen needed to talk about something dreadful that had happened, but in her own way and in her own time. Fortunately, the question was all right and Karen was able to go on.

"Lars was born for the sea. When he was little, Kelolo

rigged a harness in which he could ride on someone's back. We all took turns carrying him, so he soon went all over the ship, though I did draw the line at taking him up in the rigging. He especially liked when Peter or Kelolo took him on the bridge where he thought he was the captain and bellowed orders to the men, in baby talk, of course. He would point to the sheets when he thought the sails should be taken in or let out, and laughed when spray hit his face. Then when he was older and learned to crawl we leashed his harness to the mast so he wouldn't fall overboard. Toddlers who grow up at sea don't walk, you know, so when he was about a year old, we went back to San Francisco."

Suddenly she looked exhausted. "I don't want to talk anymore," she said.

"Why don't you rest now. I'll just sit here," Mildred replied.

Karen closed her eyes and went back to sleep. Mildred sat quietly for a time, then picked up the tray with the remains of the soup and went down to the kitchen.

Peter was home and greeted her with relief. "We're so glad that you're here."

"I'd like to talk to you," she said. "To ask you some questions."

As soon as they were settled in the privacy of the study, she said, "Please tell me about Lars. What happened?"

Peter looked at her in surprise, "Did Karen talk about ... Lars?" He stumbled over the name as if out of practice. "If it weren't for her nightmares, I would think she'd forgotten. The whole tragedy with Maia, coming right now with her time so near, has brought them back. But she won't talk about it, doesn't even mention the coming baby. All she does is cry. That's why I left. I can't stand it when she cries, and it isn't good for her to get so upset."

"Better crying than not talking," Mildred said, more tartly than she intended. "When I lost my babies to diphtheria, I cried and cried. Then I couldn't stop talking about my little treasures. My mother just listened. She said that's what I needed. She pointed out that the women who ranted and raved in First Day Meeting when they lost loved ones were those that seemed best able to pick up the pieces. Some tried to pretend nothing had happened, but they were the ones that never recovered."

Mildred waited patiently for her message to sink in, then

said quietly, "What happened when you moved back to San Francisco?"

"Lars was almost a year old. Karen wanted him to learn to walk like a normal youngster, so we rented an apartment near our friends, the Bendixens. It was as if he knew all along how to walk but was saving his first steps until he had firm ground under his feet. Soon he was toddling everywhere, as enthusiastic about exploring the city as he had been at sea."

Peter paused, his face clouded and with changed voice he continued, "A few months later, I took the *Lady Roselil* on a trip to Oregon, leaving Karen and Lars. We were blown out to sea by a storm and arrived back days after we expected."

Peter stopped speaking, his eyes pleading. Mildred nodded encouragingly but waited for him to go on.

"We were so happy, the three of us. But when they needed me, I wasn't there." With tears inching down his cheeks, he continued in a low monotone, "Karen and Lars were walking home from having tea with Elizabeth Bendixen. Lars thought he saw me ahead, coming up the sidewalk. He let go of Karen's hand and ran down the hill. 'Papa' he called and ran so fast he couldn't stop. They tell me that when he fell, he curled up like a ball, as he had taught himself to do on board ship when a wave tossed the deck about. He just rolled right down the hill and into the street. The cable-car driver never saw him."

Peter paused again. Mildred made no sound but didn't take her eyes off him. "We lost them both. Karen was only three months along. She was so upset, she miscarried, and I wasn't even there." He choked on the words and took out a handkerchief to blow his nose. Embarrassed, he stared at the floor.

There was a knock on the door. "You missed hearing the supper bell," Gudrun announced, pretending nothing was amiss. "Karen is awake and asking for Mildred."

"Please, if it isn't too much trouble, have Inger-madmor make me a tray and I'll eat with her," Mildred said and went upstairs.

Karen did indeed look much better. She was sitting up in bed and eating a bowl of porridge when Mildred came in with her tray of mashed potatoes and meatballs.

"My, that looks good," she said enviously. "Do you suppose there's enough for me to have some too?"

"They gave me more than I can possibly handle." Mildred

smiled and ladled potatoes and meat into Karen's bowl.

While they ate, they chatted quietly about Elsbeth's latest plans for the wedding and decorating her house. Mildred spoke about Maia's children, of how they were settling in.

Finally, Karen pushed aside her tray. "I can't talk about what happened to Lars," she apologized.

"You don't have to tell me anything. Peter explained. I'm so sorry—about the baby too."

"It seems so very long ago and in a different life. They wouldn't let me hold him. They said it was better. Then I lost the baby. She would have been a girl, but they wouldn't let me see her either. The doctor said I should try to forget them both. Then Peter came home. He was so upset every time I cried that we stopped talking about it."

"You said Elizabeth helped you," Mildred prompted.

"She was the only one who let me talk. She would hold my hand and let me cry. Like you."

"Did you go back to sea?"

"I couldn't face going back. I became afraid even to leave the house. The streets were so steep, the hills and the fog closed in on all sides. Peter decided we should go home to Denmark and sold our share of the *Lady Roselil's* cargo to the First Mate. We took the train to New York and the steam packet to London."

"Where did you live?"

"When we returned to Fanø, we stayed in Nordby with Peter's mother, and it was several weeks before I could face my own mother. Finally, we moved into our own place in Esbjerg in the shipping company's warehouse. Peter went back to sea, and while he was away, I went home to Millfarm."

"Did you finally make peace with your mother?"

"Eventually. We were fine as long as we stuck to the present, but we've never been good at talking about our feelings. I kept expecting her to say, 'I told you so.' Of course she didn't, but she never would let me talk about Lars or the baby. Lars was the name of her father who was lost at sea when she was but twelve. She never talked about him either."

After a slight pause, she went on, "I dreamt about her and Grandma this afternoon. In my dream we finally talked about my Grandfather Lars and his son, my Uncle Peter, who was lost in the same shipwreck. When I was a child, I thought the sinking of the *White Karen* was a family mystery, but it just turned out to be a terrible tragedy that no one ever mentioned. I didn't even know my mother had a brother. Then I also found out that she had an older sister, Karen, who died in childbirth at about the same time and that I was named for her. I wish we could have talked like in my dream when I was a child. But we never did. I only found out about the tragedies by accident."

"And you never talked about your babies, either," Mildred said softly.

Karen almost didn't hear because her head hurt again and there was a ringing in her ears. Her throat closed and she couldn't speak.

The silence cradled them. A rainbow of light crept across the bed as the setting sun came out from behind the clouds and shone through the icicles that dripped from the roof. Karen realized something. "As a child, I found out that Mother had sunk her sorrow so deep that her spirit nearly drowned. I swore I would never do the same. But I did, didn't I?"

"Buried sorrows come back to haunt us," Mildred agreed. "But they fade in the light if we only dare to let in the sun. Talk to Peter. He needs to hear the story from you, and you need to tell him that he wasn't to blame for what happened."

"But it was all my fault. I shouldn't have gone out that day. I shouldn't have let go of Lars's hand. Peter couldn't still the storm that kept him away."

"Tell him that. He blames himself for not being there when you needed him. You need to forgive yourselves—and each other."

The silence settled again. Finally Mildred rose from her chair. "You look tired," she said. "I'll leave now. But, someday you must tell me why a captain and his seafaring wife would leave the excitement of world travel to become farmers on the Minnesota prairie."

"I'm not sure that I'm ready to talk about it...yet."

"I'll be here whenever you wish."

Karen closed her eyes and was asleep even before the door closed.

25

The Aftermath of the Storm

I stood on the forecastle, looking at the seas, which were rolling high, as far as the eye could reach, their tops white with foam, and the body of them a deep indigo blue, reflecting the bright rays of the sun.

Our ship rose slowly over a few of the largest of them, until one immense fellow came rolling on, threatening to cover her.... I sprung upon the knightheads, and seizing hold of the forestay with my hands, drew myself up upon it. My feet were just off the stanchion, when she struck fairly into the middle of the sea, and it washed her fore and aft, burying her in the water. As soon as she rose out of it, I looked aft, and everything forward of the mainmast, except the longboat, which was griped and double-lashed down to the ring-bolts, was swept off clear.

The galley, the pigsty, the hencoop, and a large sheep pen which had been built upon the fore hatch, were all gone, in the twinkling of an eye—leaving the deck as clean as a chin new-reaped—and not a stick left, to show where they had stood.

Two Years before the Mast
The Pacific Ocean
Richard Henry Dana, Jr. (1816-1882)

The next morning, Peter brought breakfast. Finally slept out, Karen had been awake for a while and was lying in the warm bed watching as dawn crept over the horizon and in through the window. "I missed you," she said as he came in the door.

"Mildred suggested that I sleep in the sewing room so you could rest."

"I wasn't just talking about last night."

"I know. I've missed you, too."

"It feels like the morning after that typhoon off the coast of Japan. The air is clear and the clouds white, the waves slow and gentle; it's like being rocked in a cradle."

"This time at least, the chicken coop is still there!" He put the tray down next to her on the bed and patted the bulge under the cover. "Is the cargo dry?"

"All ship-shape and accounted for, *Kaptajn Storkeben*—and kicking up a storm of her own." Karen poured milk, still warm from the cow, onto the oatmeal and dipped the spoon into the melting dollop of butter on top. "Mmm," she murmured. "I'm starved."

Sitting down in the chair that Mildred had occupied the day before, Peter said, "You eat, while I talk. Then it'll be your turn. Mildred said we should talk about Lars."

For the first time, Peter poured out his feelings of guilt for not being in San Francisco when Karen needed him. She had never consciously blamed him; after all, even he couldn't prevent the storm that delayed him. But hearing him say the words made all the difference.

"But it was all *my* fault. I shouldn't have let him run down the hill. I should have caught him."

Wordlessly, he took the bowl from her hands and embraced her. He let her cry against his broad chest and cried with her until they were both soaked in forgiveness, of each other and themselves.

Peter laid her back down on the bed, and she moved over to make room. Lifting her head onto his chest, he placed his other hand over her stomach. "Go to sleep Rachel. Mam and I need to talk."

And they did. She told him what had happened, even though he had heard it all from others. He described arriving in San Francisco to find their life destroyed, their treasure lost, nothing left except a wife who would not be consoled. "They told me to take you home so you could forget."

"How could either of us ever forget?"

They were silent for a while; then Peter said, "Mildred told me that each time you are expecting, you re-live Lars dying and that's why you become so sad. I never realized that you needed to talk—I just thought you needed to be left alone."

"I know how you hate to see me cry, so I always felt it was better to go off by myself."

"When you get so upset, I'm afraid that you'll lose the baby. Like that time."

Karen raised her head in surprise. "Crying isn't what made me lose the baby. Big-Anne said that would probably have happened anyway. I was having cramps when Lars got away from me, that's why I couldn't catch him."

"No one ever told me."

"I'm not sure I ever told anyone but Big-Anne. She wormed it out of me, and I thought you knew. If only I'd stayed home that day...."

They were silent for a while, stunned by the damage silence had done.

Finally Peter kissed her and said, "If tears are all you need, we'll batten down the hatches and prepare for a downpour!"

"Aye, aye, *Kaptajn Storkeben*." She snuggled up against his side and the need to shed more tears was gone.

"Why do you always ask who is going to die this time?"

"Because someone always does. Each time, it's as if the price of a child born is someone's death."

Peter gently removed Karen's head so he could sit up and see her face, "How can you say that? You aren't usually superstitious!"

"But before John was born, there was Jesse's tragedy; then before Anne, Fred lost his parents; and now, Maia...." She could barely form the words and get them out of her mouth. The tears were back. Finally, she gulped, "Each time, I have to re-live all that has happened. I'm sorry, so sorry."

"But, sweet Karen, my Roselil, none of those deaths were your fault. Surely you can't blame yourself. You're usually so level-headed."

"I feel different when I'm expecting. The air is much clearer, the flowers much brighter, and the storms that much worse. The joys and sorrows are both much stronger."

She paused, suddenly understanding what she had said. A sharp kick from Rachel brought her back to the present. "Rachel says that it's time for us to get going!"

Peter chuckled. "Already she's ruling our lives! But she's right, I do have to get to the newspaper office—if you don't need me right now."

Karen could but laugh at the little-boy look on his face, so unlike her *Kaptajn*. "I always need you, but I think I'll manage until tonight. Just don't go gallivanting for a few more weeks!"

"I never gallivant!" Peter looked positively horrified.

"Oh, I didn't mean that you'd...you know. Just that I don't want you traveling."

"I'll confine my gallivanting to our bedroom—not now, of course. But just you wait until...when do you think?"

"I'm afraid we'll have to wait until May," she answered with genuine regret.

Peter looked at her with mock horror. He pulled down the cover and, kissing her navel through the lawn nightgown, whispered, "I love you anyway, Rachel. But after May you'll have to share Mam with me. I'm the captain of this bed."

"Aye, aye, Sir!" Karen tried to snap a salute, but hit the side of his head. Laughing, she struggled to sit upright, but only managed to fall back so hard that she almost bounced Peter out on the floor.

"Let's not swamp the ship. You just stay put and enjoy your coffee. Inger-madmor will cope for a few more minutes—it's good you have a capable first mate!"

She picked up the cup and stared with dismay at the scummy milk floating on top of the neglected coffee. Peter laughed and promised to send someone up with more. As he was going out the door, Karen had a sudden inspiration. "I think I'll write our story. When it is all written, I'll be able to put it away and get on with life."

"You would write about us?" It was his turn to be upset.

"We wouldn't show it to anyone else, if you don't wish. But I think it would help, just to write it all down."

Karen lay back, her head full of ideas of the story she would write. Where to begin? In what order tell what needed to be told?

There was a knock on the door and Inger-madmor stuck her head in. "Someone would like to see you, if it's all right."

"You're back," Lil-Anne exclaimed from behind Inger's skirts. Without waiting for permission, her small form catapulted up on the bed on the side where Peter usually lay, and snuggled up against her mother's side. "You're all wet," she scolded and without drawing breath, "The cat found a litter of kittens in the barn. Did you find our baby out there too?" When she saw Karen's surprise, she added, "Well, they said you weren't feeling well, and that's what they always say when someone is about to find a new baby. Is she still out in the barn?"

That child missed nothing. She might not understand the biology, but she certainly knew more than everyone realized. "No, not yet. The baby won't come until end of the month. I just had a very bad cold," Karen lied, realizing that she needed to explain about kittens and babies right away, before the moment was lost. "Like the cold Papa had last week."

"I don't like it when you go away," Lil-Anne mumbled, holding her mother's hand tight.

"But I was right here, in this room."

"Your body was in bed, but *you* weren't here."

Perhaps she was right, seeing the truth, as always. "Well, I'm back and won't go away again. Now, tell me about the kittens."

And she did. How cute they were, and funny. "But Mittens won't let me touch them. I wanted to bring one to you, but she wouldn't let me. Svend says we have to wait until they're older."

"When we finish talking, I'll get dressed and we can go down to the barn together." Then Karen went on to explain that Mittens hadn't *found* the kittens in the barn. They talked about how lazy and fat she had been lately and what had really happened. Quick as always, Lil-Anne's head swiveled to where her mother's bulk raised the covers and she looked at her with questioning awe.

Karen nodded with a big smile. "Would you like to say hello to your little brother or sister? Put your hand right here." As she had hoped, Rachel felt the light pressure and squirmed in response. Lil-Anne laughed in delight and Karen could not help joining.

"Are there six babies in there? Like in Mittens's tummy?"

"I certainly hope not. One baby will be quite enough."

She was afraid the next question would be how the baby had come into her stomach—they had had enough biology lesson for one day. Fortunately, Lil-Anne was easily distracted when her mother asked for help getting out of bed and finding some clothes that would fit. Hand-in-hand they walked down the stairs and out to the hall to pull on boots for the muddy trek to the barn.

After lunch, Karen sat down in the study to start her memoir. It was good to have something to do, for no one would let her lift a finger in the house. Inger-madmor kept everything running so smoothly that they might have been on board the *Lady*

Roselil with a good crew doing all the work. She wrote as if telling about someone else, as if it were one of her stories, letting the events speak for themselves. She began with the previous summer, that bright and joyful summer when all seemed so peaceful. As she wrote, she realized how gradually that summer faded, how the joy dissolved into despair with the fallen leaves frozen in the cold of winter.

The story would take weeks to tell, but each evening, she read out loud to Peter what she had written that day. They would laugh over the funny parts and he let her cry when she felt the need. Sometimes, he would add to what she had put down or suggest what should come next. A few times, he too had to blow his nose before they could go on.

"Perhaps when the children are older, we should let them read your journal," he said one night. "That way there'll be no secrets."

"You want them to read our personal stuff?"

"The children are different. They need to know that their parents are human too. But let's wait until they're grown—and married."

A couple of weeks before Rachel was expected to make her appearance, Mildred visited again. The weather was much better, but the roads still difficult. Using her dogcart she managed to navigate between the two farms. The cart was light enough so that the few times the two large wheels did get stuck, she could easily push them out by herself.

They ate lunch by themselves in the dining room where they could talk in peace. Karen asked how they were coping with Maia's children.

Mildred quickly brought her up to date. "I don't know how we would manage without Minnehaha. She's met the challenges of our bigger household with her usual competence, washing extra clothes and cooking bigger meals without complaint. One day she said, 'I think we have some leftover pieces of quilt fabric large enough to piece into dresses for the little ones. Their rags will hardly last through the next wash. Perhaps Olga can learn to baste. That would help take her mind off what happened better than the poor doll. While I'm using the machine, the little ones can play in the sewing room, where I can keep an eye on them.'"

The nightmares were less frequent, the tantrums rarer, and

enough order restored so that the bigger problems of the children's future could be addressed. Thomas went back to school, and Mildred talked to the teacher about having Olga attend as well. "She's six," Mildred explained. "She should have started school last fall, but Maia kept her at home to help with the baby. She speaks only the little English that Minnehaha has taught her, but the teacher's own parents emigrated from Sweden, so she feels that she can help Olga."

Karen told her about the journal. "Writing it all down makes it easier for Peter and me to talk about our feelings."

"The poor man was distraught when I was here. Everyone had told him to help you forget by not mentioning tragedy. As if that could possibly be good."

"We share everything else. I don't know how he could think we couldn't share this burden too."

Mildred spooned the last of her soup from the bowl and dabbed the corners of her mouth with her napkin. "Speaking of sharing, I'd like your recipe for this delicious soup."

Karen fetched the recipe book the girls had given her for Christmas. While she copied down Elsbeth's pea soup, Lil-Anne appeared at the door, anxious to show off her doll quilt. She had pieced together the six squares of the top and only needed to quilt them to the backing before binding.

"Mom has a big tummy because we're going to have a baby," she announced and then glanced at her mother to see if she had overstepped good manners. Mildred's delighted laughter was approval enough, and she thrust the quilt top under their guest's nose. "How do I make this big enough for the baby? Queen Antoinette says that dolls don't need quilts."

"It is lovely," Mildred answered. "Add a wide border and some corner squares and it will be a perfect baby quilt."

Lil-Anne's eyes crossed at how much work that would be. "You do it...please, will you?"

"I'll be glad to take it home and add the border. Then next time I come, we can finish it together. If we tie the layers together at each square, it will be quite easy."

"Wow, thank you."

As they waited in the hall for Svend to hitch up the cart, Mildred leaned over to give Karen a gentle hug. "You still owe me the story of why you and Peter decided to come to America," she whispered.

26
The Judge and the Tzaddik

Dear Jesse,
After the Benson tragedy last month, I had a very bad time. When Peter was away, Svend took matters into his own hands and dragged poor Mildred Bullard through the mud to cheer me up. She sat with me for most of a day and patiently listened to my misery. For the first time, I was able to talk to someone about little Lars.

After she left, Peter and I talked. We never really had, thinking that since we both knew what happened, it was better not to re-live the tragic events. That was wrong and we now both understand that we needed to share our memories, good and bad. I am also writing about this past year and what came before, telling the story as if it happened to someone else to help me understand what happened. Seeing the words on paper, it became clear that the sadness that overwhelmed me last month was the burden of the unspoken past. I somehow felt that all the deaths were the price for my having children and that I was responsible. Then when the Benson tragedy happened, I could no longer bear that burden alone and collapsed. All this makes little sense when put in a letter, but feelings are not about logic.

In this time of waiting for our Rachel, I have thought much about your loss. You are so much a part of our story that I am enclosing a copy of the beginning in the hope that reading it will be as helpful to you as it was for me to write. I have only shown it to Peter and will never let anyone else read it unless you give me permission, but I do hope that you will at least share it with dear Sarah. The doctor says that my time is three weeks away, but if I remember what Grandma taught me, it may be sooner.

I am therefore sending you what I have written so far. The rest will follow as soon as possible, but may have to wait until after Rachel is born.
I keep you always close to my heart,
Karen

Letter to Jesse Schneider
from Karen Larsen
Babel Farm, March 15, 1891

Denmark, August 1879

After Karen and Peter returned from California, they settled down to the life of a young married Fanø couple. At first, as they had before leaving for the sea, they lived with Peter's mother and his two younger siblings in Nordby, at the northern end of Fanø, where they had their own large room that had been fixed for them in the loft. Bodil Larsen was a charming woman, Erik looked up to his elder brother, and Peter's sister Julie doted on both of them; yet they wanted their own home, however small.

Karen went back to managing the family shipping company's business office, taking the ferry from Nordby to the warehouse on the Danish mainland, a trip that took but twenty minutes. At the meeting of the company shareholders that fall, there were two main items on the agenda: the future of the *Lady Roselil* and whether to invest in a steam ship.

"It makes economic sense to keep *Roselil* in the Pacific for the oriental trade out of San Francisco," Captain Fredriksen, Karen's Uncle Paul, said. "The new captain seems capable and Peter and Karen tell me they do not wish to return to California."

"No, absolutely not," Karen agreed in panic, although Peter had warned her to keep quiet.

Her father proposed investing in a steamship for the shorter European trade.

"The future is in motorships," Peter echoed. "I plan to take a course on steam engines this winter, and then, in the spring, I'll sign on as First Mate on the *MS Fortuna*, out of Varde—I've already talked to Captain Thornby. By end of summer, I'll be ready to captain our own steamship, which we can purchase with the profits from *Roselil*'s next voyage to China and Japan."

After some further discussion of the pros and cons, the shareholders voted and the proposal passed. Karen and Peter had talked of this plan many times, and she suspected that Papa had been pulling the strings behind the scenes. He'd been itching for years to modernize to steam.

Late in the summer the following year, Karen received a letter from Jesse in Lithuania. She had not seen Jesse since they had first become friends during her stay in Ribe in the winter of 1875. Soon after she returned home to Fanø, he had left for Lithuania to go to school. While studying for the rabbinate, he married the Rebbe's daughter Deborah, a marriage arranged by their parents while they were still children. The two women had never met, but became friends through the exchange of many letters over the intervening four years.

Now, Jesse wrote that he and Deborah were planning to visit his parents in Ribe and wondered if Karen would come and see them. At the time, Karen was staying at Millfarm while Peter was at sea as First Mate of the *MS Fortuna*, and she quickly arranged to stay with Aunt Ingrid and her family.

Lil-Anne, as she was still called then, watched her pack. "Are you bringing all your new clothes?"

"I only have one fashionable dress with me—you know Mam doesn't approve when I dress *foreign*. I'll just wear traditional clothes for traveling."

"I have an idea," Lil-Anne said and disappeared to the other end of the house. Soon she returned, carrying a doll. "It's about time Queen Antoinette went back to Cousin Margrethe. She's tired of living in our loft."

At fourteen, Lil-Anne was not so little anymore and had outgrown playing with dolls. The French doll belonged to Cousin Margrethe but had come for a visit four years earlier when Karen returned from Ribe.

"I wish I could come with you. Mam says I have to stay here to help with the harvest."

"Maybe next time."

Although it was a beautiful August day, it was rather windy on board the *Lene*, but Karen stayed by the railing for the two-hour sail to Ribe. The small valise was between her legs and Queen Antoinette tucked securely under her arm. As if seeing the sights for the first time, she stared at the emerging mainland, full of memories. She had been so many places and met so many people since, it felt like another lifetime since she had spent the winter there. *It's hard to believe that it was less than four years ago. Baby Villum will be a big boy. Will Jesse and Deborah meet me at the Ships Bridge? Will it be awkward?*

Deborah spoke several languages but had no Danish or English, and Karen was worried about her own rusty German. Jesse frequently wrote how good and wise his wife was. Karen would seem very silly by comparison.

"But I've been around the world," she said to the doll, seeking royal reassurance.

Aunt Ingrid and Cousin Margrethe waited for her on Bridge Street, gripping each of Cousin Villum's hands firmly while Cousin Jens ran up and down the dock waving and yelling as if he were still a boy of eight.

Jesse stood a little to one side with his sister Hanna and a small attractive woman, obviously Deborah. Excited, he bounded up the gangplank as soon as it was in place and, forgetting Jewish decorum, grabbed both her hands and looked deep into her eyes. In that one glance, it was as if he read her soul and reassured himself that all was well. Karen hoped that the dark beauty observing from the dock was not jealous.

In the confusion of embraces and introductions, Jesse and Karen had no chance to exchange more than that quick greeting and a promise to meet for tea the next day. Aunt Ingrid overheard and suggested, "Why don't you both come to the house at three o'clock. Then Margrethe can take Hanna into the garden so the three of you can have a nice long chat in peace." After a quick consultation in Yiddish, Jesse smiled and Deborah nodded agreement.

The tea party was a great success. At precisely three o'clock, the maid showed Jesse, Deborah, and Hanna upstairs to the parlor and then went to fetch the tea. Because of the Jewish dietary laws, only that would be served, although Aunt Ingrid had protested that she felt inhospitable for not having readied the customary cakes and breads.

"Welcome," Aunt Ingrid said graciously.

Deborah replied in German and handed her a platter of delicious looking cookies and finger sandwiches, as if she had guessed her hostess's quandary.

After seeing that the guests were seated, Ingrid excused herself, saying "Hanna, come with me. Margrethe is impatiently waiting for you down in the garden."

Karen, feeling very fashionable in a striped cotton frock in her favorite lavender color, studied her guests while the maid emptied the tray.

Jesse was dressed much as usual in a dark suit. His father was a tailor and always made sure that Jesse had well-cut clothes. His hair curled up around the edge of the yarmulke that, as usual, threatened to slide off the back of his head. His beard was neatly trimmed, shorter than before, and even his long side-curls were less unruly. Marriage sat well on confident shoulders and his very posture bespoke happiness. His slight body had more substance and he no longer looked as if the next gust of wind would blow him away.

Despite yesterday's brief lapse, he was scrupulous about not meeting Karen's eyes but glanced from one woman to the other as if anxious that they become friends. "I see you're in disguise today," he joked in Danish and then turned to Deborah, switching to German. "When I first knew her, Karen would wear ordinary clothes instead of the traditional Fanø costume when she didn't want to be recognized.

While handing Deborah a cup of tea, Karen discretely examined her. She was small and delicate with a serene face. Her dress was tasteful, if plain, with a matching hat that managed to be fashionable and yet to modestly cover her hair, as Jewish tradition required. Karen suddenly felt bareheaded and wished for her Fanø headscarf. But wouldn't that have looked dowdy and provincial next to this lovely creature?

Deborah withdrew her hand from Jesse's clasp to receive the cup. "*Danke schön*," she murmured politely. She had no compunctions about meeting Karen's gaze, her brown, almost black eyes crinkling at the corners to match her friendly smile.

Picking up a copy of the *Fanø Weekly*, Karen handed it to her. "*Hier ist mein Aufsatz über die Heiraten…,*" she started in halting German. She'd practiced that, but it wasn't coming out right, so she suppressed an unladylike word and continued in Danish, "Jesse, you'll just have to be the translator. Tell her this is the article about different wedding customs that was inspired by what you wrote of yours and those Peter and I saw in China and Hawaii."

What could have been awkward soon turned to a lively discussion, ably mediated by Jesse who translated Karen's Danish almost simultaneously. Deborah's German was spoken clearly and simply, so it was easy to follow.

"Jesse has told me of your tragedy," Deborah said sympathetically. "He says that you don't wish to talk about it, but I just wanted you to know that our prayers were with you during your terrible ordeal."

"Have you and Peter decided about your future?" Jesse asked. "Is he enjoying working on a steamship?"

"I don't think he likes the captain of the *Fortuna* very well, nor being a lowly first mate again," Karen sighed. "But after this trip he'll be captain and have his own ship, The *MS White Karen*, no less. Meanwhile, I'm managing the shipping company and continuing to write, so I'm content."

"I understand that your mother still hasn't completely accepted Peter," Deborah continued softly, "Surely, she doesn't blame him for what happened?"

"No, not really, but I keep expecting her to remind me that she used to say, 'marry a sailor and weep at his grave'. But Peter is all I ever wanted. I would have had trouble accepting someone that my mother picked for me, like your parents arranged for you and Jesse."

"As I wrote you, I did have a young man that wanted to marry me, but my *Tzaddik* is my true love, and my parents did know what was best."

Jesse looked embarrassed while explaining that *Tzaddik* was Deborah's pet name for him and that it meant a 'righteous man'.

"But it also means 'wise man,' and *that* you are," she reminded him.

Jesse took his wife's hand and said, "Deborah is the wise one. I call her the Judge, like Deborah in the Bible."

"Well, Your Honor," Karen laughed, "Do you and the Wise Man from the West want more tea?" She refilled the cups and passed the cakes. "When am I going to meet little Rachel?"

"We're coming next summer and bringing her then," Jesse answered. "My parents have never seen their first grandchild."

"Jesse may have a job in Copenhagen, at the synagogue there," Deborah said proudly. "It would be a great opportunity for him."

"Isn't Jesse supposed to teach in your father's school and eventually take over?"

"There is trouble in Lithuania, though it's hard to believe

that Jews will be in danger. The Rebbe found the Copenhagen job for me and is advising us to leave. Next summer, while we visit the city for my interview, Deborah can also decide if she'd want to live there."

Karen barely had a chance to congratulate them when Margrethe and Hanna burst into the room, their arms full of fragrant roses from the garden.

27
Esbjerg

Dear Mildred,
I will never be able to thank you enough for coming to visit me in that dreadful weather. You found me in the slough of despond, but now that spring promises to come soon my spirits are rebounding. I still don't have much energy, but that's hardly surprising as my time nears. No one will let me lift a finger and I daily give thanks for the capable hands of Inger-madmor. With nothing to do, I decided to answer your question about why Peter and I came to Minnesota. That part of our story really begins with Peter's transition from sailing master to captain of a steamship, our MS Karen. You will notice that Jesse and Svend were part of our lives, even then.

Please do not show the story to anyone, as there are some private parts that I'm not ready to share, other than with you, dear friend. Keep it for me until after Rachel comes, just in case.... No, I'm not being gloomy again, but one can never tell.

Affectionately,
Karen

Letter to Mildred Bullard
from Karen Larsen
Babel Farm, March 20, 1891

Esbjerg, September 1879

As Danish towns go, Esbjerg is new, having been founded after the disastrous war of 1864, when the rally-cry was to "regain at home" what had been lost to Germany. The harbor had been built as the only deep-sea port on the western coast of Denmark able to handle the ships of the burgeoning trade with England. The smaller harbors of Sønderho and Nordby were no longer adequate as modern ships needed the dock facilities, warehouses, and train access of the mainland. Sailing ships became larger and larger and by the end of the next decade were being replaced by steam.

Even before Peter and Karen married, the family shipping company had bought a warehouse in Esbjerg, thanks to Anders Andersen's foresight. That first warehouse had soon outgrown the small building in which they started and been replaced with a larger facility containing offices on the ground floor and a Mr. Rasmussen as clerk to assist Karen's father. On Karen and Peter's return in 1878, she resumed running the office and they arranged a cozy apartment in the warehouse loft. It was a convenient *pied á terre* where they could have a life independent of family scrutiny when Peter was in port and Karen could be close to her work.

By September of 1879, all had gone according to plan and Peter was due to return from England on his last trip as First Mate on the *MS Fortuna*.

While he was at sea, Karen had gone to Millfarm in Sønderho at the southern end of the island to visit her family. Svend, then the coachman for the Sønderho Inn driving the stage daily to and from the Nordby-Esbjerg ferry, was always happy to give her a ride to Nordby. Today was no different as she left her parents to prepare a feast for her husband. Tonight they would celebrate the end of Peter's 'apprenticeship' with steam. Next month he would once again captain a family ship, the motorship *Karen*.

The ferry took but twenty minutes, and Karen hurried down the gangplank as soon as it docked. She all but ran to the warehouse and up the stairs to the apartment, wanting to spruce up the place and prepare a welcome dinner.

They had only two rooms and she only needed to dust and put away the laundry. Satisfied that all was presentable, she ran back down the stairs with her market basket on her arm. Stopping in the office on the way out, she checked with the clerk to see if there was any business that needed her immediate attention. There was not likely to be much since Rasmussen was very capable and had come to Sønderho just a few days before to have her approve some bills.

"Tomorrow, I'll sign the letters to the shareholders about the meeting," she promised. "You really should learn to use that new typewriter, it would be so much more efficient."

"But hand-written letters are much more personal," Mr. Rasmussen protested, adding that he'd think about it.

Karen sat down at her desk to write a shopping list. "Old fuddy-duddy," she mumbled to herself. She did have to admit that he was very reliable and never seemed to resent working for a woman—a much younger woman, at that. "Let's see, we have potatoes, but lamb chops would be nice—Peter likes them. I don't suppose I can get any lettuce—maybe a cauliflower... and a bottle of wine, and for dessert I'll make *æblekage*."

She listed a few more purchases. "Oh, Mr. Rasmussen, I forgot. Please send Klaus for some ice and tell them and the baker to resume our regular deliveries. We also need more coal for the stove."

"He's already gone upstairs with a bucket. Then he'll do the other errands."

Karen stepped out of the warehouse door and turned up the hill to the market square. Esbjerg had changed considerably in the few short years they had been away, as fast growing as any American 'boomtown' and with the same pressure for expediency at the expense of grace. Lacking the luxury of a slow evolution to preserve beauty and tear down the ugly, it had none of the picturesque tradition of Sønderho nor the historical majesty of Ribe. With the building of the railroad spur in the mid-seventies there was no holding back development. Now, in 1879, the town was growing so fast that land was at a premium. Every day, large houses, that had only recently replaced shacks, were torn down to make way for multi-story warehouses and office buildings. At mid-century there had been only a tiny settlement of a dozen residents, no more than a ferry stop to connect the busy Norby harbor with the mainland; now a jumble of buildings squeezed between the teeming harbor and the railroad station. The grubby little town of Karen's childhood was becoming a center for the shipping industry. Of course, it would never be a real city like San Francisco, and the view over Esbjerg harbor towards Nordby at the northern end of Fanø could in no way be compared to the magnificence of the Bay by the Golden Gate. Yet, its very smallness reassured her, its low hills felt safe.

Karen hurried through her shopping and, returning home, put the last finishing touches to the table. The white linen tablecloth from Grandmother's loom looked especially nice with Mother's best beeswax candles and the bouquet of heather, picked that morning on the dune in back of the mill. The boy had already laid the fire, so she only had to put a match to the stove, peel the potatoes, and rinse out the cauliflower. As soon as the pots were boiling, she would put them in the hay-box to finish slow-cooking while she made applesauce for the cake and whipped the cream. She wanted Peter to be greeted by the smell of baking apples when he stepped in the door but, knowing that he would be hungry for other than lamb chops, she would not fry them yet and not serve dinner until later. Hearing a noise at the door, she rushed to open it, tossing her grubby apron aside, in case she had missed the arrival of the *MS Fortuna*. But it was just the cat, clawing to be let in.

"You heard we were home, eh?" she said to the tabby winding itself around her legs and purring loudly. "Mr. Rasmussen tells me you've been a good mouser." She poured a little cream into a saucer. The cat lapped it greedily. Licking her chops she looked up with a hopeful "meow?"

"Certainly not. The rest is for Peter's coffee."

Soon all was ready—except for her to dress. Every few minutes, she looked over the table out the window towards the harbor. Each time a spewing smokestack rounded the northern end of Fanø and steamed for the pier, she grabbed the binoculars to see if it was Peter's ship. Twice she rushed to the window in vain, but not until the third time did the *MS Fortuna* appear from behind the Nordby *Grønning* meadows. She would not dock for at least a half hour and then it would be some time before Peter would be free to come home. Since the Captain took a dim view of relatives meeting his ship and getting in the way of his crew, Peter would not expect Karen at dockside. She could take her time transforming herself from a dutiful Sønderhoning into a fashionable woman.

She debated between her new brown English wool suit and the older blue silk dress. "Which one, Missy?" she asked the cat, studying first one then the other in the mirror. "The brown just came from the tailor, but it's really for daytime rather than evening. Besides Peter likes the low neckline of the blue."

Missy batted a paw at the blue dress and she took that as feline approval. She piled her hair on top of her head, deliberately using just enough pins for it to stay in place, not expecting the loose pompadour to last long. Again, she looked out the window.

Her timing worked perfectly because she was taking the cake out of the oven just as Peter finally appeared. "My, you smell good," he exclaimed as he wrapped his arms around her.

"You too," she murmured into his chest while he undid her hair.

"Are you crying?" he asked tipping her chin so he could see her face and using his thumbs to wipe away her tears. "You worry too much. I'll always come home." Then he changed the subject and stepped back to admire her, "You're a sight for sore eyes. Too bad you'll be wearing that lovely dress for such a short time."

"What do you mean?" Karen started to protest. "It has plenty of wear left." Then she caught on. "You should talk, those elegant English trousers of yours are …," but she couldn't finish the sentence for laughing as he picked her up and carried her to their bedroom.

Dinner was fashionably late. "These chops are delicious," Peter exclaimed. "Much better than anything Cook can produce from the supplies miserly Captain Thornby allows."

"How *was* the trip?"

"It'll be good to be captain again. I prefer being in charge. Thornby's such a surly fellow and runs his ship for his own 'fortuna' without regard for the crew. As a result they too were surly, and it was hard for bosun and me to keep them swabbing the soot off the deck and polishing the brass. He's always in such a hurry that the stokers have to keep at it day and night to keep a good head of steam, yet he's too stingy to allow the repairs on the engine that would keep it running economically. I don't think he's really comfortable with the mechanical side of steam. He seldom goes below deck although I've become pretty good at tinkering with the clunky monster. Luckily, we had a good following wind coming home, so we could use the auxiliary sail most of the way."

"I'm so proud of you. Not many Fannikers are as modern as you and willing to transfer to steam."

"Mmm," he agreed and changed the subject. "Was that

æblekage I saw by the stove? I hope you made plenty of whipped cream."

Hunger having been satisfied, they lingered over coffee, sharing the latest gossip.

"I saw Jesse and Deborah last month in Ribe," Karen said. "They're coming back next summer, after Jesse's ordination."

"You mean, I'll finally get to meet the famous Jesse and the wise Deborah?"

"Don't tell me you're jealous! Of Jesse?"

Peter gave a slightly embarrassed shrug. When he still would not meet Karen's eyes, she added, "Why was it fine for you to meet women in every port, but I can't have even one male friend?—a Rabbi at that, and very much in love with his wife."

"Well, that's different. I was away from home."

"It's no different. I was away from home too."

Peter looked at her in surprise, finally understanding, "You're right—it isn't different." He rose from his chair and came to her side of the table. "Let's not quarrel. Did you meet Rachel last month also? Did she come with them?"

"She's too young to travel yet, but they'll bring her next summer. His parents have never seen her. She'll be five then, a year older than…" but her voice refused to continue; little Lars would never be five and would never meet his grandparents.

Peter changed the subject, "What're their plans? Will they settle here after Jesse's ordained?"

"Ribe's too small a community to support a rabbi, but he may have a position in Copenhagen starting next fall. It's a good opportunity for him."

She rose to clear the table, but Peter pulled her onto his lap and buried his face in her hair, "Leave the dishes and I'll help you later. I want to talk to you." But there was no more serious talk that evening.

It was the next morning before either of them paid any attention to the plates, whose crusted leftovers glared from the table. "I'll put on the coffee pot and clear this stuff," Karen said. "The rolls and butter should be downstairs." Peter took the hint and went down to fetch the warm rolls and fresh milk that had been delivered to their front door.

"I've had an idea," Peter finally said over his second cup, wiping the breadcrumbs and bits of marmalade from his mouth. "This fall, I'll take *Karen* on her sea trials up to Bergen and down to Berlin. It won't be very exciting, and I know you'd rather stay in Sønderho. But after that, we'll take her to the African coast for the winter and into the Mediterranean in the spring. I'd like you to come." He glanced across the table hopefully, waiting in suspense for her answer.

"Oh, I don't think so. It wouldn't be the same as before...." She hesitated, panic rising.

"I know it wouldn't be the same, but it could be a fresh start. The Greeks are hungry for Northern trade, and Morocco will be fun—and sunny. We'll pick up good cargo at every leg and think of the wonderful stories you'll be able to write." He paused and hesitated before adding, "Maybe we'll finally be lucky and become a family again."

"Luck has nothing to do with it," she replied tartly.

"You mean...? You didn't...?" Peter exclaimed in horror.

"Of course not! Grandma would never allow that! But she has lots of advice about herbs and vinegar. It sounds like an old wives tale, but it seems to work."

"Perhaps I should have words with Big-Anne?" Peter murmured ruefully. "Sometimes it isn't so great to have a midwife in the family." But he didn't pursue the matter further, as if he hoped the sun and warm waters of the Adriatic would be more seductive than the cold North.

He changed the subject. "Is that a new dress? That's a good color for you."

She pirouetted to show off the pleats gathered below the bustle in back. "There's a matching cape. It's called *en Spadseredragt*— a walking suit. I'm meeting the editor of the Fanø Weekly this afternoon, and Ernst treats me with more respect when I don't look like a Fanniker."

"And I thought you were dressed up for me."

"That too." She smiled up at him. "When do you finish today? Mam-Bodil wants us for dinner. You can join us when you're done."

"I'll catch the afternoon ferry and we'll spend the night— that gives us plenty of time to talk."

"Sister Julie wants to take a typing course this spring after her confirmation. Do you think Rasmussen would let her be his office assistant?"

"It can't believe that little Julie's so grown-up. I'll speak to her."

"Is it all right for me to wear this?" she asked, smoothing the front of her new dress. "Mam-Bodil doesn't seem to mind when I dress 'foreign.' Sometimes I think she's jealous but doesn't quite dare."

"The dress is perfect. Mam'll approve. She likes to see the latest fashions and Julie will definitely be agog. Are you going to mention Africa and the Mediterranean to Ernst?"

"Wait a minute—I haven't agreed to go—I'll think about it—Maybe."

"Good," Peter said, as if she had consented. He gave her a kiss on the cheek and went out the door, whistling happily. Missy followed him down the stairs, the tip of her tail waving ever so slightly in anticipation of catching a fat mouse.

By the following summer, Karen and Peter had returned from the coast of North Africa. Although she had only reluctantly agreed to go on the *MS Karen*, afraid that returning to sea would bring too many painful memories, they did have a wonderful time and Karen was expecting. They moved back into their cozy loft, except when Peter was at sea when she usually went home to Millfarm to be pampered by everyone. She knew they were all afraid that the birth of the baby would make her ill again, but no one dared say anything in her presence.

As promised, Peter made only short trips to England, Germany, and Holland so that he could return frequently and be with her if she needed him. After each trip he confided his growing dissatisfaction. "I'll never get used to the noise and the soot of steam. The stokers are but slaves, grubbing away in the bowels of the ship. The life of a wind-sailor may be limited, but he has the sun and the stars for inspiration. The *Karen's* a fine ship, but she's not the same as a square-rigger. On her bridge I feel like a ferry-captain, not the master of the sea."

They began to talk of emigrating to America, but she was adamantly opposed to living in a big city like San Francisco, unwilling to face memories of Lars that would haunt her at every street corner and on top of every hill. "What would we do there? Where would we go?"

Peter smiled eagerly. "When we took the train across the continent from San Francisco to go home, the open lands of the Midwest spread before us. Ever since, I've been unable to get the sight of the Great Plains out of my mind. The prairie is like the sea, reaching beyond the horizon, the grass waving in the wind, as tall as a man."

After his next trip they had dinner at Southhouse. Enthusiastically, he announced that they would move to Minnesota as soon as the baby was old enough for the trip. While everyone exclaimed in surprise, he reached up for Uncle Paul's big atlas on the overhead beam and pointed to the state in the middle of the USA. Pulling out a pile of promotional brochures, he explained, "They've just extended the railroad to the southwestern corner of Minnesota. It's ripe for development. We have our eyes on some land near the town of Lincoln that we can buy for only five American dollars an acre! It isn't much of a town yet, having only the depot and a couple of houses, but there's marvelous opportunity for investment.

"But you're no farmer!" Uncle Paul argued.

"I worked on the land in Nordby before I was old enough to go to sea. And Karen's lived on a farm all her life. This winter, I'll go to the Agricultural School—the one not too far from Askov. They have a special program for people who are planning to emigrate. You'll see, it'll work. We figure we can be ready to leave next spring."

Everyone talked at once, each with a different reason why the plan was impractical. The weather was too cold, it was too far away, children couldn't thrive in the wilderness, and wild Indians would slaughter them. But their mind was made up.

Lil-Anne hugged her sister with tears in her eyes. "I'll miss you. You're always leaving me."

"Come with us."

"Oh, I can never leave Fanø. Someone has to take care of the mill."

Only Anders accepted their decision and gave his blessing. With a sad smile and a touch of envy he examined the atlas, measuring the distance to Minnesota from Fanø.

28
Rachel

Dear Sarah and Jesse,

Thank you for your lovely note about Rachel. We are delighted that you will come to the baptism in two weeks; Saul too is welcome, though we understand that someone has to stay in St. Paul to mind the store.

After all my fuss, I am almost embarrassed to say that everything went very smoothly and we are both feeling very well. When I woke Peter up in the middle of the night, telling him it was time, he was so flustered that he could not find his boots. Svend heard the commotion and offered to go for the doctor so Peter could stay with me. By the time Doc Patterson arrived, it was almost all over and he barely had time to chase Peter out of the room and wash his hands before putting the ether mask over my face. Next I knew I woke up out of the fog with Rachel in my arms. I must say, this was the easiest of all my birthings, but I sorely missed my grandmother's quiet guidance. American doctors make me feel that only they know about babies and that mothers are a nuisance to be put to sleep. Ether may be a modern surgical miracle, but I regret missing the most important part of Rachel's arrival.

She's very well behaved and lets me sleep most of the night. During the day I have many helping hands: Inger-madmor runs the house smoothly and Kristina has surprised us all with her talent for taking care of babies. She spoils both Rachel and me by picking the baby up the minute she cries. If I did not have to feed her, I would hardly be allowed to touch her.

Dear Sarah, I am so glad that Jesse shared my story about him and Deborah. As you can imagine, I have been a little too busy to write the second part, but I have had plenty of time to think *during the midnight feedings. As I look down at my Rachel's blonde curls, I wish that I could have known her namesake. So while I am still being pampered, I decided to write about your Rachel. I started with the summer that I was expecting John, before we emigrated to America. Peter was afraid that recalling the dreadful time that shaped all our lives would bring back my sadness, but although I shed a few tears as I wrote, I am filled with gratitude when I look at my beautiful children and wonderful husband.*

Soon,
Karen

Letter to Sarah and Jesse Schneider
from Karen Larsen
Babel Farm, April 4, 1892

Fanø, August 1880

Their last summer in Denmark, pregnant Karen went home to Millfarm to be pampered whenever Peter was away, plying the short North Sea routes to England, Holland, and Germany. Though she claimed that she was feeling just fine, she was not herself and irritated by everyone's protective attitude.

One morning a month before the baby was due, Karen wandered into the Northroom and squeezed her rounded bulk onto the bench to eat breakfast. Only by farm standards was she late, the rest of the family having already finished and started their chores. Judging from the sounds coming from the east end of the house, Mam and Girl-Eva, were fussing with laundry in the scullery, while her sister was in the kitchen washing the breakfast dishes with much banging of pots and pans.

"Here your highness," Lil-Anne grumbled, plunking a bowl of breakfast oatmeal down on the table in front of Karen.

"It's not my fault they won't let me do anything. Even Granmam says I should take it easy, and she's usually the first to say that exercise is good. You all hover as if I carried a cargo of chinaware."

"It's different when it's your own great-grandchild," Lil-Anne agreed, mollified. "And you did have trouble last time...." Seeing the look of pain on her sister's face she relented and said,

"Don't mind me. It's great-washday and you know how Mam gets. She's yelled at me twice already. I had better go finish the dishes before she does it again."

"Just leave them for me so you won't be late for school," Karen called after her. "I can do that much."

She stared at the unappetizing mess in the bowl before her and thought about Lil-Anne. Already as tall as her elder sister, she looked more like Papa than Mam, solidly built like the miller and as well planted on the land. Although she had a vivid imagination that gave her a quirky view of the world, she didn't have Karen's restlessness but was content to slip into the Sønderhoning mold. It was as if her imagination insulated her from the mundane in life and gave her an independence of spirit.

She's not like me. I'm too facile, too shallow. I wish I had her depth of character, her natural affinity for happiness.

The mailman interrupted Karen's musing just as she was drying the last dish and wondering what to do with herself for the rest of the day. He brought entertainment in the form of a packet of letters. The large envelope from the office in Esbjerg was quickly disposed of since it contained nothing that Rasmussen couldn't have taken care of without approval. He continued to defer to Karen, despite the fact that he had managed perfectly fine in her absence during the winter and spring with only minimal supervision from Uncle Paul. There was a postcard from Holland, Peter writing that his trip to Hamburg would be delayed and not to expect him home for another week.

Still optimistic about negotiations, he ended, cryptically.

They had persuaded Uncle Paul and Papa that Peter should talk to the director of a shipping firm in Hamburg. During their trip south that winter, they had developed trade connections with the French colonies along the African coast, and a German firm had expressed interest in investing in the *MS Karen*.

"I don't like doing business with Germans," Papa had grumbled. "Why would they want to invest in a Danish ship?"

"Having a ship with Esbjerg registry is useful to a German company because the French don't trust them any more than you do," Peter explained. "The director happens to be Danish and has a very good reputation. We can depend on him."

Apparently Peter was expecting a successful visit but did

not want to be too specific on a postcard open to public scrutiny.

The next in the pile of mail was the new issue of the *Fanø Weekly* containing Karen's latest article, a description of their February visit to the fascinating city of Barcelona. She became so absorbed in admiring the "by Karen Andersdatter" at the top of the back page that she missed seeing the thin envelope with a Ribe postmark until it fell to the floor.

"Finally, they're here," she said, recognizing Jesse's hand. But the letter was not quite what she expected, containing as it did only a few lines of cramped writing in which Jesse pleaded, almost demanded, that Karen come and see him.

During the usual hasty washday cold lunch, she told the family that she was going to Ribe. Looking up from her plate, Mam said," Certainly not."

Even Granmam, when consulted that afternoon, advised against traveling, arguing, "You wouldn't want anything to start while you're there."

"But I'm over a month away," Karen protested. "Besides, they do have midwives in Ribe—have had for years."

"Nevertheless," Granmam said.

Karen sent a telegram: *You must come Sønderho* STOP *I cannot travel* STOP.

She feared Jesse would refuse, arguing that he could not eat the food and was therefore relieved when his reply telegram came the same evening, promising to be on the *Lene* the next afternoon.

Karen turned deaf ears to all protests that she should wait for him at Millfarm, and after breakfast she resolutely walked into town, albeit slowly. After lunch with Kirsten at Southhouse, she ambled down to the harbor and waited on the bench by the beach, knowing that the tide and wind would keep Jesse away until at least mid-afternoon. She was concerned at the terseness of his note and wished Peter were home. The letter hadn't mentioned Deborah and Rachel. Well, if they all came, Kirsten-Mos and Uncle Paul would put them up. *If Jesse comes alone, he can have Christian's bed in the loft.*

I wish Peter were here, she thought for the tenth time, her hand on her bulging stomach, rubbing gently to quiet the kicking from within. Soon her head nodded forward and the peak of her scarf pointed towards the barely visible cathedral tower across the water, as if to guide her friend. She closed her eyes in the warmth of the late summer sun....

"The struggling Moon looks ready to break forth," a gentle voice quoted from the Wordsworth poem that had led to Karen's nickname, Mistress Moon. There he was, a haggard, tired Jesse. She almost didn't recognize him, for his side-curls and beard were gone, his yarmulke replaced by a seaman's cap. She blinked sleep from her eyes and barely kept her arms from embracing him.

There was no Deborah in sight and no little Rachel. Her heart clutching in fear, Karen didn't dare ask where they were. "It's a struggle to get up, but once I make it, I can walk just fine," she said heaving her bulk from the bench. "We can talk on the way back to the mill. Christian has left for University, so you can stay in the loft as long as you wish."

They walked slowly through town. Jesse seemed far away, and she didn't know how to ask what was the matter. He stopped by the church gate and started to say something, but his voice cracked. Clearing his throat, he blurted, "Deborah's dead."

"Dear God! No! And Rachel?"

"Rachel too!"

His hand automatically went to straighten the yarmulke that he wasn't wearing; instead he rocked back and forth, *davening* as if in prayer and repeated, "Both dead! My beautiful Deborah and little Rachel."

Karen guided him through the gate and past the church and made him sit beside her on a bench hidden behind the fruit-laden branches of an elderberry bush, out of sight of curious eyes. "When? How?" she whispered; it was all she could think to say.

Haltingly, Jesse told his tragic tale. "I was returning home from *schul*, my mind full of the passage of *Rashi* that the Rebbe and I had been learning that afternoon. Rachel would usually come running out of the yard to meet me, but the gate swung from a broken hinge and terrible screams came from the kitchen."

Jesse had crept along the side of the house and grabbed the ax from the chopping block. By the time he pushed open the back door and stepped inside, the screams had stopped. They were lying on the kitchen floor, two soldiers bending over them.

"Broken furniture was thrown everywhere; our little house wrecked. I don't remember killing the monsters, just my neighbors telling me to leave town."

His head dropped between his hands, his voice barely audible. "May the Lord forgive them. I can't."

"And what about you?" Karen whispered. Her arms would no longer be restrained and she pulled his head towards her shoulder. Finally he cried, great sobs racking his slight frame.

Karen looked at the church where she had been baptized, confirmed, and married. Soon her unborn child would be carried there for his naming. She looked across the yard where a stone commemorated her grandfather and two uncles who had been lost together at sea and to where Aunt Karen had been buried with her infant daughter, years before Karen was born. She did not seek the stone for her own little Lars, because he was buried on the other side of the world. So many deaths. *What if I lose Peter? What about the child kicking beneath my apron; the child whom I already know but have never met?*

Tears trickled down her cheeks and dripped onto Jesse's cap until it was as soaked as her apron. Without volition, she brushed the teardrops from the hair that curled around the edge of his cap.

"What will you do now?"

Jesse sat up and let her take his hand. "What can I do?" he sighed. "I can't go back to Lithuania and can't stay in Ribe. Mother is hysterical, Father's crushed, Hanna clings to me, and the little ones are afraid to go outside."

"But surely, you can find a congregation somewhere. What about the job in Copenhagen?"

Again he tried to rescue the missing yarmulke from sliding down, but the knit cap was securely in place. "Not now. I can't be a rabbi. I'm no better than those monsters. I'm a killer, a murderer."

Karen started to protest, but what could she say?

They stayed on the bench in the shade, holding hands. Eventually, she made him walk home to Millfarm; it was all she could think to do. She showed him the stairs to the loft and left him to arrange the few belongings he had brought. To her parents she explained the dreadful tragedy that had befallen her friend, hoping that Mam's quiet comfort or Papa's wisdom would somehow help.

In the end, it was time and the island itself that brought solace. Jesse was so quiet that the family hardly knew that he was there. He poked at dinner mechanically, not even noticing that Karen served him only what she knew he was allowed to eat. She worried that his already slight body would simply melt away. Early every evening he retreated to the loft and appeared again late the following morning, looking haggard and eating only a few spoonfuls of porridge. The rest of the time he walked. From morning until night he walked the heath and climbed the dunes, up and down, until his feet could hardly drag themselves through the fine white sand. Every day for a week, he haunted the island.

He found the beach, a mile wide at low tide and so flat it was hard to tell where the beach ended and the sea began, and so long that it stretched the full length of Fanø. With gulls circling above and sandpipers running back and forth alongside, he walked the nine miles to the northern tip of the island and then back down to Sønderho. Scarved women digging for worms on the strand stared at him, and tourists in bizarre bathing costumes glanced after him curiously, but he saw none of them.

Karen worried that Jesse would one day keep going into the sea and disappear forever, but Lil-Anne reassured her, "He just stays on the beach. He's fine, he just needs time to work it out."

"You followed him?"

"I knew that's what you would do if you were able," Lil-Anne said. "Yesterday, I brought him bread and cheese for lunch and then we walked together."

"What did you talk about?" She should have known that Lil-Anne would do the right thing.

"We didn't talk, we just walked. Tomorrow after school, I'm going to take him to Kangaroo dune and we can sit and listen to the lark."

By the end of the week, Jesse seemed better. He began to talk to the family and notice the beauty of the old house. After dinner, Papa quietly asked him about a passage of scripture that he found puzzling. The cover on the table in the Northroom was pushed out of the way, and Father lifted the family Bible down from its place on the wooden beam over his head. The two men bent over the table, deep in discussion, the lamp above them throwing deep shadows over the table.

Soon Peter will be home. He'll know what to do, Karen thought.

Peter came back the next day. Having left the MS Karen in Esbjerg harbor to unload her German coal, he took the ferry to Nordby and then Svend's stage to Sønderho, arriving late in the afternoon.

Not even waiting for Peter to take off his boots in the hall, Karen explained Jesse's tragedy. "You have to help him. You'll know what to say."

"There's nothing I *can* say," Peter protested. "There are no magic words. You know that. Only time will help, but the pain will never go away."

"Nevertheless, talk to him," she insisted.

Peter and Jesse had never met, but it was as if they had been friends for years. The first night going up to bunk together in the loft, Peter joked that Karen's tightbed was too small for three. "Usually we both stay up here—my long legs, don't you know, but Karen can't do the ladder in her shape."

During the next few days they spent time together, often in silence, but increasingly they talked about their tragedies and what lay in the future; that is, Peter talked and Jesse listened. They walked the heath, Peter confiding his dissatisfaction with the sea and explaining his plan to emigrate to America as soon as the baby was old enough.

Jesse was very surprised. "Karen never mentioned anything in her letters. What does she think of all this?"

"I'm not sure. You know how good she is at getting other people to talk about what they want. She has been very encouraging—even found out about land opportunities, but right now, all she can think about is the baby. She's suffering from melancholia because of the other two, and we're very worried about her. I was hoping that having a new adventure to look forward to would cheer her up."

"I'm sorry to have added to her troubles at such a time," Jesse said frowning. "Her letters are always so cheerful and full of funny anecdotes, I didn't realize."

"She gets very upset when she talks about...." but Peter

couldn't say his dead son's name. "It's better if you don't mention him."

Jesse took the hint that Peter didn't want to talk about Lars either and asked, "What on earth would you do on the prairie?"

"We'll farm. The land is so fertile it barely has to be cleared — just put hand to plow and the crops grow. Beyond anything that can be done with Fanø's miserable sand."

"You can't be serious! What about your new steamship?"

"The *Karen's* a fine ship, but she's not the same as a square rigger. As soon as the baby comes, I'll go to the Agricultural School and we'll leave next spring."

Jesse shook his head. Finally he had someone else's problem with which to grapple.

"Come with us," Peter offered. He bent down to pick up a shell on the beach, but rejected it when it turned out to be broken.

"You may think you can become a farmer, but I *know* I can't. I'm a city boy."

"You never know until you try!"

That evening, the discussion continued, first in the comfort of the Southroom, then all the way up the stairs to the loft. Peter dug out the brochures and explained about the new railroad and the great opportunities. "Maybe you could live in town and help it grow!"

Jesse shook his head, but his new friend's enthusiasm was infectious and gave him food for thought.

Finally, Jesse found the answer for which he had walked so far. "I'm going to New York," he announced the next evening after supper. "I too will seek a new life in the New World."

So it was that he went home to Ribe to say goodbye to his family and pack his few belongings. He returned a week later on the day that Karen was delivered of a baby boy, staying long enough to witness the baptism of Jens Larsen, who was to be called John in honor of the his future home in America.

The day after the baptism, Peter and Jesse went to Esbjerg where Peter arranged for papers and signed Jesse as a deckhand on the *MS Karen*. In England, no one questioned the papers of the Danish sailor when he took the packet to New York, there to melt into the teeming city streets.

29
Beating the Bounds

That summer Per Hansa was carried further and further into the wondrous fairy tale in which he was both prince and king, the sole owner of all the treasures...

How could he take the time to rest? Was he not owner of a hundred and sixty acres of the best land in the world, more firmly his for every day that passed and every furrow he turned? ... He looked at the land and laughed, laughed as if at something pleasant and funny. Such soil! Set the plow and turn the sod and a field appeared. And this was not just ordinary soil, fit only for barley, oats, potatoes, hay, and the like; oh no, it was meant for much finer and more delicious uses. This soil was for wheat, the king of all grain! The good Lord had created such soil just for this noble seed; and now Per Hansa walked on a hundred and sixty acres of it, all his very own!

I de Dage—Giants in the Earth
O. E. Rølvaag (1876-1931)

Minnesota, 1881

Although John was born in September of 1880, it wasn't until the following March that Karen and Peter were ready to depart for Minnesota in the New World. At six months, he was uncommonly robust and could have made the voyage in the comfort of the Captain's cabin at a much younger age, but Karen needed time to recover from her melancholia. Tragedies haunted her dreams, and her family seemed mired in death. She had trouble rousing enough to feed John and had to be shaken awake when he cried. To make matters worse, Peter was away at agricultural school, learning how to be a pioneer farmer.

By December, the usual bustle of Christmas preparations brought her back to her senses, especially since John's lusty cries and demands for attention finally made her realize that the living needed her more than the dead. After the holidays, she was too busy getting ready for the move to worry about the past.

They prepared to leave in the *MS Karen* as soon as the North Sea was clear of ice. With Peter as her Captain and part owner, they would not be typical immigrants and would board with all the possessions, farm equipment, and animals needed to homestead on the prairie. Knowing Svend to be an expert, Peter commissioned him to go to Ribe Horse Fair and purchase a pair of horses suitable for plowing.

Svend returned that evening on the *Lene*, carefully guiding first a magnificent black stallion and then a matching mare down the gangplank. "From Horsens," he declared, naming a famous horse town up north and thereby summing up their provenance and worth. "Mare's with foal."

Leaving the reins with an impressed Peter on the soggy low-tide beach, he went back on board and returned with a protesting cow, closely followed by her wobbly calf. "Holstein," he explained unnecessarily and, pointing to her generous udder, added, "Good milker for Lil-Jens."

To Peter's surprise, Svend then handed him a handful of coins, change from his skillful bargaining. "I'm amazed," Peter confessed that night. "I can't imagine how he managed. The horses alone are worth more than he paid for the whole lot!"

As they boarded the *MS Karen* on the day of departure for America, Svend appeared again, unasked and unannounced. He was pushing his handcart, ordinarily used to transport luggage for the guests of the Sønderho Inn, but that day it was loaded with only a small chest. Making it abundantly clear that he was not there to say goodbye but meant to come along, he ordered the crew to load both into the cargo hold. When Peter tried to reason with him, he said, "A'll do for the horses." As usual when he wanted no argument, his dialect became so thick that the words were difficult to make out.

"I suppose I'm to blame," Peter said ruefully that evening when he could finally leave the bridge and crawl into the bunk next to Karen. "I did ask him to buy the horses, but I never intended for him to come with us. I hope he understands that the next few years will be nothing but hard work for little pay. As soon as we've settled in, I'll recommend him for a job at a livery stable. Meanwhile we can certainly use an extra pair of hands and a strong back."

The voyage to New York was uneventful. Once they were safely in the harbor, Peter relinquished the bridge to Captain Jørgensen, as they had arranged. Svend loaded all their baggage and animals on the train and the four immigrants rumbled across the eastern half of the continent to their new home.

At first they rented rooms in the Danish community of Tyler while their cottage was being built on the farmstead in Lincoln. They had timed their arrival for the spring so they would have a full growing season to get started. Peter rode out daily from Tyler to supervise construction and breaking the sod for their first planting. Having learned carpentry at sea, where survival depended on solid workmanship, he would tolerate nothing less, even in their first shelter. Although well built, their 'balloon' house, as they were nicknamed because they seemed to appear on the prairie overnight, was hardly more than a shack with only a kitchen-living room and an adjoining bedroom. Ungainly tall to accommodate an unfinished second floor that was Svend's temporary bedroom, the house was designed to serve until a more substantial building could grow around it.

Svend immediately took charge of the animals, staking the cow and hobbling the horses to graze. He insisted on camping out there, upending his cart and draping a canvas tarp over it to make a crude night shelter against the spring rains.

Karen too made frequent buggy trips, laden with wooden traveling boxes. Svend deposited the loads on a raised platform of planks by the entrance and covered them with oiled sailcloth to protect against spring rains.

The final move came after they had been in Minnesota for less than a month. With a habitable house, they could concentrate on breaking sod for fields and a kitchen garden. The first sowing would be wheat, the miracle grain that new settlers depended on for a cash crop.

But first, Peter wanted to survey their new land, and after breakfast the next morning he set out with Karen and Jens to walk the boundary.

Karen could hardly keep up with Peter, as his long strides

cut diagonally across the first plowed field and then through tall prairie grass. His blond hair and broad shoulders sailed ahead of her just above the parting winter-brown stalks, and baby John, his head a smaller copy, bounced on his father's back comfortably strapped in a leather harness. At the top of a small rise, Peter squatted and searched the dense spring grass near the ground until he found the wooden post that marked the northeastern boundary of their land.

Having found the first stake, he waited for Karen to catch up. He turned around and pulled her into an embrace with his left arm while sweeping the prairie with his right. "All this is ours," he said. "As far as we can see; a mile south and a half-mile west, three hundred and twenty acres of the world's most fertile land. Two quarter sections, paid for and deeded to the Larsen family."

Only a slight ripple spread behind them, a faint wake in the prairie sea, marking their path to the post.

Peter tipped his head back so that his hair caressed John's cheek. "Someday this will all be yours."

John crowed his approval, enthusiastically beating on his father's shoulders with small fists. Then, raising a dimpled hand, he pointed towards the horizon in an echo of his father's gesture.

"Born to the land," Peter bragged, and reached back to guide his son's small arm towards the southwest to where the chimney, still smoking from breakfast, was silhouetted against the cloudless sky. "There's our new house, and there to the left across the road is the Jensen farmhouse."

Karen smiled up at father and son. The two were so alike, happy wherever fate placed them, ready to tackle any obstacle in the way. Impatiently, John bounced up and down, his small heels spurring his father as if to say, "Down, down." She lifted the baby out of the harness and set him down on the trampled grass around the stake. He was completely surrounded by the towering stalks.

"Don't get lost down there," Karen laughed and squatted down next to the boy. He giggled and grabbed at the grass straws, possessively pulling the prairie towards himself.

Peter opened a mysterious sack. Lifting out three small rocks, he gave John and Karen one each. A little self-consciously, he explained that they were for the boundary marker. "For good-luck. We'll each put one next to the post and again at each of the others. If we do that every year, we'll soon have rock cairns at the four corners of our land."

At first John didn't want to relinquish his rock, but finally was persuaded that it would look grand on top of the wooden stake. Carefully he deposited his treasure in the center. The three stood back to admire the effect, John now perched on his father's arm. Feeling that slightly more ceremony was needed, Karen unscrewed the top of the water bottle that she carried and poured some into a cup. She splashed a few drops over John's rock as a libation for the spirits of the land and passed the cup to Peter. He solemnly sipped a little and offered some to John before handing it back to Karen.

"Up we go," she said, lifting John back into the harness on Peter's back. They started off again, this time heading west along the northern boundary of their land towards the next marker.

The last shingles were being nailed on the roof when the three returned from their three-mile hike around their property. Karen extricated a sleeping John from the harness and placed him on a quilted horse blanket in the shade of an old cottonwood tree. It was well away from the dangers of the littered construction site and down by the spring where Peter could keep an eye on him while supervising the digging of a well. He had promised that, after harvest in the fall, he would cut down the rotting trunk and plant a real tree in its stead, an elm perhaps. Karen would have preferred a beech to remind her of the shade trees around the Askov school building, but in her first lesson on the harshness of the Minnesota winter, she was told that a beech could not survive. A sturdy oak was her next choice, but upon inspecting the scrubby native specimens down by the nearby creek, she had agreed that an elm would be more graceful. Since neither beech nor elm would grow in the salt air of Fanø, she was grateful for any arboreal species that would fulfill her longing to possess a real tree.

"If you wanted trees, you should've bought land up north," neighbor Jensen pointed out. "But dem forests is useless for farming." Hailing from the wasteland heath of North-Jylland, he was not a man of many words but always willing to share his store of pioneer wisdom, gained from two years of farming across the road from the Larsen's new house. Enthusiastic about living on the prairie, he had been delighted to give up being a tenant farmer and the struggle to reclaim the Danish heath in favor of turning Minnesota buffalo grass into fields that he would eventually own.

Helena Jensen, equally friendly but more talkative, was delighted to have such near neighbors, especially fellow Danes. Their son, a likely lad of ten with only two younger sisters for company, was disappointed to learn that the only Larsen child was a baby, but soon attached himself to Peter. When his chores permitted, Frederik followed the glamorous sea captain about, hoping for crumbs of attention.

With Karen, he was extremely shy, unused as he was to strangers. Always willing to help, he would turn up at odd times but just stand there until she found something for him to do. The first time they met, she tried to be friendly. "I hear your name is Frederik Jensen. I have a nephew in Denmark called Frederik. I miss him very much, so you're welcome to visit any time."

Getting no response, she tried again, "Our neighbors back home are also called Jensen, so I hope we can be friends."

The boy stared at his shoes and mumbled something ending in, "... Fred."

"What did you say?" she prompted, straining to hear.

"I like 'Fred'," he repeated, still barely audible. Seeing Karen's frown, he corrected his manners by adding, "Mrs. Larsen."

"Fred it is then. And I like to be called Karen." The boy still stood there expectantly so she added, "Peter went to town to fetch more nails, but Svend is in the pasture checking the horses and I'm sure he would like your help."

The boy happily scampered off and was soon to be seen feeding the mare a handful of grass. Thereafter, whenever Peter was not around, he would trail after Svend and soon showed a talent for working with the horses.

On this, the first day of their official residence on the farm, Karen was anxious to begin settling her new kitchen. She removed the tarp from the boxes, but found them too heavy for her to even shift.

Svend appeared uncalled at her side with the familiar cart. "Let's start with these three," she instructed. "Those five can go in the bedroom. The rest have nothing we need for now and can be brought upstairs to the loft when Peter can help you. That one has more blankets, if you want one. It must get cold up there at night."

"No, *Mistress Moon*, A's fine. The loft is snug, and the heat rises from downstairs. Better than many places A've bunked in my day."

Karen looked affectionately at the little man who was moving the boxes onto his cart as if they weighed no more than bales of hay. His coming along had made such a difference in getting them settled, his devotion a gift that could never be repaid.

Grateful for his help on this fine April morning, she preceded him into the kitchen and surveyed her new domain, hands itching to bring order to the chaos of boxes piled around the floor. She looked forward to the day Peter would build a real kitchen with an iron stove, so she wouldn't have to cook on an open hearth, but first things first.

In previous trips from town Karen had arranged her small supply of bowls and dishes on the waiting shelves, but some of them were now sitting on the dining table with the remains of breakfast and begged to be washed. *If we're to have bread in the house, I need to put up the dough. Now.*

Lifting the kettle from the fire and using her apron to protect her hand from the heat of the handle, she poured a bit of water on the new worktable under the window, found a scrub brush, and scoured the freshly sanded wood. While it dried, she piled the dirty dishes into the washbasin to soak in hot water and a shaving of yellow soap. With luck, she would be able to finish kneading the dough before John awoke and demanded to be fed. She looked out the window down towards the spring and was reassured to see Peter going about his work but near enough to where John slept on the ground for him to keep an eye on the baby.

Without being asked, Svend had already emptied the bag of flour into the galvanized bin under the worktable. Karen piled several scoops onto the table and made a well for the sponge that had been left to rise overnight. Helena Jensen had thoughtfully brought over a cup of starter last night as a house present so she wouldn't have to wait the several days needed to capture wild yeast and grow her own. She added a pinch of the salt that Helena had also brought, grateful for the ancient traditions of welcome that had supplied the essential staple, forgotten in the rush of the move.

Svend was still shuttling back and forth to the tarp, hauling boxes into the kitchen and bedroom. "When dat big one is unpacked," he mumbled, as if speaking to himself rather than appearing to give orders to his mistress. "A'll stuff it with dry grass, for the haybox." Filled with hay, the box would provide a place to slow-cook potatoes or porridge so the fire on the hearth could be banked when not otherwise needed.

"You think of everything," Karen approved, wondering if she would ever get used to having a retainer at her beck and call.. "I'll unpack the box as soon as I finish with the dough and feed John."

Svend went back out the door, his monologue trailing behind. "Then A'll stack some boxes in the bedroom for your clothes. If'n A lays dem sideways it'll be like a chest."

Karen checked out the window again and hurried to finish as it appeared John had woken up and was demanding his mama. Folding the dough into a ball, she put it in a bowl, covered it with a dishcloth, and placed it on the hob next to the hearth. With perfect timing, Svend came back with a squalling John under one arm and a bundle of dry prairie grass in the other.

Relieving him of the live burden, Karen said, "I'll take the noise-maker if you'll finish unpacking the haybox. It has mostly pots that can hang on the rack over there. Anything else you can stack on the table." She held the soaking boy at arm's length and carried him into the bedroom to change his diaper. Recognizing the necessary prelude to being fed, John ceased wailing and looked up at her with patient blue eyes. *I have to boil the diapers. Good thing I remembered to buy that enamel pot—another chore before making dinner.*

She returned to the kitchen and settled into the brand-new rocking chair that Peter had triumphantly brought out on his last trip from Tyler and undid her bodice. "No biting," she admonished with a smile. John grinned back releasing her nipple with a soft whoosh and displayed his offending teeth. "You look just like your Papa," she crooned softly, unsuccessfully suppressing the memory of another armful with a ready smile.

As she bent over the baby, a lock of her hair came lose from the bun at her neck and dangled over his face. He laughed aloud and batted at the toy, like a kitten playing with yarn. Her heart squeezed; she hoped it would become easier when he was a little older. Good thing that John's lanky frame promised to become another *Storkeben*. Unlike the other image that haunted her—a miniature of her stocky father.

"Now get back to work," she said, trying to keep her lips in a prim line so as to discourage another responsive smile. "We have a busy day, and Papa'll want to have his dinner soon."

Later that afternoon, as Karen was putting together leftovers and slicing bread for their cold supper, there was a knock on the door. Little Fred stood on the stoop, his arms full of newspapers and envelopes.

"Is that our mail?" she asked, relieving the boy of his burden. One letter was from New York, and she put it aside to savor later.

"We was in town. Postmistress let us bring your mail. She says to write permission for next time."

"John and I were just having milk and a *tvebak*. Please join us," she said, handing the baby an oven-warm rusk and another to the boy, thickly smeared with home-churned butter. What a joy to share the first fruits of her kitchen with a neighbor, albeit he was only a child.

The boy was not known to ever turn down an offer of food. He mutely crunched on the treat and rinsed it down with the accompanying mug of milk, swallowed in one large gulp. Licking his creamy mustache, he said shyly, "You're to come for coffee tomorrow afternoon. And the Captain."

"That's very kind. Did your mother invite us?"

The boy stared at his feet and noticing that the shoes that he so rarely wore were dusty, polished them by rubbing first one then the other against the back of his pants. Emboldened by her friendly voice, he finally looked up and blurted, "And the baby. And Svend. It's my birthday, you see. I'll be eleven."

Supper that evening was a silent affair; the far end of the table was cluttered and the floor piled with half-unpacked boxes. Only the baby still had the energy to make contented gurgling noises, sitting in his own little chair next to the hearth and munching on a *tvebak*. Finally even he flagged and sleepily rubbed nose and eyes with a pudgy hand, smearing soggy biscuit over his face.

"You and John just settle in your chair," Peter offered. "Svend and I will tackle the dishes."

Gratefully Karen did as ordered and soon both of them closed their eyes. The next she knew was when Peter gently lifted the boy out of her arms to tuck him into bed. "You stay there and read your letter."

"Go'nat Mistress Moon," said Svend bringing the lamp closer to her chair. Without waiting for a response he climbed the ladder to his nest in the loft, another lamp in his hand.

"It's from Hanna," she called to Peter, delighted that the letter was from Jesse's younger sister. "She and Saul have arrived safely in New York where Jesse's found a small apartment for the three of them."

Hanna and Saul had been married back in Ribe only a few months earlier. He was the younger son of a family friend from Russian Poland where Jesse was born and the Schneiders lived until they moved to Denmark. The young people had met when Saul came to visit Ribe to investigate job opportunities there. They had fallen in love, and both families had blessed the union although Hanna was barely eighteen. Saul, when he learned that he had a brother-in-law in New York to pave the way, had decided they should emigrate and they departed Hamburg a couple of weeks after the *MS Karen* left Esbjerg.

Peter pulled up a chair on the other side of the hearth, placing the newly arrived stack of Danish newspapers next to his feet. "Listen to this," Karen said.

On board ship we made friends with a young woman from Lithuania, not far from where Jesse used to live. Sarah is quite beautiful and very quiet. She lost her whole family in a cholera epidemic and decided to go to America—all by herself. Can you imagine being that brave? It is hard enough for a man like Jesse to be alone. I am so glad I have Saul to take care of me.

New York is a very large place with over a million people, they tell me. It is noisy and dirty, but Jesse says I will come to like it after a while. It is lucky that Jesse talked my parents into letting me study English with your cousin Margrethe. Although everyone on our street speaks Yiddish, it is much easier to get a job if you know English. Tomorrow I am going to apply for a position as a salesgirl in a department store not far from here. It is ten times as big as my father's little shop in Ribe. Some of the customers are American so they need someone who can speak English and it will help that I have sales experience.

Poor Sarah is living with a very grouchy aunt. She is working in a Jewish clothing factory sewing dresses and taking English classes at night. She is quite smitten with Jesse and I am hoping that he will soon notice how lovely and brave and smart she is. Would it not be nice for both of them if something developed?

Please write as soon as you are settled. I am dying to hear what life in the wilderness is like. Have you seen any Indians?

"She's so funny." Karen sighed. "I've already explained to her that we're quite civilized out here and no Indians. In her own quiet way she's a schemer. I don't think Saul realizes that going to America was really her idea! She'll have Jesse and Sarah married before they know it. But it would be nice for them."

"Now we'll only have to talk them into moving west to the fresh air." Peter laughed. "Maybe you can explain to Hanna that Marshall is an up and coming town—lots of business opportunities. Saul sounds like a real 'go-getter,' as they say here. Persuade her and she can whisper in his ear...."

30
Dwelling Together

The shared road is beautiful
For two who want to be together,
Then happy times are twice as joyful
And sorrow half as heavy.
Yes, there is joy in dwelling together
When the trip hammer is love.

All places are home, be they large or small;
When there is one goal
And that which pulls the great load
Is at the heart's core.
Truly, there is joy in being together,
When yes and amen
Are the language of the heart.

Wedding Song
NSF Grundtvig (1783-1872)

Babel Farm, April 1891
At the annual beating of the bounds ten years later, John and Lil-Anne could hardly keep up with Peter's long strides, his blond hair and broad shoulders sailing ahead of them down the road. The children, their heads smaller copies of their father's, walked hand-in-hand stumbling over the unevenly graded dirt road.

"Hurry up, Lil-Anne," John said, "or Papa'll start without us."

Peter turned around to reassure them, "Don't worry, the wagon is behind us and no one else has even left the farm."

It was a far larger party that set out on this cloudy Saturday morning towards the northeastern boundary post of the Larsen farm than when Peter, Karen, and John had made their way through the tall prairie grass ten years earlier. It had become a family tradition to celebrate each anniversary of their arrival in Minnesota by walking the bounds. Peter, as always, led the group, but was now followed by the two older children, while Karen and Baby Rachel rode in the wagon, driven by Svend. Fred and Elsbeth, whispering romantic nothings, straggled at the rear, and the four "girls" were to catch up with them at the first post.

Helga and Olaf Iverson had, as usual, declined the annual invitation, protesting that they weren't family. "You're as much part of the Larsen Tribe as Svend or Fred or the girls," Peter always said, knowing that they would not change their mind.

This year, Helga pointed out that someone should stay behind to ready the barn and cook for Fred's birthday party. She looked pointedly at Inger-madmor who quickly promised that she and the girls would return on the wagon after the special ceremony at the first boundary post.

There had been many other changes in the intervening years. First and foremost, the little family had grown. John was no longer an infant but a tall ten-year old; Fred had joined them six years earlier shortly before Lil-Anne's birth, and, just a week ago, little Rachel had been born. The property and the Jensen farm had also been transformed. The prairie grass on the ruler-straight border between them had been replaced by a dirt road that continued alongside the old Johansen place and on north. Where the three properties joined, smaller green roads extended west and east towards the next boundary posts where they made right-angle turns north and south to eventually outline the rectangles of each of the three farms. These roads, whose main function was to give access to the fields, were hardly more than parallel ruts made in the grass by wagon wheels, but walking on them was considerably easier than making way through the man-high grass, as they had the first year. The land on either side of the road had also changed from wild prairie into fertile fields. It was still too early in the year for wheat and corn to have been planted, but weeds and wildflowers had optimistically raised green heads, little suspecting that they would soon be chopped to pieces by the blades of the harrow preparing the soil for seeding.

Peter had also added new buildings to the growing enterprises. When they adopted Fred Jensen upon the tragic death of his family, they had arranged to lease his farm. The center of the farming activities had then shifted across the road, where now larger barns, stables, and the new silos added to the landscape. Meanwhile the main house had expanded around its basic shell to provide living quarters for the Larsen family and the four girls. The yearly walk around the combined properties had grown from three to five miles, and only those with strong legs and a stout heart made the complete circuit. Every year as they walked in a figure eight around the two farms, Peter made it clear to Fred that his family's property would eventually be returned to him.

This April morning was Fred's twenty-first birthday and today he would become the legal owner of his farm. However, with the acquisition of the abutting Johansen land, he and Peter had agreed to a swap whereby the old Jensen farm was to be merged into the Larsen property while Fred would be the proud owner of his own quarter section to the north. During the coming week, they would sign the legal papers at the Lincoln County offices in Tyler, but today they would mark the great event with a more elaborate ceremony than the yearly beating of the bounds.

It was therefore a large group that assembled at the first meeting point, consisting as it did of nine adults, two children, and a newborn baby. Peter walked to the wagon and helped Karen down, handing Rachel to Kristina. Taking a good-sized rock from the pile in the back of the wagon, he indicated that the others should do the same. He and Karen walked hand-in-hand to the Larsen boundary post, where they each placed a rock on the top of the ten-year pile that completely covered the post. Karen placed a second rock for Rachel and helped Lil-Anne find a good place for hers. John and Fred were next, followed by the rest of the company and Svend at the end.

According to tradition, Karen then opened a stone jar and poured water over the pile, saying solemnly, "May the Angel of the North watch over this land by winter, so that it may rest from its labors." As if she had voiced a prayer, the company responded with a solemn but enthusiastic "Amen."

Peter jumped up to stand on the floor of the wagon where

he could be heard by all and called Fred to join him. Looking very much the captain on his bridge, he held up a paper scroll saying, "I have here the deed to the Jensen farm which has been held in trust for Frederik Jensen until his coming of age on this day of his twenty-first birthday." He handed Fred the deed asking those assembled, "Do you bear witness to the return of this trust?" To which all shouted enthusiastically, "We do!"

They repeated the laying of rocks around the adjacent Jensen post, but this time Fred poured the water libation, echoing Karen's words.

Peter jumped back on the wagon, pulling Fred up with him, and again brandished a scroll. "I have here the deed to the former Johansen Farm; henceforth to be called 'Jensen Farm.'"

Fred followed suit, raising his own scroll and calling out proudly, "I have here the deed to the former Jensen Place; henceforth to be part of the Larsen Farm."

Peter and Fred exchanged scrolls, saying in unison, "Do you bear witness to this exchange?" and again everyone shouted affirmation.

They then placed rocks around the base of the third marker, to begin a new pile at the southeastern corner of the Jensen farm-to-be. Elsbeth, as future mistress, was supposed to say the first blessing, but at the last minute she panicked. "We'll say the words together," Fred whispered. While Elsbeth slowly poured the water they invoked the angel to guard their southern boundary and bring a bountiful harvest.

The company roared their approval with a loud "Amen!" Rachel, who had been peacefully asleep in a basket on the floor of the wagon, awoke and let it be known that she was ready to return home. Peter helped Karen onto the wagon seat and Kristina handed her the baby. Inger-madmor corralled Gudrun and Katinka to pile into the back. Peter instructed those who were planning to complete the walk to select a burlap bag and fill it with enough rocks for each of the upcoming posts.

"I want those big ones, "Lil-Anne piped up, pointing to the back of the pile."

"You dolt," John pointed out. "You should pick the smallest ones like I do, because you have to carry them yourself."

"Are you sure you want to walk that whole long way, Lil-Anne?" Karen asked.

"I'm six now, I can do it," she answered stoutly. "And Papa

said I get to do the blessing at the next post—the one to the rising sun! I like the sun one best."

"I'll look out for her," John said protectively. "It's only a mile and a half until we get back to the house. She can always stay there while Dad and I complete the walk."

"It's going to rain," Svend predicted gloomily in Danish, looking at the thickening clouds from his high perch. "Baby Rachel will get wet if we don't hurry home."

He snapped his whip and the loaded wagon lumbered home while the remaining five people walked the half-mile east towards the next posts, again under Peter's leadership. Lil-Anne said the blessing, only needing a little prompting: "May the Angel of the Rising Sun bring the new day to this land." Then Elsbeth repeated the words for the Jensen farm.

There the party split again. Fred and Elsbeth went north hand in hand to walk counter-clockwise around his new land, while Peter, John, and Lil-Anne went south and then west until they were back at the main house. There, Peter and John again turned south, without Lil-Anne, and walked clockwise on the three-mile boundary around the original Larsen half-section and the added Jensen quarter.

The rain held off until almost noon, but turned into a gully washer when Peter and John were on their last leg. It was, therefore, a bedraggled man and chilled boy who shook out their hair and took off their boots in the back hall. A pot of soup was simmering on the stove, and dry clothes were draped over the back of a chair.

As they helped themselves to soup, John looked up at his father, "Dad, will you give me my own farm when I'm twenty-one?"

Peter was taken by surprise. It was not like John to doubt his place in life. For the first time Peter wondered if his son felt usurped by his foster-brother. "We only returned what was always Fred's. Don't begrudge him the little we've given him to make up for losing his own family. All we have will be yours—if you want it. Time enough to worry when you've decided what you want to do." Putting his arm around John's shoulder he added, "For now, let's go celebrate your brother's birthday.

That evening in their bedroom, Peter watched while Karen nursed Rachel. He leaned back in his chair and stretched out his stocking feet to the heat of the stove. "*Det var en god dag*—that was a good day," he said contentedly. "What a fine family we have."

He took the satiated baby while Karen buttoned the front of her nightgown. Putting the white bundle over his shoulder, he rubbed her back, his large competent hands completely covering the small frame and wobbly head.

"We had a letter from Sarah, today," Karen said. "They're coming to the baptism Friday morning. Jesse, Sarah, the boys, Hanna, and the baby are all taking the train—everyone except Saul, who is staying in Saint Paul to mind the store. Jesse finally convinced Sarah that they can stay at Fred's place for the weekend and that the kitchen is so new that there's no problem with it being *kosher*. We just have to make sure there's enough bedding, they'll bring everything else."

"Mmm," Peter mumbled, absorbed in listening to the small sounds coming from his shoulder. He finally collected himself and said, "I'm so glad. It wouldn't be the same without them. They'll be quite cozy at Fred's place. It's small, but Elsbeth has already made it a home." He placed Rachel on the bed and watched as Karen changed the diaper.

"I just wish they could stay for the wedding, but they have to take the train back Sunday night. They seem so happy with their new house and living in Saint Paul. There's something funny about Sarah's letter though, as if she were not telling everything."

"Do you think there are problems with their new store?"

"Oh no, she's all bubbly, as if she has a happy secret that she's dying to tell. Do you suppose she's...?"

But Peter's attention had again wandered. He picked Rachel up and savored the smell and feel of her warm body. Humming softly, he placed his youngest daughter in her cradle and tucked the covers around her.

"Is that the wedding hymn, you're singing?" Karen asked walking over to her dressing table and picking up a hairbrush.

"Fred and I were going over the music for the ceremony with Pastor yesterday, and I can't get the words out of my head! Can you believe that it's been fifteen years that we have 'dwelled together'? Old Grundtvig had it right. The joy *is* twice as great!"

He took the brush from her hand. Pulling out the pins, he gently ran his fingers through her hair to untangle the bun at the back of her neck. With long slow strokes he started to brush.

"Was it a good day for you too?" he asked. "Are you happy?"

"Mmm," Karen murmured, feeling liquid all over. "What have we done to deserve such happiness?"

"Are you never satisfied?" he asked, impatiently. "I daily wonder what I've done to deserve all this. But you! You work so hard for everyone. Don't you realize how many lives you touch, how many you have transformed? You deserve the best there is. Wait a minute, I want to get something." He disappeared out the door, and she heard him on the stairs and then as he climbed back up.

"Take a good look," he said, putting the book of recipes that the girls had given Karen in her lap. "Look at how many there are. Remember each one, what she was like when she came and how she changed. The fearful became brave, the timid bloomed, the bumbler found her skill."

"But they were here to help me and just needed to grow up a little, to mature. They have made their own lives," she protested.

"That's not the way we all see it! You have a way of making a difference." He picked up the brush again and slowly counted the strokes.

Her muscles untangled, and the remaining feelings of guilt dissipated. She closed her eyes, half asleep. *Does he really think that I work hard? That I have transformed lives? He certainly transforms mine.*

She remembered her doubts when she took the train to Rotterdam to meet him those fifteen years ago. When he had proposed on the Marianne, filling his small mate's cabin with branches from which he had hung golden bangles. Like in the folk song about Sir Peder and Roselil, he had swept all doubt away. She had felt so sophisticated then. Yet now, she knew that she had been but a child with a world of experience before her. *I too needed to grow up.*

"98, 99, 100. There," Peter finished. He bent down and nuzzled her neck. "Each of my women has her own smell," he murmured, "Anne is apples and cinnamon, Rachel is warm milk, but you are my lavender lady."

"Mmm," she hummed. "And you are Sir Peter who fills my garden with gold."

She turned her head to meet his lips, a ringing in her ears. Like the faint jingling of golden bangles.

31

Peace in the Land

I am the LORD. If ye walk in my statutes, and keep my commandments, and do them; then I will give you rain in due season, and the land shall yield her increase, and the trees of the field shall yield their fruit. And your threshing shall reach unto the vintage, and the vintage shall reach unto the sowing time: and ye shall eat your bread to the full, and dwell in your land safely. And I will give peace in the land.

Leviticus, 26: 3-6

Lincoln, Minnesota, April 1892

The following Friday afternoon, the train carrying Jesse and his family pulled into the Lincoln station. Billows of black smoke enveloped Svend on the platform where he was waiting to bring them to Fred's new farmhouse for the weekend. He had left the big buckboard nearby, and the famous Larsen blacks stood with their noses buried in feedbags, their coats and silky manes rosy in the early afternoon sun.

Jesse jumped down the steps to help the rest of the family down to the platform. Sarah peered out from behind him and smiled at the stocky bow-legged Svend, knowing immediately who he was.

"*Velkommen, Rabbi,*" Svend said in his usual Danish greeting as he formally doffed his tall hat.

Sarah expected Jesse to protest that he wasn't a rabbi; instead, he seemed to acknowledge the title by switching to German and introducing her as '*Rabbitzim Sarah*'. "And these are our two boys, Jonathan and David. And you remember my sister Hanna from Ribe. This is her baby, Abraham."

Svend bowed to each of the guests in turn, giving Hanna an extra grin of recognition. "*Bitte,*" he said, also switching to German. Waving towards the wagon, he suggested that they should wait there while he retrieved their luggage from the baggage car. "Schneider," he cried to the attendant, raising his voice to make sure this dimwit, who spoke neither Danish nor German, understood which bags to unload. He showed the boys how to carry a large wicker food hamper between them. Awed as they were to be allowed to help the famous Svend, they lugged first one, then the second hamper over to the wagon, while Svend shuttled back and forth with several large valises and a packing crate.

"*A ta'r jer lige til Jensen's gaard,*" Svend said to Jesse in Danish.

Jesse pointedly translated that they were going straight to Fred's new place.

"*Gewiss,*" Svend acknowledged the change in language. "You'll be there in good time so's you can settle in for your Sunday."

"Svend always calls *Shabbat* 'the Jewish Sunday'," Jesse explained. He's taking us straight there so we'll have time to prepare."

"I was hoping we could see baby Rachel first," Sarah objected. "We have plenty of time before sunset."

"Karen will bring her tonight, and you know there's no arguing with Svend!"

"We're over here," Karen called from the small buckboard, amused at their surprise. "We couldn't wait until tonight!"

Lil-Anne jumped to the ground and ran to Jesse to be picked up. "We snuck out," the little tattletale reported.

Everyone clustered around the carriage, exclaiming at Rachel, saying how healthy she looked, "and you too," Sarah said to Karen. "Jessele, why don't you and everyone go with Svend. I'll ride with Karen."

Climbing up, she helped Lil-Anne to sit between them. "Be careful of the crate with the china," she called, then apologized, "Look at all our baggage. You'd think we were staying for a month instead of three days." She pointed to the hampers of food, dishes, and utensils. For a Jewish family, travelin—even if they were only camping in a house for the weekend—required a lot of baggage.

"It is so good of Elsbeth and Fred to let us use their new

house. The china is a present for them. We'll just borrow it for the few days we are here."

"The house is still empty until the wedding at the end of the month," Karen answered. "Svend sometimes spends the night, but he takes his meals at the Iverson's and the kitchen is so new, it's still *kosher*. Even the pots and pans are new—a wedding present from her parents—she's letting you break them in. We appreciate how much planning you had to do to come."

"Playing pioneers for a few days will be fun," Sarah insisted. "The boys are very excited, and Jesse would not have missed Rachel's baptism for anything."

"Why can't you stay for the wedding?" Lil-Anne interrupted.

"We can't be away from the store that long, and the boys have school."

"I sensed from your letter that you're excited about something else," Karen said.

Sarah looked at her in surprise. "How did you know? But I can't tell you, Jesse wants to tell you himself." She changed the subject to the evening's dinner.

"I'm not allowed to come," Lil-Anne interrupted. "They say there isn't enough room, but I take up less space than John! It ain't fair."

"Isn't," her mother corrected automatically. "Fred set up a trestle table in the kitchen and Peter brought over extra chairs. But once we're seated, no one will be able to move. As it is, the boys will have to eat on the bedroom floor. Elsbeth has made a braided rug out of old wool trousers—she's turned quite domestic now that she's to be the mistress of her own place!"

As far as sleeping accommodations, Sarah, Hanna, and Baby Abraham would share the bedroom and Jesse would bunk with the boys in the loft. "Fred loaded it with bales of hay for them to sleep on. It's likely to be cold during the night but Svend will be there first thing in the morning to fire up the stove so you don't have to touch it for the Sabbath. He'll also bring fresh milk and cheese—Jesse's seen how we make it and says it's alright for you to eat."

"I'm sure everything will be fine," Sarah reassured. "You take such good care of everyone."

"That's what Peter says. But I've been such a nuisance," Karen protested.

"It's about time we took care of you for a change."

They had arrived at the entrance to Babel Farm. Karen would have driven Sarah all the way to Fred's place, but Rachel was beginning to fuss, for it was time for her to be fed.

"I don't mind walking," Sarah insisted. "Isn't it just down the road?"

"I'll show you the way," Lil-Anne volunteered, jumping down to help the guest from the carriage.

As the two walked deep in animated chatter, Karen called after them, "Lil-Anne, you come right back! Sarah, there are potatoes and carrots in the sink for you to use." They didn't even turn around to answer, merely waved their hands in the air to show that they had heard.

When Sarah and Anne entered the renovated house, Svend and Jesse had already unloaded the wagon. Svend pointed to himself and, not realizing that Sarah was fluent in almost as many languages as her learned husband, said loudly in Pidgin-German, "*Auf morgen, Milch und Kase, Ich bringen zu Rabbitzim.*"

Sarah nodded to show she understood about the milk and cheese, but before she could tell him to just call her Sarah, he was out the door.

He lifted the child onto the wagon seat and clambered aboard. "*Auf wiedersehen,*" he called with a cheery wave as they drove off.

Adding to the confusion, John arrived to greet the guests. He was clutching a bouquet of prairie grasses, which he handed Sarah with a smart bow and a cheery welcome.

He turned to Jonathan and David, and soon the boys were pummeling each other in greeting. "Where'll everyone sleep?" he asked. "There's only one bed in there." At ten, he was already worrying about everyone's comfort. Like his mother?

"Us men are sleeping in the loft," Jonathan said grandly. "The bedroom is for the women and babies."

David pointed to the ladder and dragged at his brother's arm. "C'mon. I've never slept on a hay bed. We can pretend we're pirates."

"But sailors don't sleep on hay, they've got hammocks," protested John, a seaman's son.

"Hammocks; hay; what's the difference? Then let's be Army scouts on lookout for Indian war parties."

The three boys happily scampered up the ladder. From the

way they were brandishing imaginary tomahawks and shrieking, it wasn't clear whether they were Indians bent on scalping or an avenging troop of soldiers.

Relieved to have the boys out from underfoot, Sarah studied the unfamiliar and primitively equipped kitchen. Since they would be nine adults, three boys, and two babies for dinner, she would have to improvise. She assured Hanna that there was so little space it would be better if she just took care of her baby.

"Reb Jessele" she called up the ladder to where her husband was helping the boys make up beds on the hay. "Please take the chairs outside. We'll bring them in when we're ready to eat."

Deftly, she browned pieces of chicken and set them to braising at the back of the stove, while potatoes and carrots simmered at the front. Two large *challah* breads and bottles of wine would complete their meal, good company making up for its simplicity. Meanwhile, she popped a brisket into the oven for the next day's dinner, and soon delicious smells filled the little house.

"What can I do?" Hanna volunteered again, squeezing through the door that was partly blocked by the improvised trestle table. "Abraham's sound asleep—for now anyway."

"Send John home and have the boys clean up. Then find the candles. It's about time. Everything should be ready as soon as we've finished setting the table. There are three oil lamps, so you can light them now and hang one in the bedroom and one in the loft."

"It looks very festive," Hanna said, admiring the table, although the tablecloth was only an old sheet and jelly glasses were to be used for wine. The new china had a narrow border of little flowers. It was plain for everyday use, but pretty. The soft light from the hanging lamp brought out the subtle colors of the prairie grasses in the jar and blurred any imperfections.

Jesse went over to his wife, and with a wink in Hanna's direction put his arms around her waist and kissed her neck. "Thank you for putting up with my crazy notion to spend the weekend as pioneers," he whispered.

"It's fun. I know that being here for little Rachel means a lot to you. Now please bring back the chairs and sit down. There isn't room to stand, and dinner will be served as soon as everyone is here."

32
L'Chaim — To Life

These then are my last words to you: Be not afraid of life. Believe that life is worth living, and your belief will help create the fact.

Address to the Harvard Young Men's
Christian Association
William James, (1842-1910)

Svend drove the Larsen family in style later that afternoon. It was ridiculous to take the wagon for such a short distance, but they were loaded with extra chairs, not to mention Peter, Rachel, John, and Karen. Fred was picking Elsbeth up at her house and the Bullards too were expected.

While the men unloaded chairs, Karen carried Rachel into the small bedroom off the kitchen. Karen had just fed Rachel and hoped that she would sleep. John followed with the wicker basket that was the baby's traveling bed, the two Schneider boys trailing behind to watch from the door.

"What can I do to help?" Karen asked, returning to the kitchen.

"We're all ready, please just sit down."

As if they had overheard Sarah's invitation, the prospective bride and groom walked in hand-in-hand followed by the sound of the Bullard carriage on the road.

"Boys, come down," Hanna called. "We're ready to eat." A loud scramble on the ladder greeted Mildred and Obadiah, as they came in the door. Sarah showed them where to sit and handed yarmulkes to the bareheaded male guests. Obadiah self-consciously perched one on top of his head.

"Jonathan," Sarah instructed, handing her eldest son a washbasin, a cup, and a towel. "As soon as Papa has washed his hands, you can pass the bowl and show our guests what to do."

Jesse rose to say the blessings. His chair scraped on the floor and would have overturned onto the stove, except that Sarah neatly intercepted it. Karen smiled. *He looks like a Biblical prophet, our very own prophet.*

Jesse, lifting his glass of wine, chanted the *Kiddush* in Hebrew, followed by a translation in English for the visitors' benefit. "And there was evening and there was morning, a sixth day...," he began and ended, "Blessed are You, Lord, our God, King of the Universe, who sanctifies the *Shabbat*."

Elsbeth had blushed red and stared at her plate during the Hebrew chanting. Fred had confided to Karen that she was very nervous about attending a Jewish dinner, afraid that she would be uncomfortable with peculiar rituals. At the English words she looked up in surprise and whispered to Fred, "But that's all right, not strange at all, quite lovely!"

"I told you not to worry," Fred whispered back. "Jesse is fine. He's a nice guy." Karen glanced at Sarah and Mildred. Both were smiling. They might not know Danish, but obviously they understood.

Jesse, undistracted, gestured to Jonathan, who brought the cup and bowl of water and poured water over his father's hands. Jesse chanted a blessing for the washing of hands, then Jonathan, solemn with responsibility, squeezed his skinny body around the table, carrying the bowl to each person in turn.

Jesse removed the cover from the two loaves of bread and chanted, *"Baruch atau Adonoi...."* He broke the bread into pieces and passed the plate down the table. Sarah was about to rise to take dinner off the stove, but he held up his hand saying, "One more prayer." Raising his glass, he chanted once again, *"Baruch atau Adonoi...,"* but this time he ended, "Blessed are You, Lord our God, King of the Universe who has given this land and this house to Fred and Elsbeth for their use. May He keep them in the hollow of his hand and bless their marriage that it will be happy and fruitful."

The rest of the bread and wine were distributed, the plates filled with chicken, potatoes, and carrots, and the boys sent to the bedroom with heaping plates and admonitions to keep quiet and not wake the babies.

Jesse rose again, but this time to toast the guests. Beaming at the assembled company he said, "*L'chaim*—to life!" The faces around the table, gleaming softly in the light of the candles, turned expectantly towards him. "*L'chaim!*" he repeated, rescuing his yarmulke from sliding off with one hand and raising his jelly glass with the other. "We welcome you, dear friends, to this our temporary home." Then turning to Elsbeth and Fred, he added, "We are honored to borrow your new house and to initiate this cozy kitchen with a Shabbos meal. I propose a toast to Fred and his bride-to-be: may your life be happy and prosperous in this lovely place."

"Skaal" and "*L'chaim*" echoed around the table. Mildred joining as enthusiastically as the rest of the company and Obadiah adding a soft "Amen."

Before Jesse had time to eat more than a couple of mouthfuls, Sarah leaned towards him and whispered loudly enough for all to hear, "Tell them Jessele, tell them your great news."

"Yes, yes, tell them," Hanna echoed.

"I was going to give everyone a chance to eat first," Jesse protested in a whisper, but his friends would not be put off. Turning to everyone, he added more loudly, "The news that Sarah is so anxious for me to share is that I've been asked to organize a new congregation in Saint Paul and serve as its Rabbi and Director of its Hebrew school."

"That calls for three long, three short, and three long," Peter prompted. A traditional Danish round of nine-fold 'hurrahs' bounced off the walls and brought the boys running from the next room to see what all the shouting was about. Even Mildred and Obadiah, quiet until then, added their voices to the acclamation. Abraham and Rachel, who had been peacefully sleeping on the bed, started to cry, and it took some time for everyone to settle down again.

Finally, the babies were snug on their mothers' laps, and the boys were allowed to remain in the room for dessert. Mildred, having checked with Karen about what was *kosher*, had brought apples, stuffed with honey, cinnamon, and walnuts. They had been baking in the oven during dinner and were now brought to the table.

Karen turned to Jesse. "How did all this happen? You didn't write a word in your last letter!"

"We wanted to surprise you," he answered. "Our synagogue, 'Sons of Jacob,' is growing so fast that some of the younger families asked me to start a new one. It'll be very small and to begin with we'll have to meet in a tent."

"He won't tell you the important parts, he's too modest," Sarah interrupted. "His learning group began to turn to him more and more because he's such a scholar. Then when they found out he had *smicha*—ordination—from the famous Slobodker Yeshiva in Lithuania—boy were they impressed!"

"Yes, and how do you suppose they found that out?" Jesse asked patting his wife's hand.

"It just slipped out one day when I was talking to Mrs. Bearman," Sarah confessed, looking innocent. "She's such a gossip..."

"As you well know," Jesse interrupted with a grin.

Karen was stunned. "But...You always said you couldn't...."

Jesse laughed, "Everyone ganged up on me and said I'd be a much better rabbi than storekeeper. I'm forever forgetting what I'm supposed to do and start to check a scripture passage or give the wrong change because I'm arguing with a customer on a point of law."

Hanna interrupted, "He's not as bad as all that, but we can manage the store while he puts his gifts to better use. It's a great honor, and we're all so proud of him!"

Karen asked Mildred about the two older Benson children.

"Minnehaha is such a wonder with them. Most of the time they sleep through the night. Thomas, the eldest, only wakes up occasionally with a nightmare since we encouraged him to speak through his fears during our evening meeting for worship. At first that seemed to make things worse, but over time, it helped a great deal."

"What about Minnehaha? Has she heard more from the divinity student?"

"He came to visit us once and was a very polite young man." Mildred chuckled, "I fear that we may lose her soon. I think he has designs on her when he graduates and has a job. I heard them whispering about her becoming a teacher at the mission school."

"Minnehaha is interested in a young man! Will wonders never cease?" Karen exclaimed.

The meal having concluded, Jesse induced David to chant grace, his treble rising over the sudden silence around the table. Then he sang again—a traditional Sabbath hymn, Sarah explained. Hanna taught everyone a sprightly round in Hebrew, beating time with her baby's small hands.

Danes aren't the only people who like to sing, Karen thought. She was about to ask what Mildred would do if Minnehaha left. Perhaps Kristina could take her place. Baby Rachel was getting restless on her lap, so she rose to make her way into the bedroom.

Sarah followed. "Such a beautiful baby," she whispered so as not to waken Abraham, again sound asleep on the bed. "They make a lovely couple," she chuckled.

"Rachel looks like Peter, except she's a lot prettier," Karen agreed, unbuttoning her shirtwaist. "Let's hope she has his disposition."

Mildred appeared in the doorway. "May I join you? I would like to know what happened to Jesse to make him change his mind about being a rabbi."

"It all started when he received Karen's letter last month," Sarah said. "What Karen wrote us about how ill she had been and how Mildred had helped her to talk, it made a deep impression. Then Jesse read her story about Deborah aloud to all of us."

"He had told me about her, of course, but only the basic facts, without details. He never wanted to talk about how she died—even to me. Then I had a series of strange dreams."

In the first dream, Deborah had appeared. She did not speak but gestured for Sarah to follow and then vanished. "I told no one what I had dreamt. Then it happened again the next night and I told Hanna about my dream."

The third night Deborah was carrying a little girl that Sarah knew must be Jesse's Rachel. Sarah again tried to question her, but the apparition disappeared in a swirl of fog leaving only an echoing, "Ask the *Tzaddik*...."

"I don't believe in ghosts, but I was haunted by these dreams. At first I thought she was telling me to see our Rabbi at Sons of Jacob, but that didn't seem right. Hanna and I talked it over, and she reminded me that Deborah used to call Jesse 'the *Tzaddik*'. She suggested I try to get him to tell me what really happened."

"But I thought he couldn't remember anything," Karen said.

"At first all I could get out of him was the story as you later wrote it, but even that was more than he had ever told me before. He claimed he was trying to protect me—that he didn't want me upset. That he would forget."

"That's what everyone told me about my children—'don't talk about them and you'll forget,' they claimed. I always wondered if Jesse would ever find peace."

Sarah nodded. "I think his roaming the prairie was really a search for just that. At first it was necessary to get the business started, but he was never meant to live in the country away from a Jewish community. In some strange way, your asking to call your baby Rachel helped him decide to move to Saint Paul. Saul had been urging him for a long time."

"He always said that he couldn't be a rabbi because he was a murderer. Did he change his mind?"

"He had never said that to me in so many words, until we talked. I almost laughed. Gentle Jesse killing not just one but two soldiers! With an ax!—I couldn't believe it, couldn't see him doing such a violent thing."

Jesse had finally remembered. His landlord, who lived at the front of the house, was a blacksmith—a big burly fellow with an even larger apprentice. They and a neighbor came running when they heard the screams and made Jesse leave. The neighbor helped Jesse down to the harbor where he escaped on a Danish fishing boat. "Jesse truly doesn't remember what happened to the soldiers because he wasn't there!"

"Did Jesse feel guilty because he *wanted* to kill them, even if he didn't actually do anything?"

"If we were judged on our thoughts rather than our actions, we'd all be murderers! That's not the Jewish way."

The women fell silent while Karen changed Rachel's diaper and tucked her in the middle of the bed next to the sleeping Abraham. Then, before rejoining the rest of the company, Mildred whispered, "But didn't anyone ever write Jesse and tell him what really happened?"

"He never asked. At first he didn't want to upset his father-in-law or get his friends in trouble. Then Deborah's father died and Jesse lost contact with the school. He did write to the yeshiva last fall, but no one answered because most of those who knew the whole story left a few years later during the *pogroms*—the killings. Then, just last week, he finally received a note from one of his classmates who now lives in New York. He said the blacksmith killed one soldier and the other one ran away. He was later hung for raping the wife of a Russian army officer. The smith was put on trial but his lawyer managed to convince the judge it was self-defense. Jesse's only crime was to evade his compulsory army service. That's why the soldiers were at the house—to bring him in."

"Jesse must be so relieved!"

"He's a changed man! We're so grateful to you."

"But I didn't do anything," Karen protested. "Mildred was the one who helped me, and I only wrote the stories because Peter suggested that I should."

"But you were the one that got up from your bed to take up life again. That courage inspired Jesse. Your Rachel has become a symbol to him of new possibilities and new life."

At that moment, they heard renewed singing from the other room, young David's treble rising clearly over Jesse's deep tenor and accompanied by enthusiastic clapping.

"We should go home before Peter teaches them all a sea-chantey," Karen laughed.

"Or they start dancing the *hora* on top of the table," Sarah agreed.

As they squeezed back into the room, Peter rose to propose yet another toast. "Here's to friends and family, to dear ones present and absent, but most of all to Karen, who brought us all together. To new beginnings: *Skaal* and *L'chaim!*"

Acknowledgements

The story of the Larsen family first came to me when I visited Danebod in Tyler, Minnesota and Karen whispered that she wanted to move to this lovely Danish heritage community. Having received my orders, I spoke to Elsie Hansen, co-author of *A Century at Danebod* and Margaret Madsen. Both were extremely helpful and I was allowed to copy several memoirs of early settlers and *Lincoln County Minnesota, 1873-1973* from the archive at the Tyler Public Library. Thus the fictional town of Lincoln, Minnesota and its newspaper, *The Lincoln Pioneer*, emerged somewhere between Tyler and Lake Benton, Minnesota, undiscovered by any mapmaker.

Jesse, "the Prairie Rabbi," was inspired by a family story told by my former colleague and long-time friend, Professor Jacob "Pete" Bearman. I am also indebted to Dr. Stephen Feinstein of The Center for Holocaust and Genocide Studies of the University of Minnesota for his suggestion that I meet with Linda Schloff, Director of the Jewish Historical Society of the Upper Midwest. Director Schloff added dimension to Jesse's character with her thoughtful insight about Jews in Lithuania and St. Paul in the nineteenth century.

Dorothee Aeppli gracefully corrected my German, but I translated the epigraphs by Aakjær, Andersen, and Grundtvig from Danish and those by Rølvaag from Norwegian.

The reference library of the Minnesota Historical Society was an invaluable resource for the history of the nineteenth century. Special thanks go to Ruth Bauer Anderson for answering my arcane questions and pointing me to exactly the right archive or text, including the portion of Mary Carpenter's letter which is quoted, with permission, at the beginning of Chapter 8, and the letters of Thomas and John Williamson about the dismal displacement of the Sioux Indians after the rebellion of 1964. The exhibits and staff at the following other sites of the Minnesota Historical Society were also incalculably helpful:

Mill City Museum in Minneapolis explained about the milling of grain, while Fort Ridgeley, Birch Coulee Battlefield, and the Lower Sioux Agency helped me visualize the terror of the Sioux uprising and its dismal aftermath.

Dr. Eric Buffalohead, Chair of American Indian Studies at Augsburg College added depth to my superficial knowledge of Sioux history and pointed me towards the Minnesota Valley. The remarkable Henry Benjamin Whipple, first Episcopal Bishop of Minnesota, came alive at the Rice County Museum in Faribault, Minnesota. His staunch support of the Sioux Indians and his timely petition to President Lincoln at the end of the uprising earned him Chief Good Thunder's respect and the name of *Straight Tongue*. Robert Neslund, teacher at the Shattuck and St. Mary's School in Faribault originally founded by Bishop Whipple and his wife Cornelia, kindly helped me create a historically credible back-story for Minnehaha.

Last, but not least, searches in Google provided links to innumerable websites of libraries, historical biographies, museums, tribal councils, agricultural practices, and maps. GoogleArt also found Sara Davenport's lovely watercolor that inspired the cover and was adapted with permission.

This is a work of fiction. All of the characters are products of my imagination or are used fictitiously, although the events and personalities associated with the history of Southwestern Minnesota and the Sioux uprising are presented as accurately as I can. Any errors of fact are my responsibility and not that of the many who gave so generously of their time and expertise; they are certainly not to blame for the flights of fancy I took with their contributions.

Please visit my website: *www.AnneIpsen.com* for an extended bibliography.

About the Author

Anne Ipsen was born in Denmark, but grew up in the Boston area and then settled in Minnesota. Intrigued by the state's ethnic diversity and social consciousness, she explores these values in her latest novel about Karen and Peter. Leaving her professorship at the University of Minnesota to devote more time to her writing, she researched the Danish-American heritage community around Tyler and the tragic history of the Sioux Indians from the nearby Minnesota Valley. Her special interest in the difficult adjustment of immigrants is reflected not just in the stories of the Larsen family and their Jewish friend Jesse, but in those of Karen's Scandinavian, Irish, and Indian Girls that work on the Babel Farm.

Anne has published two memoirs and a novel that draw on her Danish heritage, as well as innumerable professional articles and several essays and book reviews for The Danish Pioneer. Anne and her husband now live in Massachusetts, the location for her next project about Puritan New England. For more information visit her website at: *www.AnneIpsen.com*.

NORMANDALE COMMUNITY COLLEGE
LIBRARY
9700 FRANCE AVENUE SOUTH
BLOOMINGTON, MN 55431-4399